Book VIII of the Locket Saga

Book VIII of the Locket Saga

Cygnet A Brown

Chapter 1

"Well, if it isn't my old pal, Andrew Mayford."

The year was 1809. Dirt streets, rutted and rocky during the dry season and muddy during the rainy season, wound between the red brick buildings of Silver Street at Natchez Under the Hill. Andrew walked up to the storekeeper, Daniel Moses. Daniel was sweeping the dust from the front step of his store on Silver Street. Daniel was sweeping the dust from the store's front step.

Saloons, hotels, warehouses, grocery stores, a coal yard, an ice house, a quarter-mile race track, a ten-pin alley, and even a few private residences lined Silver Street. Many of the businesses existed primarily to service the flatboats, keelboats, and steamboats that docked at Natchez.

Natchez was a city with a dual personality. "Natchez Under the Hill was 'Natchez improper,' and Natchez above the Hill was 'Natchez proper.'

'Natchez Improper' had gambling dens, saloons, and houses of prostitution that were popular with the rough boatmen and travelers at the waterfront. Known as Natchez Under-the-Hill, part of Natchez was one of the rowdiest ports on the Mississippi River. Here, the keelboats and the flatboats docked after coming downriver from as far away as Pittsburgh, Pennsylvania.

"Hello, Daniel! How's Natchez under the Hill been treating you?"

"Fair to middlin'. I see you made another successful trip down the Mississippi."

"It's not a lot of money, but it's a living," Andrew answered.

"What are your plans?"

"I just finished my business at the warehouse. I'm now looking for a long soak and a bite to eat before heading down to the boarding house. After that? I haven't got a clue."

The Spanish built Silver Street about 1790 to connect the town above to the riverfront below. In the 1800s, Natchez Under-the-Hill had already become a major port on the Mississippi River. It exported and imported agricultural goods, with cotton being the primary export. As the city became richer, the imported goods grew more luxurious. Natchez is one of the oldest European settlements in the Mississippi River Valley. It was the center of economic activity for the young state. Its strategic location on the high bluffs on the eastern bank of the Mississippi River enabled it to develop into a bustling port. At Natchez, many local plantation owners had their cotton loaded onto steamboats at the landing known as Natchez Under-the-Hill to be transported downriver to New Orleans or, sometimes, upriver to St. Louis or Cincinnati. The cotton was sold and shipped to New England, New York, and European spinning and textile mills.

Down the street, the door of one of the bars opened a man flew through it and lay sprawled out on the street.

"And stay out!" a big, burly man stood at the door. He put his hands together like he was dusting the man's presence from his hands and turned and closed the door. He stood arms crossed outside the door. The man in the street stood up and staggered up the street.

"If it happens once, it happens ten times a day. Natchez under the Hill is the most licentious spot on the Mississippi River." Daniel Moses said. "Sometimes I want to leave it all. If it weren't for the money, I'd be somewhere else."

Taverns, gambling halls, and brothels lined the principal street. Here, rumors were that the only thing cheaper than the body of a loose woman was. Unless, of course, it was a man of color.

Enslaved people were also sold at the landing at Natchez-Under-the-Hill, as well as on the city streets and at the Forks of the Road. Natchez Under the Hill had become the second-largest slave market in the South.

"Where would you go, Daniel, if you weren't here?"

Daniel shrugged. "I don't know. Maybe New Orleans, or maybe I'll do what the wealthy people of Natchez do and move up the hill. I might do that. I'm making enough money."

More genteel of Natchez lived on the top of the hill, but they also liked a little vice. The men from the hill came down where they could gamble their cotton earnings at the racetracks or the poker tables.

"So, will you be heading up the trace, Andrew?"

Both men knew that after he finished his business in Natchez, Andrew would make the long trek back north to their homes overland on the Natchez Trace,

"Yep, I'm sure that my father has another load of grain heading down this way in a few weeks, and he's counting on me to deliver them."

"The trace is dangerous. Two men were found murdered on the trail just last week. There wasn't a coin between them."

Andrew shrugged. "I'm not worried. I have a well-armed and loyal crew."

Daniel nodded. "See you later, Kaintuck."

Both men laughed. It was a standing joke between them. Many of the men who made this trip were locally called "Kaintucks" because they were usually from Kentucky, although the entire Ohio River Valley was well-represented among their numbers.

Andrew was not, however, from Kentucky. He was from Pennsylvania, and his parents lived in Pittsburgh. A person couldn't tell by his dress that he was from a well-to-do family who lived in Pittsburgh. He wore the same buckskins and boots that all the frontiersmen wore. After traveling downriver for several weeks, he even smelled like them.

For years, the Natchez Trace had been an Indian trail, and even earlier, animals, including buffalo, used it for migration. Natchez was the starting point of the Natchez Trace overland route. This trace, or trail, ran from Natchez to Nashville. From there, Andrew took overland roads through Ohio to his family's home.

The trace was the only way keelboat men had to return upstream. These keelboat men maneuvered flatboats and barges to transport all kinds of goods down the Mississippi River. When they arrived in Natchez, they traded their cargoes for money. Like the others, Andrew sold his wares and the lumber he used to construct his boat at Natchez and took the overland route to Nashville.

Natchez had been part of the United States territories since before Andrew's cousin Isaac went west with the Lewis and Clark Expedition. The US. and Spain signed the Treaty of San Lorenzo, settling their decade-long boundary dispute. On October 27, 1795, all Spanish claims to Natchez were formally surrendered to the United States.

A week later, Natchez had become the first capital of the new Mississippi Territory, created by the Adams administration. On March 10, 1803, the territorial assembly incorporated the town. After it served for several years as the territorial capital, in 1802, the territory built a new capital, named Washington, six miles to the east, but this didn't diminish Natchez's growth.

"Word has it that up north, they are building steamboats that can sail upstream! Have you ever seen one?"

"I have not," Andrew replied. "I can't imagine how any boat could travel upstream."

"Can you imagine how much a boat like that can move upstream on its own power, could change everything here on the Mississippi?"

"I have heard that these steamboats are successful in the east, but I can't imagine any boat being able to move upstream under its own power on the Mississippi or even the Ohio, for that matter," Andrew replied.

"What if they could?" Moses asked him.

"What I wouldn't do to be part of that experience," Andrew stated. "Having the ability to travel upstream would certainly be better than dodging cutthroats and thieves on the trace."

"That it would. That it would," Daniel replied.

Chapter 2

The leaves were tiny bug-sized bits of green on the trees by the time Andrew arrived back home at his parents' home in Pittsburgh, Pennsylvania, a few weeks later.

The hired servant let him in the door and into the entryway. His mother, who had been in the parlor, came out to see him.

"Thank God you're home!" she exclaimed. "I worry so much about you!"

Andrew raised his arms wide. "Well, here I am safe and sound."

"I don't know why you don't settle down with some nice girl, You're almost thirty years old! It's time you settled down instead of going traipsing down the river like some river pirate."

"It's good to see you, too, Mother."

Andrew was used to her complaints about his choice of enterprise. If she had her way, he'd be sitting behind a desk in his father's stuffy office, working on financial records like his brother Charles was already doing at just eight years old. That just wasn't the life he wanted to live. He enjoyed the freedom that life on the river offered him. Someday, he might settle down, but now wasn't that time.

The stench of his travels must have suddenly hit his mother because she turned up her nose. "Go take a bath now! You reek!"

After a bath in his copper tub in the bathhouse behind the house, he changed into more civilized clothes. Once he was "presentable," his mother allowed him in the main rooms of the house.

The next morning, Andrew went down to the river where keelboats, barges, and flatboats were moored.

At the dock, he found his friend J. P., who was painting the name of his new boat, "Evergreen," on the boat's bow.

"You clean up nice, Andrew," P. J. said. You even smell nice."

"Thank you very much," Andrew replied.

"I didn't mean it as a compliment."

"I never said you did, but I take it any way I want."

P. J. smirked. "If I didn't know you better, I'd think that you were a local dandy."

"My mother would give anything to turn me into a city boy," Andrew said drily.

P. J. slapped Andrew on the back. "Great to see you back, friend."

"It's always good to survive the Natchez Trace." Andrew smiled back. He and PJ had known each other since they were young boys. They sometimes traveled to Natchez together but hadn't for a couple of years because PJ was as good at building flatboats as he was at piloting them. There was as much money in building them as there was taking them downstream and without the dangers that the river system entailed.

They talked for the next few minutes about Meriwether Lewis' death, and then PJ changed the conversation back to Andrew's plans. "Are you going back up north to take your relatives some more manufactured goods again?"

"No, I won't be doing that anymore. They've been getting their goods from Waterford or Erie lately. The area has developed a lot, and those communities offer more reliable service than I ever could."

"So, are you making another trip back south?"

"Without a doubt. It looks like I won't be taking grain this time, though. My father thinks he may have a special project he wants me to pilot."

"You get some of the best shipments thanks to your father. What will it be this time? Corn licker?"

Andrew shrugged. "I couldn't tell you exactly. I'll let you know when I have more details."

"Why the secrecy?" P. J. asked.

"I'm not secretive. I'm just not exactly sure yet, but as soon as I know, you'll be among the first I tell."

"I guess I can accept that answer," P. J. said.

A comfortable silence fell between them. They stood here at the edge of the river by the dock watching the flatboats, keelboats, and barges ascending and descending the stream. They did this often.

There were numerous plain box flatboats. The plain box design made the craft easy to dismantle for the lumber it contained when they arrived at their destination, which was either Natchez or New Orleans.

Several keelboats were moored nearby. Keelboats were long and slender, sharp fore and aft, with a narrow gangway just within the gunwales. Unlike flatboats that could not be maneuvered upstream, the boatmen could pole or warp upstream. They could also use oars with the aid of the eddies whenever they found them. Andrew had done his share of keelboat poling when he had gone to the northwestern corner of the state. He would not miss those trips.

At one pier, men were loading a barge. When the keelboat was covered with a low house, lengthwise, between the gangways, it received the dignified name of "barge." The only claim of the flatboat, or "broad horn," to rank as a vessel was because it floated upon water and was used as a vehicle for transportation. Keelboats, barges, and flatboats had prodigious steering oars. The oars of the same dimensions hung on fixed pivots on the sides of the last-named, by which the shapeless and cumbrous contrivance was, in some sort, managed. Ignorant of anything better, the people of the West were satisfied with these vehicles of trade. They would keep using them until something better came along.

Andrew knew that his father was betting money that something better had already come along.

That afternoon, Nicholas Roosevelt, his wife Lydia, and her maid carrying Lydia's luggage arrived at the Mayford home. They arrived by a hired coach from the East.

Nicholas Roosevelt exited the coach first. He was tall and built like Andrew's father. He was dressed in a similar business suit. His hairline was receding. His eyes were blue. The hair on his curly head and his well-groomed beard were medium brown and as yet didn't appear to have hints of gray like Andrew's father's hair did. He had a confident smile.

Nicholas helped his wife from the coach. Andrew was surprised that Roosevelt's wife was much younger than he was. She couldn't have been more than in her late teens. Lydia Roosevelt was a petite woman dressed in a high-waisted dress, the latest fashion. She had dark hair and pale skin. As they came closer to the house, Andrew saw that she, too, had blue eyes, and she looked exhausted after her coach ride from New York to Pittsburgh.

After Lydia, another woman stepped out of the coach. She gathered the satchels from the coach, so Andrew guessed that she was Lydia's maid. Lydia's maid had to have been a couple of years older than her mistress. She was thin, but not too thin. Like any good maid, she did not look at anyone in the eye but simply kept to her duties.

Lydia spoke to the butler who had let them in. "Could you direct Susanna here to our rooms so that she can put away my gowns?"

"Indeed, ma'am," Instead of just showing Susanna to the rooms, the butler tried to take the bags from her.

Susanna gently resisted his help and shook her head. "No, I can handle these."

The butler led the maid to the room.

Andrew watched them ascend the stairs. Susanna, huh? She was pretty. She may not have looked him in the eyes. There was something different about her. Unlike many of the servants of visitors to their home, she held her head high.

It was at that moment that Lowri Mayford stepped forward and took Lydia's hand. "It's so nice to meet you," Lowri said. Something about the younger woman must have alarmed her because she seemed taken aback. "My dear, you look exhausted. Come, let me show you to your room so that you can rest."

"Thank you," Lydia replied. "This trip was particularly exhausting. I don't know what's wrong with me. I don't quite feel myself today."

"Madeleine, can you show Mrs. Roosevelt to her room?" Lowri turned toward the housemaid who had just come into the room from the dining room.

Madaleine curtsied. "Yes, ma'am."

The housemaid ushered Lydia Roosevelt up the stairs to the guest room while Jonathan and his sons ushered Nicholas straight to the study.

Andrew had spent so much time down south that he knew southern men were not that direct in their actions. Nothing in the South moved rapidly. He expected that the hot weather was what kept things slow in the south. The men there took their time, smoked a cigar, drank a brandy, and relaxed before returning to business. However, like any good Yankee here in the Northeast, Nicholas Roosevelt went straight to business.

"I suspect you're wondering what this is all about," Nicholas replied. He sat dignified in the seat across from Jonathan.

"My son and I speculated last night that perhaps you might be considering putting steamboats on western waters."

"You assume correctly," Nicholas replied. "We are looking to build a steamboat to go from here in Pittsburgh to travel down to New Orleans."

Andrew shook his head. "Can't be done. Most of the year, barges can't take the Falls."

"The Falls?"

"Yes, there is a terrible series of shouls in the Ohio River that we call "The Falls". Much of the time they are impassible by barge, and often in the dry season, even flatboats can't manage them either."

"I'm sure we can figure something out," Nicholas replied. "That brings us to why I am here today. I would like to arrange to have a pilot take my wife, her maid, and myself down the Ohio River and the Mississippi River to New Orleans. I would like to hire you, Andrew, to be that pilot."

"You, your wife, and her maid?" Andrew shook his head. "No, it's not safe to take women down the Mississippi by land or by boat. Coming back up the Natchez Trail is dangerous even for us men."

"Rest assured, we will not be traveling up the trail," Nicholas replied. "We will be returning to New York by ship so that I can prepare the supplies I would need to build the steamboat in Pittsburgh."

"So, you'll be needing a place to build your steamboat here in Pittsburgh, then?" Jonathan asked.

"I see you are most perceptive, Jonathan," Nicholas replied. "Yes, we would need a shipyard on one of the rivers here in Pittsburgh."

"Then call it done. I would be happy for you to use my shipyard on the Monongahela to build your steamboat."

"Splendid," Nicholas replied. "And you, Andrew? Will you pilot our flatboat down to New Orleans?"

Andrew opened his mouth to object to going when his father said.

"He'd be happy to," Jonathan answered for his son, something that he never did.

Andrew's jaw lowered, and he glared at his father. His father glared back at him. Andrew sighed deeply.

Nicholas observed the exchange and assumed correctly that Andrew's reluctance was due to having women on the trip. "If you're worried about my wife or her maid Susanna, they're both tougher than they look."

"Yes, sir," Andrew replied. He wasn't entirely convinced. "I will take responsibility for the boat, but the women would be your concern. I don't mean to be blunt, but I'll have enough problems getting a barge to New Orleans in one piece."

Andrew had taken trips down the Mississippi River long enough to know that rivers were dangerous places. Rivers were dynamic and changed regularly. Sometimes changes came fast, such as a flood, while other changes were more gradual, like the gradual erosion of a shoreline. In either case, gradual or fast, changes posed problems for anyone who ventured onto the Mississippi. Where the water was once deep, it might be shallow, hidden debris could quickly sink a boat, and the bends might not be in the same places that they were during the previous trip. Despite these problems, the Mississippi River and its tributaries were a superior means of travel throughout the frontier to the west of Pittsburgh.

Jonathan gave Andrew a wide-eyed, disapproving look, but Andrew ignored it. Jonathan Mayford may have been his father, but his father wasn't the one taking a flatboat downstream with two potentially squeamish women aboard. For the safety of his crew, he had to make his conditions clear.

"I respect your bluntness, Andrew Mayford, but you don't have to worry about my wife or her maid. They can take care of themselves." Nicholas Roosevelt held out his hand, and Andrew put his in Mr. Roosevelt's. The firm handshake sealed the deal, and Andrew was committed to this endeavor.

"Well, now that we have that settled, let's move on. I understand that Fulton and Livingston obtained a U.S. industrial patent for their "steamboat" design," Jonathan said.

Nicholas Roosevelt nodded.

"Yes, they hope to increase their profits by obtaining exclusive rights to steam navigation along the Mississippi River. They have already been granted exclusive rights from New York State to steam navigation along the Hudson. They've asked me to handle the western side of things." Roosevelt handed Jonathan a sealed letter. "Here's the letter verifying what they want."

Jonathan unsealed the letter and studied it for a moment.

"I would be happy to help finance this project too, as long as when Andrew returns, he agrees that it's possible. I have the docks and access to raw materials. You're welcome to any of my contacts that you'll need."

"Splendid, that's good to know. I can assure you that your cooperation and assistance will be well compensated. Rest assured that both Mr. Fulton and Livingstone realize the great potential for steamboat traffic on the western waters. Less than two weeks after Clermont's first successful voyage, they had already begun to plan for this steamboat on these western rivers. They certainly believe that it is possible, and I aim to prove that it is."

"What is it that you do, Mr. Roosevelt?" Andrew asked. "I mean, when you're not planning to build steamboats."

"I'm an inventor who's interested in steamboats. It's as simple as that."

That evening at dinner, Lydia Roosevelt and Lowri Mayford joined their husbands and Andrew at the dining room table. Jonathan and Lowri sat at either end of the table. Lydia sat on one side of the table and Nicholas sat on the opposite. Lydia appeared refreshed after her afternoon nap. Andrew sat beside Nicholas.

Andrew was disappointed that Lydia's maid was not with them. He would have loved to have heard what she knew about the Roosevelts during dinner conversation. Of course, there was no reason that she would be with them. She was a servant. She was eating dinner in the kitchen with the Mayfords' servants. He didn't understand why, but he felt intrigued by this young woman. She was Lydia's maid and belonged to the lower working-class society, but something about her seemed out of place. As he thought about it, he tried to analyze exactly what was out of place.

She didn't carry herself like most servants he had seen. Not that he usually paid attention to his mother's servants or the servants of her friends. He usually didn't, which was also strange. Why did he care now? He had to know what was different about her.

He turned his attention back to the conversation at the dinner table. His mother was prying Lydia Roosevelt for information about herself.

"Have you and Mr. Roosevelt been married long, Lydia?" Lowri asked her house guest.

Lydia blushed. "No, we have not. We've been married for less than six months. However, we had been engaged to each other for four years before we were married, so it seems like we've been together forever."

"You had been engaged for four years?"

"Yes, we knew we belonged together as soon as we met, but my father insisted on a long engagement. Nicholas was 37, and I was just 13 years old, but we knew we belonged together. We were willing to wait until my father agreed to allow us to wed."

"Your father?"

"Yes, Henry Latrobe is my father."

"Your father is Benjamin Henry Latrobe?" Andrew could hardly believe his ears. Everyone knew about Benjamin Henry Latrobe. He was known by almost everyone in the country. He was one of the men responsible for building the capital building.

In August 1796, commissioners focused on building the Capitol's north wing so it could be used by the legislature. Some of the rooms on the third floor remained unfinished when the Congress, the Supreme Court, the Library of Congress, and the courts of the District of Columbia occupied the US. Capitol late in 1800.

In 1803, Congress allocated funds to resume construction, and a Superintendent of the City of Washington replaced the commissioners. He made Benjamin Henry Latrobe the architect who oversaw the construction. As the first professional architect and engineer to work in America, Latrobe modified the original plan created by William Thornton, a Scottish-trained physician living in Tortola, British West Indies, by redesigning the south wing for offices and committee rooms and simplifying its construction.

"Yes, my father-in-law helped finance the Clemont, and he plans to finance our steamboat as well," Nicholas answered.

"It sounds like celebrities are contributing to these steamboats," Jonathan Mayford replied, "Robert Fulton developed the first commercially successful steamboat in America. Robert Livingston assisted in drafting our Declaration of Independence, and Lydia's father helped design the US. Capitol."

"Indeed," Nicholas cut his piece of roast and savored the morsel. After swallowing his mouthful, he said. "Mrs. Mayford, I must compliment your cook. This roast is divine."

"It's a venison roast, Mr. Roosevelt. It came from just outside one of the communities up the Allegheny. Our chef, Paul, will be pleased to know you enjoyed it."

"It is excellent. It is finer than many beef roasts I have eaten in New York."

When the Mayford maids came out to clear the dishes at the end of the meal, Jonathan suggested they take dessert and coffee in the sitting room.

Andrew had had enough of these social pleasantries. He much preferred hanging out with people who didn't know a salad fork from a dessert spoon. He needed to abandon this fancy dinner party to get some fresh air.

"Excuse me," he said. "I think I'll call it a night. If you'll excuse me, I must step outside for a little bit before bed."

As Andrew expected, his mother explained Andrew's planned exit. "My son has spent so much time on the river that he hates being shackled to the conventions of civilized life."

Andrew rose to his feet and nodded. "If you'll excuse me."

He pushed his chair back under the table as his mother had taught him and walked through the kitchen toward the back of the servants' area. His mother's maids were cleaning the kitchen and washing dishes. He exited the back door where Paul was smoking his evening pipe.

"I see your mother finally let you escape for the evening," Paul said. He had known Andrew since Andrew was a child and knew the young man's struggles with his parents' lifestyle.

"Yes," Andrew said.

Andrew saw movement in the shadows of the corner of the backyard. He recognized Susanna's silhouette in the shadows. She didn't seem to be aware that anyone had just left the house through the kitchen door. Instead, she stood looking up at the full moon above the gas streetlamp. She seemed oblivious to anything but her thoughts and that full moon.

There was enough light for Andrew to see that she had changed out of her traveling outfit and was dressed in a light frock. Even in this light, her dark features intrigued him. She wasn't wearing a hat. Her hair was pulled up into a Grecian style like Lydia's. Her dark tendrils framed her face.

Andrew crossed the yard. He ducked under a clothesline. At that moment, she must have heard him coming because she turned towards him.

"Well, good evening," Andrew said to Lydia's maid. "Did you have a pleasant dinner?"

Susanna shrugged.

"It was filling," she replied. "Paul is a good cook."

"Thank you, Miss Susanna," Paul said. He seemed entertained by the interaction between the two younger people. The bowl of his pipe glowed as he took a long draw from his pipe and observed the two as they interacted.

Susanna's thick French accent was recognizable, but her English was flawless.

Her hair wasn't as black as he had thought. She had dark brown hair. "Is there something I can help you with, Mr. Mayford?"

Paul laughed. "She called you Mr. Mayford."

Andrew replied. "I'm not as highbrow as my mother wants me to be. When I'm not in my mother's presence, you can call me, Andrew."

"That's the truth," Paul exclaimed. "We all call him Andrew when his mother isn't around. His father doesn't care. However, don't use his given name when Andrew's mother is nearby. She would have a fit."

"Isn't that the truth?" Andrew replied. "I'm not much for high society. I can't wait to head back down the river to Natchez. Don't you have something better to do, Paul? I would like to talk privately with this young lady."

"I can see that," Paul chuckled.

Paul finished the pipe that he was smoking and tapped the pipe stem on his finger. Embers fell to the ground, and Paul snuffed them out.

"I must attend to preparations for tomorrow's breakfast," he said. Andrew and Susanna watched Paul re-enter the house.

"You haven't always been a woman's handmaiden, have you? You wouldn't happen to have a last name, would you?

"Of course, I have a last name," Susanna replied. "My last name is Bouvier."

"Just what I thought. Based on your name and your accent, you are French. Based on my experience with the upper class, I could assume you were also once French nobility."

"That is true," Susanna replied. She shrugged. A sad look passed her face. "How did you know?"

"I recognize your noble airs. My mother was of Welsh nobility. As I'm certain you're aware, she has her own airs."

Susanna chuckled.

"Based on your current situation and the fact that you are French, I would also guess you escaped France during the French Revolution."

Susanna got a sad, faraway look on her face. "Yes, you guessed correctly, but it wasn't quite that simple."

Under the flicker of the gas light, he saw that her eyes were the darkest brown he had ever seen.

"My parents were killed during the revolution, and I escaped to America with my grandmother when I was a child."

"Oh, I'm sorry," Andrew replied.

Susanna leaned toward him. "You've never lost anyone. Have you?"

"No, I've been lucky that way. I guess." Andrew leaned toward her. He could smell the soap on her skin. The soap was his mother's perfumed soap that they kept in the guestrooms.

"I was secreted out of the country by my grandmother and was brought here to the United States. We lived quite well for a while, but when she died three years ago, I learned that she was deeply in debt because she tried to maintain the lifestyle we had in France. I was penniless. If it weren't for Mr. Latrobe's generosity in hiring me, I might now be in the poor house."

"It would be a shame for such a pretty young woman to live in the poor house."

A line furrowed on Susanna's forehead.

"Don't frown, Susanna. It takes away from your beauty."

Susanna's eyes fluttered nervously. She took a step back.

"So, flattery is how you choose to spend your time with the help?" Susanna asked. She was trying to change the subject.

"I wouldn't say that exactly. It is just that I find people who work more real than the ones sitting there in the parlor drinking coffee and eating pastries."

"I don't know why you say that," Susanna replied. "Those people in the parlor are the ones who give us the ability to eat regularly. I am grateful to Lydia for keeping me on after her marriage."

She lowered her head. Her long, dark lashes draped over her eyes.

"How long have you worked for Mrs. Roosevelt?" Andrew wanted to touch her chin and raise it and make her look at him with her beautiful brown eyes again.

"I've worked for her since my grandmother died. I've gotten to know her quite well. She's with child, although I don't think she realizes it yet."

Andrew's jaw dropped. "She's having a baby. My father and Mr. Roosevelt want me to take her with us downriver. I wasn't sure whether I wanted to take her with us or not. Now I know I do not! I cannot!"

"You don't have anything to worry about with Lydia Latrobe Roosevelt. You don't know her like I know her. Believe me, she can handle herself as well as I can."

"You? What does a pretty thing like you know about how difficult it is to go down the Mississippi?"

"I know a lot about tough times, Mr. Mayford," Susanna looked him in the eye. Her brown eyes grew dark and angry. "You can be sure of that."

He saw fire in her eyes, and he felt invigorated that she was coming out of her shell with him. He liked this side of her better than her demure personal maid side.

"I told you to call me Andrew. My father is Mr. Mayford."

He looked into her brown eyes. Her lips pressed tightly together.

"Lydia and I can all take care of ourselves."

It wasn't just the fire he saw in her eyes. He also sensed the pain she had endured. Yes, she knew difficulties. He didn't know why, but he instinctively knew he believed her.

"All right, she can come. You can both come."

Later, Susanna lay in her bed and thought about her reaction to Andrew.

In some ways, he reminded her of Derrick Pitt. She had met Derrick while she and her grandmother lived in New York. She remembered the way he looked and how he unsettled her. It was exactly as Andrew looked at her, now. Men like him weren't afraid to take advantage of women like her. Women who no longer had standing in the community, even though they did nothing wrong.

Derrick had the same red hair as Andrew. Andrew was even more handsome than Derrick had been. Derrick was not the man that Susanna thought he was. When he realized, when Susanna's grandmother died, that Susanna wasn't getting any inheritance and, deeply in debt, he was gone before the household auction used to clear that debt. She hadn't started working for Lydia before he was courting another wealthy young lady.

Henry Latrobe had paid off her debt and put her in charge of making his tiny, but tomboyish, daughter into a New York debutante.

Susanna instinctively knew that Mr. Latrobe wanted the marriage between his daughter and Nicholas Roosevelt to occur, but he also knew that his daughter wasn't ready for the New York social scene. He needed a girl like Susanna to smooth off Lydia's rough edges.

Susanna had not disappointed Mr. Latrobe. He was pleased with the progress Lydia made toward becoming a lady.

Susanna doubted Lydia's transformation had as much to do with her as it did with the fact that Lydia was head-over-heels in love with Nicholas Roosevelt, a man who was more than twice her age. Susanna knew Lydia's transformation from the lanky tomboy to the lady; she now had more to do with Nicholas Roosevelt than her tutelage.

Andrew's face came back up in Susanna's mind. Andrew was not Derrick. Andrew wasn't after her money because she didn't have any, and there was no reason he would think she had any. He seemed to be a kind enough man. He came from money, but he didn't act as though money was his main objective.

Who was she trying to fool? His family did have money. He was probably just bored with his wealthy life. He was probably just looking for a woman with whom he could have a few laughs. When he was bored with her, he would move on. That's what rich men did with women like her.

Andrew Mayford would soon learn that Susanna was not that kind of woman. She may be alone and down on her luck, but she was a survivor. She would not let anyone make her think otherwise.

Chapter 3

Andrew found Nicholas's obsession with planning every detail of the flatboat he built. His attention to detail was beyond tedious in Andrew's opinion. Andrew usually just eyeballed how he put boats together, but Nicholas Roosevelt had to do things perfectly. His education as an engineer made him check and double-check everything to make sure that everything about the boat was perfect.

Andrew didn't understand why Nicholas thought it important to have every aspect of the boat be perfect. It wasn't as though they would be traveling in the boat for a long time. When they reached New Orleans, they would have to break up the boat and sell the lumber just as every other boat crew had to do. Nicholas' calculations made the boat-building take ten times as long for any barge that he had ever taken down the Mississippi.

In addition, Nicholas studied the details of the navigation maps with Andrew to determine the ideal channels for the steamboat to travel.

One day after dinner, Nicholas was poring over the map of the Mississippi River near Little Prairie. Nicholas was asking him about the depth and width of the river in that location.

"You do know that the channels could change over time. One hard flood and the whole area will be different."

"I guess I can see that as being the case," Nicholas replied.

None of the ready-made keelboats, barges, and flatboats had been good enough for Roosevelt. Nicholas Roosevelt didn't want a flatboat that was built for speed. Instead, he wanted a flatboat that offered all the creature comforts that he and his wife were accustomed to in their home back in New York.

For the next three weeks, Andrew, his friend PJ, and their crew feverishly worked together and finished the flatboat that would be Roosevelt's home as they followed the current of the Ohio and Mississippi Rivers from Pittsburgh to New Orleans.

Finally, the boat was finished. The boat was flat and had an awning. A rowboat was attached to the back of the flatboat so that Roosevelt and Andrew could take it to examine and record information about the ripples and currents.

The flatboat supported a huge box that acted as a comfortable bedroom for the Roosevelts, and there was a dining room where Susanna slept on a cot near the pantry. Another room was built at the front of the boat to serve as the crew's quarters. A fireplace was built in this room. Roosevelt had hired a cook to prepare the meals for the Roosevelts and the crew.

In May 1809, everything was finally ready to begin their journey. The women were down in the parlor when Nicolas came down the stairs. He had exchanged his black suit for a pair of Andrew's buckskins.

"Well, don't you look like the frontiersman?" Lydia smiled at her husband. She then turned to the butler, who stood nearby. "Would you get my trunk from up in our room?"

The butler nodded. "Yes, ma'am."

He directed Paul, the cook, to help him carry the trunk down the stairs. A few minutes later, they returned carrying the trunk

"What are these?" Nicholas asked.

"These are our fancier dresses," Lydia replied.

"What do you need them for, Lydia?" Nicholas asked.

"You don't expect us to wear these clothes when we arrive in New Orleans, do you?" Lydia asked. "I packed a suit for you as well, Mr. Roosevelt."

"Thank you, Mrs. Roosevelt."

Even though he wasn't so sure about the need for the fancy dresses in New Orleans, Andrew was pleased to see that, like Nicholas, the women wore simpler clothing for the trip downriver on the flatboat. Lydia Roosevelt wore a simple light blue cotton dress, and her dark brown hair hung in a long braid down her back. For head covering, she wore a light blue cotton under-ruffle bonnet covered with a wide-brimmed woven wicker bonnet. It was tied on with light blue satin ribbons.

He couldn't help noticing that Susanna wore a simple high-waisted dress that was not made of cotton. She wore a darker blue linsey-woolsey blend dress in the same style as Lydia's gown. A sign that she was a servant, not equal in stature to the Roosevelts.

She turned toward Andrew and saw that he was watching her. She quickly turned away and offered to help Lydia with her sachet.

Andrew shrugged and helped PJ prepare to shove off. He was more than ready to go back down the river. He had grown impatient with Nicholas' demands for the flatboat. They would have been ready sooner, but Nicolas was a stickler for what he wanted. It had quickly become clear that whatever Nicholas wanted, Nicholas got.

Now he was in his element, and with this he was happy. He served as the pilot, while his friend PJ and two others served as the rest of the crew.

The other two of the crew were the Williams brothers: Jerrod and Marcus. They were tall, burly men and had crewed for Andrew several times.

"Are you ready, Mr. Roosevelt?" PJ asked.

"Ready as I'll ever be!" he called out.

"Then push off!" he exclaimed.

The men pushed the boat away from the dock and poled the flatboat into the stream.

Starting a new river journey was nothing new to Andrew. However, having two women onboard the boat was. This part of the river did not challenge Andrew at all. He had known these waters his entire life. His men knew these waters as well as he did, so he mused at Lydia and Susanna as they giggled at the idea that they were floating down the river.

The newness of the experience quickly wore off. The women turned to activities that they seemed to know best. They pulled out sewing samplers, stitched, and watched the landscape pass by them.

Just a few miles downriver, Nicholas asked Andrew to lower the anchor.

"You want to check the water depth already?" Andrew asked.

"Yes," Nicholas answered. "I need to see how deep the water is here, away from civilization. This area has not likely been dredged like it has been around Pittsburgh."

Andrew nodded. "Very well."

Nicholas and Andrew got into the rowboat to check the river's depths.

"Good, good," Nicholas exclaimed. "This is perfect."

When Nicholas finished his work in that spot, they continued their journey to the next narrower channel in the river, where he repeated the process.

Fortunately, the water in the Ohio River was deeper now than it had been years before when Andrew first went down the river with his cousin Isaac and Captain Lewis. Because flatboat travel was becoming more common, men in flatboats had dug out deeper channels so the boats could easily maneuver the river without bottoming out.

Chapter 4

This trip was not just a fact-finding mission but a way for Nicholas to announce to the river communities that a steamboat would soon be traveling in the western waters. Not that there were many villages along the route. Most of the terrain between Pittsburgh and New Orleans was wilderness. Roosevelt carried letters of introduction to all the important people along the route, and those people lived in Cincinnati, Louisville, and Natchez. Only Cincinnati and Louisville on the Ohio River and Natchez on the Mississippi were home to more than two hundred people.

With a population of 2540, Cincinnati was the biggest town on the Ohio River and its first major stop. When their flatboat arrived in Cincinnati, Roosevelt located the town's leadership and discussed his plans with them. He explained that he planned to take a steamboat from Pittsburgh past Cincinnati. He also explained the steamboat's success on the Hudson in New York. The community received them kindly and hospitably entertained the members of the fancy Roosevelt flatboat.

The men listened intently to Roosevelt's proposal, but these gentlemen, gathered to hear what Roosevelt had to say about the steamboat, were hesitant to offer their support for a steamboat service down the Ohio. They would have to see it to believe it.

At the dock in Cincinnati, however, the boatmen and pilots mulling about at the pier were not as polite with their objections. They scoffed at the idea that a steamboat could ever traverse that part of the river.

After they left Cincinnati, Andrew stood by Roosevelt as they waved goodbye to the city inhabitants and took the rowboat back to their massive flatboat.

"Do you really think that you'll be able to build a steamboat to travel on these waters?" He asked.

Nicholas turned to the younger man. "Those other pilots don't believe it can be done, do they?"

"That's right," Andrew answered. "I have to admit, they do know these waters."

"I see that you still have doubts, too. Let me tell you. Nothing can shake my confidence in knowing that steamboats will soon be hauling manufactured goods down the rivers. Mark my words. Cotton and farm goods will soon travel up and down the Ohio and the Mississippi faster in a week than all the keelboats, barges, and flatboats that have ever gone down these rivers. It will change the way we do business in this country. Towns will sprout up in places you never thought possible. Just you wait and see."

"I wish I had your confidence in this project," Andrew said.

"You will, Andrew. I know you will."

I'll do my best to help you succeed, Mr. Roosevelt."

"Mr. Roosevelt? Don't call me that. Mr. Roosevelt was my father's name. Call me Nicholas. You and I are at the beginning of something big. We're undertaking the mysteries of the Ohio and the Mississippi, and by Jove, I won't leave them until they reveal all their secrets."

"I don't know anything about secrets that the rivers might hold, Nicholas. However, I can navigate the river for you."

"That's all I ask."

Back at the boat, Lydia and Susanna were sitting in chairs on the deck, and the cook had a fishing pole in the water.

"Look here," said the cook. He held up a string full of river catfish. "I've got a mess from the river enough for dinner tonight! You would not believe the size of these things."

Andrew nodded. The fishing in Ohio was good, and it would be even better on the Mississippi River, which lay beyond the other side of the Falls of the Ohio River.

As they continued downriver, Andrew showed Nicholas what he knew about the river. He had been running the river for so long that he knew every shoal in both the Ohio and the Mississippi Rivers. There were only a few surprises.

Andrew saw that Nicholas applied his best engineering skills to understanding those rivers. He gauged the rivers' depths and measured the speed of the water. He obtained all the statistical information that the communities along the rivers could give him and jotted that information in his notebook.

As Andrew assisted Nicholas with his work, he too began to visualize the future of this country west of the Allegheny Mountains once steamboat travel took over these waters. It was an exciting dream. However, he still didn't see the endeavor as anything more than just a dream.

"It's going to take a lot of firewood to keep the steamboat running on the river," Nicholas told Andrew. "We'll have to stop every night and bring on a load of firewood."

"I hear that coal burns longer and hotter. I know where there's some coal a few miles down the river," Andrew replied. "It's not as good as the stuff around Pittsburgh, but it will do us better than firewood, at least for a few days."

"Where's that?" Nicholas asked.

"They have coal available at Shippingport."

"Shippingport?"

"Yes, it's on the other side of the falls. Many barge captains unload some cargo on their barge at Louisville so that the barge isn't as heavy when it goes over the falls. They then reload after they have cleared the shoals."

The village of Louisville had first been surveyed by Captain Thomas Bullitt in 1773. During the American Revolution, George Rogers Clark, his militia, and 60 civilian settlers settled on Corn Island on May

27, 1778. There, they constructed Fort-on-Shore. The town became a key point along the Ohio River because it stood at the headwaters of the falls. Here, heavily loaded flatboats were unloaded and reloaded down in Shippingport. This didn't help the town's population grow much. Louisville was just a transportation stop, not a place to settle. The population remained at less than four hundred people.

In 1780, Louisville was chartered, and Jefferson County was established with Louisville as the county seat. The Louisville Gazette newspaper soon began its publication.

The shoreline along the Ohio at Louisville was an ugly scar on the landscape. Already, deforestation, erosion, and the mining of Louisville's limestone caused the island's land mass to shrink. The absence of trees near the river created deep ruts along the riverbank on either side of the wooden pier. The Louisville Cement Company extracted rock for cement near the riverbank, thus compounding the problem.

When the Roosevelt flatboat arrived in Louisville, Nicholas shared his information about the steamboat with the local leaders. They seemed cordial, but again, Andrew could see that the community leaders didn't believe any steamboat would ever arrive in Louisville. Like Andrew and the citizens of Cincinnati, the residents of Louisville would have to see it to believe it.

Andrew had known Nicholas long enough already to know that Roosevelt would build a steamboat and that he would take it at least as far as the falls. However, Andrew feared that any huge steamboat would break up as it attempted the falls. He believed that if, by some miracle, it did clear the falls, it would not be able to fight the current of the Mississippi to go upstream. Plus, no way existed where a steamboat could travel up over the falls from Shippingport to Louisville. He was certain that Nicholas would realize that after they cleared the falls.

After their visit to Louisville ended, it was time to go over the falls. Andrew discussed preparations for their descent with Nicholas.

"I want the women to stay back in the cabin when we go over the falls," Andrew told Nicholas as they were getting ready for their descent over the falls.

Lydia must have overheard him say that because she came over. With her hands on her hips, she stated. "I will not stay in the cabin. Susanna can go back to the cabin, but I will not!"

Nicholas looked helplessly at Andrew and then at his wife. He then turned his attention back to Andrew.

"I'm certain she won't be any trouble.

Andrew threw up his hands. "Suit yourself. It's your boat."

Andrew half expected Nicholas to reprimand him for being an insulant, but all he said was. "As you wish, Lydia."

"I think Susanna should have the right to choose whether she wants to go back to the cabin," Lydia replied.

Susanna decided she would join Lydia and experience the trip near the bow of the boat.

As they went over the falls, waves pounded the deck, and by the end of the trip, everyone on board was soaked to the skin.

Andrew glanced over Susanna's slim form under her thin, soaked gown. He turned away.

At least he showed discretion, she thought.

Susanna saw that Andrew noticed how her wet clothes appeared transparent, and noticed that he turned away.

Susanna followed Lydia's lead. After passing the falls, the women sat in the sun. Neither woman changed from her wet clothes but allowed the fabric to dry on her. Lydia seemed oblivious to the men aboard as they removed their braids and brushed their long hair as they sat in their deck chairs.

Susanna knew Lydia's behavior was improper but chose not to mention it.

As the women dried in the sun, Susanna saw that Lydia's baby bump was prominent now. No one could question now that she was pregnant.

Lydia's morning sickness had subsided, and her contentedness made Susanna envious.

Susanna imagined having a child of her own. She imagined that she was pregnant herself. She imagined what it would be like to have a baby bump. She then imagined having given birth to a child. She imagined the midwife handing her a blanket, which Susanna knew held her child. Susanna imagined smiling and taking the baby. She imagined pulling the blanket off the baby's face into the baby's face, and she saw a baby's face that looked like the one she imagined Andrew must have looked like when he was a child.

What was she thinking? Susanna shook her head as if that would shake those thoughts from her mind. She should, could not, think those thoughts! Thinking thoughts like this was not at all proper.

Once Lydia's long, thick hair was dry, Susanna helped her braid it.

At the same time, on the river's northern bank, Andrew and Nicholas rowed out to Shippingport in the rowboat.

They saw a small cabin near the river on the outskirts of town and followed the path to it.

Andrew knocked on the door. A man answered.

"Andrew, it's great to see you!" the man exclaimed.

"Great to see you too, William. I brought my employer by to meet you. He has a proposition for you," Andrew replied. "William Landers, meet Nicholas Roosevelt."

"Good to meet you, Mr. Roosevelt," William Landers put out his hand, and the two shared a hearty handshake.

"Call me Nicholas," Nicholas replied.

"Alright, and you can call me William. What can I do for you, Nicholas?"

"Andrew here tells me you have a hillside full of coal."

"I sure do. I don't have much use for it, though. There are so many treetops lying around for firewood hereabouts that no one uses it except for maybe a few blacksmiths. They usually dig it up for themselves."

"Well, I just might have a use for it," Nicholas said and then explained about his plans for the riverboat.

"I guess I can get some of my men to dig some up for you. When do you plan to need the coal?"

"That I'm not sure. I must build the craft first."

"And you think coal is a better option than wood?"

This time, Andrew spoke up. "Coal offers a hotter fire that lasts longer than wood does."

Nicholas continued. "It would be a better option than wood because we wouldn't have to stop to refresh our fuel for the steamboat every day."

Mr. Landers nodded. "We do use some coal for heating in the winter, but it's not the best coal I've worked with."

"It still would last longer than wood," Nicholas said. "I imagine that we'll find a lot more uses for coal's efficiency as time goes on, whether we have wood or not. I'll want to be able to load as much coal as possible onto the boat from the mine that we open here when I bring the steamboat past Shippingport."

William Landers was quiet while Nicholas and Andrew talked. Andrew was certain that he was listening intently to what was being said.

"Well, let's go," William finally said. William grabbed one of his shovels and led them out to a hillside by the river. He forced the shovel into the ground, dug out a piece of rock from the soil, and handed it to Nicholas, who looked at it. He then handed the rock to Andrew to examine.

Andrew rolled the dirty rock around in his hands. The coal was brown with black streaks. This coal came from resins, spores, waxes, and cutaneous and cork materials of terrestrial vascular plants. This coal accumulated in ponds and shallow lakes in peat-forming swamps and bogs. These coal seams were shallow and were found above other deposits, while the coal itself, rich in oils, burned long, with a bright yellow flame and left little ash.

This coal had a lower fixed carbon than typical bituminous coal. It included various amounts of vitrinite and inertinite, and some inorganic materials, but Andrew could see an organic component too. It wasn't perfect, but it would still last longer than wood.

It's coal alright, but it doesn't look like the coal available around Pittsburgh."

"Like I said, it's not the same. This coal is called Cannelton coal. Another name for it is candle coal. It's a type of bituminous coal due to its low mineral content. This rock is coal, but by its texture and composition of the organic matter, it is a type of oil shale. It's a lot like bog-head coal, too."

"I see," Nicholas replied. "I would still like for you to consider digging and selling me some of this coal."

"No, but I will sell you the land where the coal is located. I could then have some of my men dig it for you. If you're willing to pay them."

Nicholas looked at Andrew. Nicholas's mouth was set in a stiff line. "How much do you want for the land and your employees' services?"

William Landers named his price. Nicholas didn't even flinch. He reached into his pocket and pulled out a bag of coins, and handed them to Mr. Landers. Landers took the money. After William returned his shovel to its place in his shed, the three men went to the courthouse where Landers signed the title over to Nicholas. Landers returned home, while Nicholas and Andrew returned to the flatboat.

After they returned to the flatboat in their rowboat, Nicholas and Andrew winched the rowboat onto the flatboat.

"Why did you let Landers cheat you on the price of the land? That land wasn't worth that much. You could have talked him into selling the property and hiring men to do the work for less than half that amount." Andrew said as they tarped the rowboat so that it wouldn't take on water if it rained

"I might have been able to get it for less. Then again, I doubt he has any idea of the value of the coal along that riverbank. I'll probably recoup what I paid for the men and the land in just coal. Once steamboats make regular stops in this area, that coal will be worth more than I paid for the land," Nicholas replied. "Plus, I figure that by paying him what he wants, he's more likely to follow through with his end of the bargain and get his men to dig that coal for us."

"Do you think so?" Andrew asked.

"I do. There's more to my decision than just gaining access to that coal. I believe that once steamboats run between Pittsburgh and Louisville, this riverside property will be worth more than I paid because it lies along the Ohio."

"You think so?" Andrew asked.

"Is that all you can say? Of course, I believe it. I'm surprised you doubt me."

Andrew shook his head. "It's all just theory to me. You've seen a steamboat run upriver. I have not."

"In other words, you'll believe it when you see it. I'm certain that many others feel the same way you do. I look forward to the day that you view the steamboat on the Ohio and Mississippi as more than just a theory. If all goes well. We will all see steamboats on all the major rivers in this country in a few years."

Days later, they stopped at the small village of New Madrid to supply fresh produce, a town along the Mississippi known for its fresh vegetables and fruit.

"Do you know much about this village?" Nicholas asked as he threw the mooring rope up to Andrew, who fastened the boat's rope.

"I have been through this town many times. The Spanish granted the District of New Madrid to Colonel George Morgan."

"How big of an area is it?" Nicholas asked.

Andrew knew that this wasn't simply a casual question. Nicholas was also trying to determine where future steamboat landings could be located.

"The land extends from the Cinque Homme, south to the mouth of the St. Francois, and west a distance of ten or fifteen miles, though the western boundary. The northern part of this district is the District of

Cape Girardeau. Later, the New Madrid District was created, bounded on the north by Tywappity Bottoms. The exact property line between the Cape Girardeau district and the New Madrid district is a gray area right now. No one is sure exactly who owns what. No one even seems to care."

"Has there been a settlement here long?"

"Since 1783, but before any settlement existed here, there was a temporary trading post called "L'Anse a la Graise"."

"What does that mean?"

"It means 'cove of grease". Don't ask me why they chose that name. Some say that it's because they had a lot of stores of bear meat, and others say it was named because hunters killed a lot of game here, and a lot of them were bears. Others say that it is because of the richness of the soil. Any of those could explain why, but they might all be wrong."

"So that's when the settlement started to develop?"

Andrew shrugged. "I guess. People began settling here in 1783 when two Canadian trappers, Francois and Joseph LeSieur, who regularly came to the territory to hunt and trade with the Indians, decided to lay down roots here. Other trappers and traders started doing the same thing."

Andrew had never seen the trading post, but he had heard about it from long-time settlers in the area.

The trading post had been situated on Chapoose Creek's east bank. The creek's name had since been called St. John's Bayou. It couldn't be a better place to put a town. The town extends along the great ridge from the foothills to the mouth of the St Francois River. This is one of the most fertile areas along the Mississippi River. This ridge touched the river. It had immense quantities of the best quality timber. A lake of clear, limpid water was within a short distance of New Madrid. The woods were swarming with game. Andrew had taken time to go hunting in the area several times.

He couldn't think of a better climate anywhere. The soil is rich and productive.

"I believe this place to be the most attractive site along the whole course of the river, Andrew said. "I might even consider settling here myself."

Andrew threw the rowboat's tow rope up to a local man on shore.

"Hello there! Well, if it isn't Andrew Mayford," the local said. "Mighty fine boat you have there. Who's this fellow?"

"Thank you. Let me introduce myself. I'm Nicholas Roosevelt," Nicholas replied.

"I'm Jeremiah Williams," he replied. "I'm pleased to meet you."

The two men shook hands.

"Andrew was just telling me about your settlement here. He said he might want to settle here."

Williams smiled. "I can't think of a better place to live. The Indians seemed to think so, too, because there is evidence of a past civilization here. The whole country around here is dotted with Indian mounds. I think New Madrid was once perhaps the seat of government for the extensive empire."

"Andrew tells me that the LeSieurs lived and traded in the area for several years, and other hunters and traders came."

"Yes, and then Colonel George Morgan had a dream of founding a great city here."

Who was George Morgan?" Nicholas said.

The local man replied. "Morgan is an American. He's fond of the life of the woods and has an adventurous spirit. He's one of the boldest, daring, and far-sighted men I've ever met. He visited this area about the time of the transfer from France to Spain, paddled up and down its rivers, selected promising sites for settlements, and decided to establish an empire here."

Didn't you tell me once that he took part in the Revolutionary War?" Andrew asked.

"He did," Williams answered. " At one time, he had been a man of considerable influence and had a high position in the United States. However, he became indignant about how the United States treated him. He had acquired a large tract of land from the Indians, enough to make him independently wealthy, but the United States government policy never recognized the validity of an Indian transfer. They don't believe that Indians have any power or authority to alienate any lands. Because he lost his lands, he was practically penniless. He tried to gain access, but he was denied. That's when he decided to create this settlement here within Spanish territory."

"He sounds like a man not willing to give up," Nicholas replied.

"He's not!" the man exclaimed. "He was moved by a desire for wealth, and partly by a desire to avenge himself on the United States by helping to build up the power of Spain. He came into correspondence with Don Diego Gardoqui, the Spanish minister at Washington."

"How do you know so much about Mr. Morgan?" Nicholas asked.

"He's my neighbor," Williams answered and then continued his story. He seemed like the type of person who loved talking, especially about his wealthy neighbor. "Morgan pointed out to the minister the immense importance to Spain of colonizing her territory west of the Mississippi River and of inducing settlers from America to emigrate there. He knows the West, and he has a real ability to induce settlers into the area. This caught the fancy of Gardoqui, who agreed to his scheme. Under the arrangement they entered, Morgan was to receive a land grant that reached from the Cinque Homme to the mouth of the St. Francois River, a distance of about three hundred miles. The grant was to extend some twelve or fifteen miles westward from the river and thus to include between twelve and fifteen million acres of land. Morgan pointed out to the minister that if Americans were to be induced to settle on these lands certain things must be granted to them. It was accordingly agreed that Americans should be exempt from taxation and that they needed the right to govern themselves. In addition to these inducements, Mr. Morgan offered prospective colonists cheap land, because he expected to sell parts of his enormous holdings for small sums."

"Sounds reasonable," Nicholas nodded.

"Part of Morgan's scheme was to induce Indians from east of the river to settle in Spanish territory. This was to be done, in part, on account of trading with the Indians, and, in part, so that they might serve to protect the Spanish territory, especially against the Osage Indians who lived along the Missouri River. Morgan promised Gardoqui that if the grant was made on the terms they agreed upon, within a very few years the population of the district should have at least one thousand persons."

"That sounds like a paying proposition."

"It would have been, but sadly, the Spanish government was no better to Morgan than the United States government. It seems he was deceived about Gardoqui's authority to make the land grant. He believed that he had secured the land grant from the Spanish government. In the winter of 1789, he descended the Ohio River with a huge party of American and Indian settlers. He selected this site for his town. I was among those people. We named the town New Madrid to honor the Spanish government. He left a large part of the expedition here while he and some others went upriver to St. Louis, to meet the lieutenant-governor of the district who resided there. The lieutenant governor received him with great favor and agreed to Morgan's plans. Morgan returned to carry out his plans for this settlement. He laid out the village site and had the surrounding lands surveyed."

Nicholas listened intently to Williams' story. Like Morgan, Nicholas was a visionary who thought years ahead of other men.

Williams continued talking about Morgan and New Madrid. "Because the soil was so good around here, Morgan planned to grow great quantities of corn, tobacco, hemp, cotton, flax, and indigo. He believed the land was too rich for wheat. He saw the land as perfect for farming for over a thousand miles. I agree, the country rises gradually from the Mississippi and is a fine, dry, agreeable, and healthy land, superior, we believe, in beauty and quality to those of any part of America. Morgan planned to extend New Madrid about four miles south on the bank of the St Francois River and two miles to the west of it, so that it is divided by a deep lake of the purest fresh water. The banks of this lake, called Santa Anna, are high, beautiful, and pleasant. Its water is deep, clear, and fresh. Its bottom is clean sand, without logs, grass, or other vegetation, and it abounds in fish."

"Sounds like a great basis for a community."

"He had great plans for our town. On each side of this fine lake, streets, one hundred feet broad, have been marked out, and a road of equal width about the same. Trees have been marked, which must be preserved for the health and recreation of the citizens. Another street, one hundred and twenty feet wide, has been marked out on the bank of the Mississippi."

"Impressive," Nicholas said. He was getting tired of the man's talking, but Andrew knew that this was the kind of conversation that Nicholas thought could lead to important information.

Williams kept talking.

"Uh-huh," Nicholas continued listening.

Andrew didn't know how long this man would continue talking. They had things to do. They were there to get fresh fruits and vegetables, not to hear this man talk. Nicholas didn't seem to notice.

"We constructed cabins and a storehouse for provisions, and we made gardens and cleared one hundred acres of land in the most beautiful meadow in the world to sow corn, hemp, flax, cotton, tobacco, and potatoes."

"Sounds like it was a good plan."

"We had some issues, though. The timber here is different in some kinds of trees from that in the central states of America. However, we have found white oak, high and straight, of extraordinary size, as well as black oak, mulberry, ash, white poplar, persimmon, and apples in abundance, and larger than those which we have hitherto seen. We have hickory and walnut trees too. The sassafras here is very straight and extraordinarily large. Most of it can't be less than 24 inches in diameter. The shrubs around here are mostly cane and spice wood. Some of the timber here is unknown back east. The timbers include juniper, pecan, coffee, cucumber, and some others. Juniper grows on the lowlands at the edge of the river. I'd say that its quality is equal to that of white cedar. We have a fine grove of these trees in our neighborhood."

"We'd like to visit Mr. Morgan?" Nicholas asked.

"Oh, certainly. I'll take you there."

The man continued talking as they walked through the town.

The Street we're walking on is King Street. It's the continuation of the middle road and extends to the Mississippi River."

Nicholas nodded.

Andrew noticed that the streets north of King Street, extended from east to west, were called First North Street, Second North Street, and so on, reckoning from King's Street. The streets south of King Street were named First South Street, Second South Street. The streets extending north and south were distinguished by First River Street, Second River Street, and so on.

"If you'll notice," Williams said. "The two lots No. 13 on each side of King Street are hereby given forever to the citizens. On the south side was the Roman Catholic school, and on the north side of the street is the Roman Catholic church."

"So the city here has church sites for various denominations?"

Jeremiah Williams explained. "Two lots on the south side are for an Episcopal school if it gets built, and on the north side for an Episcopal church. Another two lots on the south side were given to the Presbyterian school and church. Another two lots were given on North Street to a German Lutheran school and church. The German Calvinistic school and church were also permanently given lots."

"Sounds like a welcoming place," Nicholas replied.

"We want everyone to feel like they have a home here," Williams said as they continued inland. Every landing on the river opposite the city is equally free for everyone and is patrolled by the police magistrates."

Nicholas looked around at the tree-lined streets.

"It looks like a park here."

"We planned New Madrid that way. We don't allow indiscriminate tree-cutting here. No trees in any street of the city, nor along any road throughout the country, can be damaged, or be cut down, but under the direction of the police magistrates, or an officer that they appoint, who shall be accountable on the premises. No timber can be injured or cut down in any street or road, and it is not available for private use under any circumstances."

A tiny log cabin came into view.

"That's my place," he said. "Morgan's place is just over that rise."

He pointed to a hill just beyond the cabin. As they climbed the hill's steep bank, he continued his narrative.

"The banks of the Mississippi, throughout the territory, are considered a highway and will keep open forever as such. Thanks to George Morgan, every navigable river throughout the territory has been determined as a highway, and no obstruction to navigation can be made at that part of the river system."

"Good to know," Nicholas replied.

Andrew could see Nicholas' mind churning. He imagined that Nicholas was picturing a steamboat landing here."

As Williams, Nicholas, and Andrew crested the hill, they saw a cabin similar to Williams' cabin. It was not at all what they expected of a wealthy landowner.

Williams called out to the front door of the cabin. "Hey, Morgan! It's me, Williams."

"Hey, Williams, what's up, my friend?"

"I met these two men at the river, and they said that they wanted to meet you."

"Well, come in. Come in," Morgan said. He opened his door wide and invited the men in. He offered them a seat and poured whiskey for everyone, and straddled a chair. "What brings you out to these parts?"

"I'm researching to find out where we can port future steamboats," Nicholas answered.

"I've heard that they had them back east. What makes you think that they're stout enough to handle currents on the Mississippi?"

"I'm confident that I can build one that has enough power to go up and down this river or any river, for that matter."

"That's a pretty big order," Morgan stated.

Nicholas shrugged. "I'm up to it."

"I assume that Jeremiah here filled you in on how things work here in New Madrid."

Nicholas nodded. "He was telling me all about how wonderful this place is."

"I figured he would. We haven't been without our problems. Many settlers were attracted by the generous conditions on which land was granted and by the site's desirability, and I accomplished much of what I wanted. My plans, however, conflicted with Governor Miro, the Spanish governor of Louisiana's plans, whose headquarters were in New Orleans and who was engaged in an intrigue with General James Wilkinson."

"But you had the land grant."

"True, but Wilkinson was an officer in the United States Army in command of the district along the Mississippi River. He planned with Miro to incite a rebellion among the people of the United States west of the Alleghenies, to separate this territory from the United States and join it to the Spanish territory. Wilkinson drew a pension from the Spanish government and hoped his efforts would secure that territory of the United States for Spain."

"A troublemaker, huh?"

"Indeed. My plan of drawing settlers to New Madrid and making that a prosperous and flourishing center of trade for Upper Louisiana directly opposed Wilkinson's vision. He was my rival, so Wilkinson sought to thwart my plans. He wrote to Governor Miro that he had applied for a grant in the Yazoo country to destroy my claims here. He told Miro that I was an educated and intelligent man, but a thorough speculator. He also told the governor that I had been twice bankrupted. He said that I was very poor but very ambitious. He said that he had a spy researching my agreement with Don Diego Gardoqui. He said he was convinced that my scheme would be successful unless they, he and Miro, took steps to counteract it."

"A regular scoundrel," Williams said.

Morgan continued his story. "Wilkinson assured Miro that their plans would be greatly hindered if I carried out my plans for my settlement. Acting on this information, Governor Miro sought to put an end to my operations. On May 20, 1789, he wrote to the Spanish government protesting against my grant. He said that it formed a state within a state and asked the government to cancel this grant."

"That's terrible," Nicholas said.

"At the same time, Miro wrote to me himself and charged me with having exceeded my authority and dared to accuse me of acting in bad faith. He said that I had no authority to lay out a town and provide for a government. He informed me that he intended to construct a fort at New Madrid and place a detachment of soldiers to control the situation. I saw that this interference would ruin all my hopes. I wrote back, saying that if I had, indeed, exceeded my authority, I had only done it because I was anxious to serve the King of Spain."

"And you had all those settlers from back east there to prove Wilkinson's point," Andrew replied.

"Right, I could not conceal this fact from those colonists who had come and were still coming to New Madrid, that I had fallen out of favor with the government. The colonists complained about some of the regulations and finally sent an agent, John Ward, to present a petition to Governor Miro. Acting on this petition, Miro carried out his threat and sent a company of soldiers with orders to construct a fort at New Madrid and to take entire charge of the government of the post. This practically destroyed my influence, and with its loss went my settlement at New Madrid. The post continued under the government of Spanish officials."

Morgan continued telling them about New Madrid.

"Many of the early settlers stayed anyway. In 1795, fever struck the inhabitants. The settlement of Fort St. Fernando occasioned a hasty cleaning out of the little corn in the colony. Kentucky furnished a little, and Saint Genevieve supplied a great deal, even to New Madrid, which fell short after exhausting her supply. This example struck the inhabitants. They saw that they could sell their surplus if they had harvested extensively. The inhabitants desired to create farms to raise stock and to make crops."

"Which is why you have crops available to sell today," Andrew said.

"Exactly. Several American families came to New Madrid; some of them became farmers. They began cultivating in 1796. The first attempts at farming were difficult, but the inducement of disposing of their crops with ease made them work that much harder. It was not farmers who came and laid the foundation, it was tradesmen, cooks, and others who lived there with little expense and labor. Once white men fixed there with their lands and cattle, the Indians left the area and no longer traded near the settlement. It didn't matter much because by then we had the produce to trade with the towns downriver."

"Sounds like the settlers had a good thing going."

"Not that the government made it easy. An officer, Lieutenant Pierre Forcher, in charge of thirty soldiers, came to take charge of a post that was set up near the town between Bayou St. John and the Decyperi. The fort, built on the bank of the Mississippi River, was named Fort Celeste. It was named in honor of Governor Miro's wife. Commandant Forcher was an energetic man. His administrative ability reigned in the community. Eighteen months later, Thomas Portell took over the post. Portell was a man better suited to the place, governed with justice, and was able to satisfy most of the people. In 1798, Pierre Antoine La Forge took command from Charles Dehault De Lassus was appointed military as civil commandant of the post and district of New Madrid. La Forge was a resident of the post."

"When was the road built between New Madrid and St. Louis?"

"It was built around 1789. The Spanish government laid out the road connecting New Madrid with St. Louis. This road crossed Big Prairie, passed through the "Rich Woods" across Scott County to Cape Girardeau, past Saint Genevieve, and on to St. Louis. The road followed the old Indian trail along which the Spanish explorer Hernando de Soto probably traveled. The Spanish decided on this route because the Indians used its great sandy ridge to skirt the "Big Swamp" south of Cape Girardeau to Caruthersville in Pemiscot County. The Spanish called this road "El Camino Real," the King's Highway. In 1803, De Lassus led an expedition to New Madrid to widen the road. Last year, the Territorial Assembly of the District of Louisiana ordered that a road be opened between St. Louis and New Madrid. This road, doubtless, followed that same old Spanish road, the King's Highway."

"It still seems like New Madrid is a nice little place to settle."

"I agree. Not that it's without its problems. The town contains about a hundred houses scattered on a fine plain two miles square. However, erosion along the river has encroached on the town during the twenty-two years since it was first settled. The bank is a half mile behind its old bounds, and the inhabitants had to move away from the eroding shore."

"That does sound like a problem that could be rectified with good engineering. What kind of people live here?"

"The inhabitants are a mixture of French Creoles from Illinois, United States Americans, and Germans. They have plenty of cattle, but others see them as very poor. There is some trade with the Indian hunters of furs and pelts, but it is no longer of any consequence. Because we are so far from civilization and everything must be boated in, dry goods and groceries are enormously high. That's why the inhabitants have to charge travelers immense prices for any fresh commodities such as milk, butter, fowls, eggs, etc. There is a militia, the officers of which wear cockades as a mark of distinction, although the rest of their dress should be only a dirty, ragged shirt and trousers."

"Perhaps when the steamboat services become available, we can change all that."

"It would be wonderful to see this community grow. Few settlers live outside our small settlement. Too many robbers and counterfeiters. They make it difficult for honest folks to make a living around here. You know how it is, Andrew. Your flatboaters descending the river must travel in well-armed convoys and under the lead of some experienced commander, like yourself. If you didn't, you are certain to be attacked, killed, or robbed of your effects by these robbers who were settled at different points on the river."

Andrew nodded. He did know. River pirates were common along the Mississippi. Not a day passed that some innocent man, the owner of some flatboat loaded with produce, had been tricked into accepting counterfeit money.

"Scarcely a day passes when some tradesman isn't offered some of those counterfeit bills," Morgan said. "I keep telling them to accept nothing but gold or barter goods, but the newcomers don't always get the message until it's too late."

Andrew nodded. The whole country from Evansville, Indiana, to Natchez was filled with such people. They ruled and controlled the country. Andrew knew better than to trade his goods for paper money with anyone, especially along the river.

Morgan told them that other settlements had begun to be settled within the territory of New Madrid County. Some were made on Lake St. Ann, along the St. Johns Bayou, at Lake St. Mary, and on Bayou St. Thomas. The district of New Madrid included not only New Madrid County but also Pemiscot, Mississippi, Scott Counties, and even the counties lying further west.

The first settlement in Pemiscot County was made at Little Prairie. The settlement was made in 1794 by Francois LeSieur, who came to Little Prairie from New Madrid, where he had previously lived. On receiving the grant of land laid out about two hundred arpents (he informed them that an arpent was a French unit of measurement used before the metric system. An arpent was equal to about 78.15470 yards) into a town divided into lots, each containing an arpent. Here, a fort was also constructed called Fort St. Fernando. Little Prairie's site was well chosen because it was situated on a great ridge and touched the river, and the surrounding country was rich in soil, timber, and game. There was considerable trade with the Indians. Because of these advantages, the town prospered. The population was seventy-eight in 1799, and in 1803 it numbered one hundred and three.

Besides this settlement at Little Prairie, there were other settlements within Pemiscot County, but Morgan didn't know much about them.

When King's Highway was built from Saint Genevieve to New Madrid in 1789, several settlements also sprang up in Scott County. Captain Charles Friend, a native of Virginia, founded one of these early settlements in 1796. He received a grant from the Spanish government and moved his family there. He had nine sons and two daughters in his family, and most continue to live close to the land of that Spanish grant.

Another town founder, Joseph Johnson, made the first settlement in Mississippi County around 1800 near Bird's Point. Another early settlement was called St. Charles Prairie. He sold his land in 1805 to Abraham Bird, and he renamed the settlement Bird's Point."

Chapter 5

Morgan and Williams directed Nicholas and Andrew to families he knew in the area who had produce, eggs, and milk to sell, and that night, the crew and passengers of the flatboat shared in the fresh bounty.

The travelers on the flatboat continued downstream.

We're in Chickasaw country, now," Andrew told Nicholas on the day after they left New Madrid. "I have never had trouble with them, but a friend of mine once said that they tried to board his keelboat once."

Nicholas appeared uneasy. Just the mention of Indians seemed to put the man on edge.

They were now below the small villages and above the more densely populated areas around Natchez and New Orleans. They were in the most desolate part of the Mississippi. The most dangerous, too, because here there were not only Indians, but river pirates that Morgan warned them about. The crew remained watchful on this stretch of the river for any possible attack.

One day, as she worked on her needlework, Susanna saw a darker-skinned woman dressed in a knee-length deerskin dress and leggings. The woman cautiously came to the river with a bucket. When she saw the flatboat, she dipped her bucket into the water and scurried and hid in the tree cover.

As the flatboat passed, she looked straight at Susanna. She was tall and her face was angular and high cheekbones. She had straight black hair. Her eyes were brown. Both women stared at each other. Susanna wondered if the woman was curious about her lifestyle in the same way that Susanna was curious about the woman's way of living.

As they passed the place where the woman was hiding, she realized that Andrew stood beside her and that he was also watching the woman. She felt a chill run down her spine at the idea that Andrew was so close.

Without turning toward him, she asked, "Who are they?"

"Indians, of course," Andrew answered.

"I know that they are Indians. What tribe do they belong to?"

"They are a tribe we call the Chickasaw. Look over there. Can you see beyond those trees there?"

She followed the direction of his pointing finger. Beyond the trees, she saw houses built on stilts.

"Those are their homes. They call them Chickees."

Susanna saw that these Chickee stilt houses had no walls. The homes were built on thick posts supporting a thatched roof and a flat wooden platform raised several feet off the ground.

Andrew continued telling her about them. "These homes are where the Chickasaw live during the summer. These shelters are built along riverbanks, marshes, and waterways. They are built on stilts because of spring flooding. Their winter village homes are further inland, away from the areas that normally flood in the spring. Those homes are made of wattle and daub."

"Where do they get their tools for building?" She asked

"They used to build with stone axes, but now they trade furs for metal tools. My cousin Robert, up in Pennsylvania, made some axes for me a couple of years ago as pay for my services to their community. I sold the axes to the Chickasaw, and I made a fair profit. However, going all the way up there was not worth the effort to get axes. If I wanted to sell axes for trading posts to sell along the Mississippi, I could find blacksmiths nearer the river. However, rather than do that, I have found that taking goods down to Natchez is much more profitable for me. Plus, the area where Robert lives has become much more settled. He found that he can do more business locally, so it's not worth it for him to send his tools down this way."

"What other changes has trading with the white man created for these Indians?"

They have begun building their village homes with American-style log cabins and have even started fortifying them with palisades to guard against attack."

"Attack from whom? The white man?" Susanna felt a chill run down her spine. Andrew touched her on the shoulder.

"Don't worry, the Chickasaw have peace treaties with us. Mostly, they need protection from other warring tribes."

"I always thought that the Indians were all under the same treaties."

"That's a wrong assumption," Andrew replied. "Although there are similarities, each tribe has its individual traditions, culture, and even language."

"What language do the Chickasaw speak?"

"They speak in several related dialects of the Muskogean language family, similar to the Choctaws, but, of course, many now speak English, French, and Spanish."

"Hmm, interesting. It might be fun to speak my native language with an indigenous tribe."

"Indigenous tribe? That's a fancy word." Andrew smiled. "Not one I would expect from a lady's maid."

Susanna blushed. "Don't try to make this conversation about me. I want to know more about the Chickasaw. What kind of food do they eat?"

"Pretty much like most of the people who live in the frontier. For that matter, the whites on the frontier started eating what the Indians had eaten for centuries. Frontier food comes from the Indian traditions. They eat beans, corn, and squash that they grow in what they call a three-sisters' garden."

"Why do they call them the three sisters?"

"It's because they grow together on the same land."

"Does it produce more growth that way?"

"That's a good question. The answer is a little complicated. If they grew just one crop on the land, they would grow more of that one crop, but when they grow all the crops together, they produce more than any single crop would produce on the same land."

"Really? So, do they eat only vegetables? Do they raise livestock?"

"Well, they don't keep livestock like we do, but they don't just eat vegetables. The Chickasaw hunt deer, bears, wild turkeys, small game, and fish that they obtain on long hunting excursions throughout the Mississippi Valley region. Some even travel to the plains to hunt buffalo. Their diet is also supplemented with various nuts, fruits, and herbs. They know how to live off the land."

"Do you know all their ways?"

"Not as well as some of my relatives do, like my cousin Isaac and his father Luke."

"Oh, does he live in Pennsylvania?"

Andrew shook his head. "No, he and his wife's family are settled north of St. Louis."

"You have a sister who lives in Boston, right?"

Andrew nodded and then turned and looked at her questioningly. "How do you know this? I don't remember my mother saying anything about this when you were nearby."

Susanna chuckled. "Servants do talk too. You know."

Andrew chuckled. "Yes, I do know."

"You seem to be the only person in your family who sees the servants as people. Everyone else I know treats us like property. Sometimes I have to remind myself of that."

"Don't you let Lydia hear you say that," Andrew warned.

"Lydia is somewhat different, too. Sometimes she sees me as a mentor, but other times, she views me as a servant. I must always adjust to her moods."

"I find you an amazing person, Susanna."

Susanna experienced that overwhelming sensation that her entire world was suffocating her. Andrew had become an integral part of it, and she was afraid of what would happen if he no longer wanted to be with her. His world was not her world. Although he came from a rich family, he was a riverboat man. She did not know his world. She couldn't imagine him settling down in a house like his parents' home just to be with her.

He seemed to be infatuated with her now, but what would happen when this trip was over and she returned to New York with the Roosevelts? Would he still think of her then?

His face came closer to her face. *Was he going to kiss her?*

Susanna would not find out because at that moment, PJ yelled. "Hey, Andrew! Can you come to the boat's bow?"

PJ called Andrew to the boat's bow. Susanna continued watching the shoreline.

Andrew seemed so easy to talk to, but Susanna wasn't enough of a fool to think that he was being anything but kind to her. He was the son of a wealthy man and had earnings of his own. If things went the way her employer thought, Andrew would be rich in his own right. He was a river man who was never likely to settle down, especially with one of the hired servants.

Susanna continued to watch the shoreline. On the shore, she saw many different species of birds. She watched a deer come to the water's edge to drink. Further downriver, she spotted a bear clawing at a tree a few yards from the riverbank.

She could see what Andrew saw in this river. Its natural beauty drew her in like the silky soft baths in the copper tub they had when she was a child. She had led an innocent life back then, but now, like the deer, she had to be wary of the dangers that life away from the safety of her life back in France had offered. Fortunately, she had learned without too much pain that life away from their chateau was as dangerous as that bear she had seen a few minutes earlier.

The dangers of the serenity of the natural world was overtaken by another potential danger. Further downriver, Susanna saw a man whose lower half of his body was with deerskin. He wore deerskin boots. He had no beard. His head was shaved except for a strip of hair on his head. His head and face were painted with snakes and other imagery.

She felt chills run down her spine when she saw him. She guessed that the markings on his body must have been tattoos, but she had never seen anyone with a tattoo before. *He wore a headdress* with red feathery material sticking out from it. On his upper body, he wore a long-sleeved linsey-woolsey shirt like she had seen other men wearing on the frontier. He was laying traps along a creek that spilled into the river.

Andrew came up beside her.

"Is he dangerous?"

"No, now, if he had a canoe, I might be concerned, but he's too busy trapping to pay us any mind."

"Good to know. What kind of headdress is that?" She asked.

"It's a roach-style headdress."

What's it made of?"

"Near as I can tell, it's made of the guard hair of a porcupine or the tail hair of a white-tail deer."

"But why is it red?"

"It's dyed red as a symbol that he's a combat veteran."

"You mean he…"

Andrew nodded. "Yes, he's fought against other tribes and probably white men."

Susanna gasped. "What kind of weapons do they have?" Susanna asked.

Andrew smiled. Their traditional weapons include war clubs, knives, bows and arrows, maces, and axes. That said, they now have muskets and rifles. Like we have."

He saw Susanna's eyes widen when she heard they had European weapons. "Don't worry. We're at peace with them right now. They are friendly with the United States. He probably never has battled against an American. The Chickasaw do have numerous Indian enemies, though, like the Choctaw, Creeks, Caddo, Kickapoo, Shawnee, Osage, Quapaw, and Yuchi. They are great military strategists, and their strength was to employ unexpected tactics."

"So, they are friendly with us." Susanna sighed and felt her body release the tension she was feeling.

Andrew nodded. "And I hope it stays that way. Things could change if some American makes a seriously wrong move. The Chickasaw people believe that the ghost of a dead warrior would haunt his relatives until he was avenged. They will seek retaliation and revenge - the only question is when and where they will come after whoever took that warrior's life."

"That's not reassuring."

"Maybe not, but I would never lie to you."

Andrew rested his arm against the railing next to Susanna. He could feel her warm arm against his. They both watched a pair of Chickasaw women dressed in knee-high buckskin dresses. One woman dressed in a simple linen and woolen dress came down a path toward where the women were washing clothes by beating them on rocks.

Further down the path, they saw two men wearing breech-cloths with thigh-high deerskin boots. These men had no body hair, and both had tattooed torsos and faces. Both men had scalp locks with a roach-style headdress adorned with feathers. They were wearing shirts like white men of the frontier.

"See that one man there? Those are swan feathers. He's highly honored among his people. Not just anyone can wear them."

"You know a lot about these people."

Andrew nodded. "I have had enough contact with them to respect them."

"You seem to know a lot about them for someone who doesn't know much about them."

"I said I didn't know as much about Indian tribes as some of my relatives did."

"Oh, I see."

A few nights later, Andrew was on watch when he observed some movement at the aft. At first, he thought it was one of the men going ashore to relieve himself, but soon, he realized that these were two people dressed in dark clothes and black painted faces.

They were trying to break into Roosevelt's quarters!

Andrew acted quickly. He grabbed his pistol and ran toward the back of the flatboat. He entered Roosevelt's dining room. There he saw Susanna dressed in her nightgown, standing in front of the pantry door. In front of her stood two Chickasaw Indians.

Immediately, he felt he needed to protect her. At that same moment, Nicholas came out of the bedroom wearing his nightclothes.

"What is going on here?" Nicholas asked.

"Whiskey, we want whiskey," one of the Indians said.

"No," Andrew replied. "No whiskey."

Nicholas turned toward Andrew as if to ask, "*Why not*?". Andrew shook his head. He had seen too many Indians act crazy from drinking even a little alcohol. "There's no whiskey here for you. Go away. Leave now!"

One of the two men pointed at the jugs under the table. "You no tell truth. You have whiskey. We want!"

Andrew raised his gun and pointed it at the Indians. "I told the truth. We have no whiskey for you. You must leave now."

The Indian who had spoken to them in English spoke to the other one in his native language, and the two of them left the boat.

Nicholas was shaking. "They were on the boat. I thought you said they were friendly."

"The Chickasaw are like any other people," Andrew replied. "There are good ones and some who are not so good. These were the second type. Now that they see that we will defend ourselves, they won't return. Let's go back to bed."

Susanna returned to bed, but Nicholas stayed up with Andrew because he wanted to be sure those men would not return with more of their friends to overtake the boat's crew.

Andrew had never seen Nicholas so worried about anything as he was after this encounter with the Indians.

"Are you okay, Nicholas?"

"I just didn't expect anyone to come onto the boat. What if they had harmed Susanna or barged into our quarters? I would never have been able to forgive myself."

"It didn't happen," Andrew said. "As you saw, they left. I'll just have to keep a better watch."

After they passed Chickasaw Bluffs, they came to a section where many gravel bars and small islands dotted the river. Andrew had to pay close attention to the channels.

"It's good that you know the river as well as you do, Andrew. I couldn't imagine maneuvering this stretch of the river without you."

"Fortunately, I have been here many times, but conditions do change, so I still have to keep a sharp eye out," Andrew said.

They finally arrived in Natchez

"Well, if it isn't Andrew Mayford," the man said. "

"Hey, Gilbert!" Andrew replied.

"What kind of load are you carrying this time?"

"We don't have a load this time. I'm taking these folks to New Orleans," Andrew replied.

"Is that a fact? Are you moving to New Orleans?" Gilbert asked Nicholas.

Nicholas shook his head. "No, I'm on a fact-finding mission. My name's Nicholas Roosevelt."

"Is that a fact? Well, I'm Gilbert Winters. What kind of fact-finding mission are you on?"

"I'm evaluating the feasibility of running a steamboat on the Mississippi."

"What's a steamboat?" Gilbert asked.

Nicholas explained what a steamboat was in more detail than Andrew thought was necessary. He could tell that Gilbert was faking interest in Nicholas's detailed description.

"And you think you can make a boat powered by steam powerful enough to run between Natchez here and New Orleans?"

Nicholas pressed his lips together and nodded. "I do."

"You're joshing me," Gilbert slapped his knee. "He's pulling my leg. Isn't he, Andrew?"

Andrew shook his head.

"Then you must be crazy, but then there are a lot of crazy folks in the world. Why, not so many years ago, a man made a cotton gin, and now we've got a fledgling cotton industry in the area."

Gilbert turned toward several other boatmen who were sitting around a fire. "Did you hear? This man is planning to put us out of business using a steam-powered boat."

All the men laughed.

Andrew expected Nicholas to become red-faced over the way that the boatmen poked fun at his plans. Instead, Nicholas didn't say a word. He just stood there listening to their banter and then said. "We made a successful navigation trip using the steam engine on the Hudson three years ago."

One of the boatmen, whom Andrew only knew by the name Pete, replied. "That may be true back east, but it can't be done on the Ohio and Mississippi. I can't imagine an engine made that can make a boat go upstream on its own."

Andrew was amazed at how they could not shake Nicholas's confidence. He did understand their disbelief, however. Nicholas may think that he can accomplish this amazing feat, but they wouldn't believe it until they saw it.

"From what Andrew tells me, the river becomes deeper with fewer hazards from here to New Orleans. I do not doubt that I can maneuver a boat down the Ohio and onto the Mississippi. I can get my supplies along the way. I have measured the river depths as I went along, and I've measured the currents and obtained all the information. I also made estimates as to the future development of the country. When I found coal banks along the Ohio, I purchased and opened them. I ordered coal to be mined and hope to have it laid aside when my steamboat, not yet built, should come along. All I need to do is get back east, get financing, and build the steamboat. It's that simple."

Andrew could see that the pilots and other boatmen were still not convinced that this venture could in any way possibly succeed. He knew that none of them would give him any words of encouragement. These people had spent their lives making their livelihood on traveling up and down the rivers. Many had developed chronic physical pain from years of poling upriver.

Some of them may have heard what he said about Fulton and Livingston's experience on the Hudson, but none of them thought that steamboats would be viable on these waters.

"Okay," Pete said. "So, let's say that you can take a boat up and down the Mississippi or the Ohio, but what about the choppy waters at the falls of the Ohio. There's no way that any boat can go up and down those falls regularly."

"I admit, the falls are a problem that we must conquer."

"See, I told you that it won't work. You can't make me believe that a steamboat will ever be able to resist the turbulent and whirling waters of the Ohio or the Mississippi. I would have to see it to believe it."

Andrew, too, began to doubt that Roosevelt could pull this steamboat enterprise off.

He had known these men for many years, and between them, they had a lot of experience.

After a hearty breakfast, Roosevelt's flatboat continued downstream.

That same afternoon, dark clouds gathered in the west. These foreboding clouds were typically found along the leading edge of a front or an outflow boundary from a collapsing thunderstorm.

"It looks as if we're going to get some rain," PJ said to Andrew.

Andrew evaluated the angry, dark cumulonimbus clouds. The shelf cloud was rolling toward the river. "It's more than just rain. We're going to be facing some strong, possibly damaging winds. Andrew nodded. "It looks like we're in for a bad one."

PJ squinted. The muscles on his forehead furrowed.

"Do you think there could be a tornado?"

Andrew shook his head. "While they can look scary, these clouds are not usually associated with tornadoes. The women should head inside until these winds pass."

"Should we tie up to something on the shore and wait out the storm?" Nicholas asked.

Andrew shook his head. "No, we'd be better off anchoring here in the center of the river. There are too many rocks in this part of the river. If we tie up to the shore, the winds could easily dash us against the rocks and ground the boat."

Nicholas nodded. "It's your call."

They stopped the boat by lowering the boat anchors.

Though he had piloted many boats down the Mississippi, Andrew had never piloted a boat this big before, and he wasn't sure how this one would react to a huge storm on the river. He wasn't sure this solution would work if the storm grew too extensive, but it was the only option that would allow the boat to survive if it was as bad as Andrew thought the approaching storm looked like it might become.

No sooner had the men lowered the anchors than gale-force winds shook the craft. Waves beat against the sides of the boat. The trees on the shore bent one way and then the other. Even though the shore was a hundred yards away, green leaves and small branches from the battered trees on shore whipped onto the barge's deck.

Despite Andrew's recommendation, the women did not take shelter in the ship's cabin.

"You need to get in the shelter!" Nicholas told Lydia. His voice could hardly be heard over the wind's roar.

Lydia shook her head. The wind blew her hair, and her skirts wrapped around her with every gust.

"No, there's got to be something that Susanna and I can do to help."

Andrew marveled at her tenacity.

Hail began to hit the deck and the roofs of the cabins on board the boat. Ice balls the size of silver dollars pinged off the water.

"Get to the shelter, everyone! "Nicholas yelled to the women, and he ducked into the men's quarters in the front of the boat as the hail pelting the deck varied from the size of musket balls to the size of apples.

Lydia stepped into the shelter of the cabin, but the intense wind prevented her from closing the door. She and Susanna watched from inside the Roosevelt cabin.

One giant ball of hail crashed and severed one of the ropes holding one of the anchors in place. It released the anchor from the boat. The loss of one anchor added pressure on the other anchor. The boat whirled round and round helplessly in the middle of the river.

The hail stopped suddenly and was replaced by torrents of rain that washed over the deck in waves. Water came from every direction. Waves from the river swept over the deck. At the same time, the clouds dumped buckets of water from the sky.

"What can we use as a replacement anchor?" Nicholas yelled. Andrew could barely hear Nicholas's voice over the wind's roar.

Andrew yelled back. "There's not much that we can do!"

"What if..." Nicholas started.

Suddenly, they felt a lurch and heard the crash and crunch of timbers underneath the boat.

"The boat?" Nicholas asked.

"It grounded!" PJ called.

"But we're in the middle of the river!"

"Sandbar," Andrew exclaimed.

The boat listed slightly to one side. The rain that came on as quickly as it came slowed to a drizzle.

"We have damage on the stern, starboard side," Andrew replied. "We'll have to abandon the boat."

Andrew then saw the sandbar where they grounded. It was far enough out of the river that they would be able to get out onto dry land rather than into the dark and choppy river waters. He also saw the gaping hole in the side of the flatboat. He knew there was no way to repair it.

The men lowered the rowboat onto the muddy waters where it bobbed with each crashing wave.

The wind stopped as quickly as it came up. Rain poured on them as they took the tarp off the rowboat and lowered the smaller boat onto the sandbar bank. From there, they began removing personal items from the boat and placing them in the rowboat.

"Can you men grab this trunk?" Lydia asked. Susanna had dragged Lydia's large traveling trunk to the cabin door.

"We got it," PJ exclaimed and nodded to Andrew.

"I don't see why we need that trunk," Nicholas exclaimed.

"We can use the trunk to sleep on," Lydia replied.

"Good thinking," Nicholas said.

"It's also a way I can guarantee my clothes make it to New Orleans," Lydia laughed.

She instructed Andrew and PJ to place it between the rowboat stern and the first seat. She then threw a buffalo robe over it.

"We probably won't need it," Andrew replied. "We're far enough downriver that we should be able to find shelter. I have lived all my life as a boatman on these waters, and from here to New Orleans, we should be able to find lodgings for the few nights that we have before we reach that city."

"It would be wonderful to sleep in a regular bed again," Lydia replied. She waddled when she walked. She put her hand on her back as though to indicate that her pregnant body was feeling the stress of the change in her comfort level.

Andrew and Nicholas decided to find a place for them to stay for the night.

The first place they stopped at was a small farmhouse several miles upriver from Baton Rouge. A middle-aged woman answered the door. "What do you want?"

Andrew was taken aback. He had not expected this kind of reaction from anyone along this part of the river.

"We just need a place to stay for the night," he replied. "Our flatboat was destroyed upriver."

"Sorry, I can't help you," she said.

"Please, we have two women onboard, and one of them is pregnant."

"That's not my problem," she said abruptly and slammed the door in Andrew's face.

When Andrew returned, they rowed downriver to another home where they got a similar response. A pouring rain and strong wind came up again that evening. They tried to reach Baton Rouge, which they did at nine at night.

They came upon a landing where Andrew knew that the people there had a small cottage and a barn. He was certain the couple who lived here would allow them to spend the night there, at least under the barn's shelter.

Andrew and PJ, who had been there before, went up to the house. The family dog was barking as they came up to the house. The woman of the house peeked out of the door.

"What do you want?"

"Is your husband home?" Andrew asked.

"No, he's not here. Don't come any closer. I have my gun."

"But, Mrs. Ruez, it's me, Andrew Mayford, and my friend PJ. We've stayed here before."

"I don't care. I ain't taking anybody in. I have had too many people try to mooch off us, and I am done with that. Besides, like I said, my husband is not here, and I'm not taking anyone in."

"But we have two women with us, and one of them is with child."

"Look, I don't know why any woman would come downriver who was going to have a baby, but that ain't no concern of mine. I am not opening my house to anyone anymore. I have been imposed upon by too many travelers."

Wearied from the search, Andrew and PJ shook their heads at the women in the rowboat. "I'm sorry. No one seems to want to take us in."

"I guess we'll just have to camp out here on the shore," Lydia said.

They spent the night in the rowboat. Lydia and Nicholas slept on the trunk while the rest of the crew and Susanna slept between the seats on buffalo robes.

Finally, they arrived in Baton Rouge. It was a miserable place at that time, with a single wretched public house. Yet they felt thankful that they had found a shelter from the storm. But when Lydia Roosevelt and Susanna were shown to their sleeping room, Susanna wished to return to the rowboat.

The hovel was a little forlorn place. Its door opened directly into the bar room. It held two tiny beds covered with linens that had not been changed in weeks and smelled of male sweat. The men shared the room next to them. The room had one window opening into a stable yard, which had neither shutters nor fasteners. The smell of horse manure was unsettling. Other than the bed, the only other piece of furniture was a rickety wooden chair.

On the other side of the door, they could hear rowdy men in the tavern. The men yelled and used foul language. As the night went on, the noise grew louder. At one point, a man sang at the top of his lungs. Later, a fight broke out. The men sounded like cutthroats. Susanna threw their cloaks on the bed, and they lay down to rest. Neither woman could sleep because of the fighting and the noise in the barroom on the other side of the door prevented that. They rose at the dawn of day and reached the boat, grateful that they had not been murdered in their sleep.

The next night, they found lodging with an old French couple who allowed them to spread their buffalo skins on the floor before a large fire, where they felt safe. Twice during the night, the couple disturbed them when the old people came into the room they occupied. The old couple knelt before a crucifix that stood on a shelf.

During the next evening, they slept on the boat that they drew halfway onto a small sandbar and out of the water.

During the night, they heard alligators scratching on the sides of the boat. "Why are they doing that?" Susanna asked.

"I think they are doing it because they think that the rowboat is a log," Lydia answered.

"Well, I'll show them what kind of log our boat is!" Susanna exclaimed, and before Andrew could warn her not to, she picked up one of the rowboat oars and struck the side of the boat. This alarmed the long, green, and scaly reptiles, and they slashed down into the water.

"It's a good thing they are more afraid of you than you are of them," Andrew exclaimed.

Susanna shrugged.

Andrew had not expected Susanna or Lydia to be as strong as they were during this trip. He knew men who would have whined about their situation and complained the whole time. Andrew couldn't imagine how his mother would have reacted to such primitive conditions, but he was impressed that neither of these two women maintained their countenance throughout the trip.

6

Chapter 6

They spent the remaining three nights sleeping under buffalo robes on the sandy beach.

Andrew was anxious about his ability as a pilot. The flatboat that Nicholas had him build was about the size of what the steamboat would be, and it had not survived the trip. What made him think that they would complete a trip down the rivers with a steamboat of equal size? Was he up to the task? Would Nicholas want him to take a steamboat downriver after the flatboat was destroyed? They had not discussed anything about what had happened. He probably wanted them to arrive in New Orleans before he told Andrew that he would no longer require his services as his pilot.

Susanna, too, was deep in thought. She imagined that at any moment, something terrible would happen before morning. Susanna imagined that the alligators would come up out of the water and attack them like they had in the rowboat. She imagined that river pirates would come and steal their rowboat, trunk, and all, and they would be left stranded on that beach. Finally, the mornings came, and they set off again down the Mississippi toward New Orleans.

They arrived in New Orleans on December 1, 1809, but Nicholas still hadn't dismissed Andrew as pilot.

As they floated into the big city of New Orleans, Andrew couldn't help watching Susanna's face. He wondered if she was thinking about what she had left back in France because she had a wistful look.

"Are you thinking about your life back in France?"

She nodded. Her face looked sad. "The houses remind me of the peasant homes around Versailles. I used to visit the poor who lived in those hovels."

"So, you miss France?"

"Yes, I'm sad. When I was a child, I believed that we were helping people. Now I realize we were just making ourselves feel better." She turned and looked at him. "I wish I had known better."

Andrew laid his hand over hers. "You wish you had known what?"

She pulled her hand away. "I'm not as good as I imagined myself to be. It's not that I was any better than anyone else. It was just that I was living a privileged life. Now, I'm just like everyone else. Excuse me, I need to help Lydia."

Andrew knew that it was just an excuse. Why was she trying to avoid him?

That evening, they stayed in a boarding house on Bourbon Street. The next morning, Andrew showed them around the city.

New Orleans was an eclectic melting pot of different ethnicities, creating a unique cultural tapestry. The city's French roots were evident in its architecture, language, and cuisine. The Spanish influence can be seen in the city's street names, such as Bourbon and Chartres, as well as the Spanish Colonial architecture style. African traditions and customs, brought by enslaved people, also played a significant role in shaping the city's culture.

It's amazing," Susanna said. "I never dreamed New Orleans would look like this."

"It's quite a city. It has numerous theaters, opera houses, and galleries. It attracts both local and international artists. You'll have to try the food before you sail away, too. Why, dishes like gumbo, jambalaya, and beignets are synonymous with New Orleans, reflecting the city's diverse heritage and culinary ingenuity."

"Surely the city's economy can't be based on the arts," Lydia Roosevelt said.

"That is true. Like all our cities, New Orleans' economy is heavily reliant on agriculture. Cotton has already become its primary crop. The city serves as a hub for shipping and processing cotton, making it a major player in the lucrative cotton trade."

"There's also sugar cane cultivation, and molasses is also a major economic activity," Andrew replied.

"Which should make it even more so when steamboats travel these waters," Nicholas replied.

While Andrew took Nicholas to find out about the next ocean-going ship returning to New York, while they were gone, the women took turns bathing in a copper bathtub. The ladies dressed in the fancy dresses that they had kept in the trunk on their trip downriver from Pittsburgh.

The men, too bathed, met the women in the gallery downstairs.

"Well, well," Nicholas replied. He smiled at his wife as she came down the stairs. "This moment is worth rescuing that trunk from the flatboat."

Lydia smiled back. "And the comfort of a bed on the boat's stern wasn't enough for you?"

Susanna also looked radiant that evening. She was dressed in a gown that had no doubt been Lydia's at one time but was made over for her. She wore long white gloves and carried a silk fan. Andrew couldn't keep his eyes off her.

That night, they ate at one of the finest restaurants in the French Quarter and drank some of the finest wines grown in France.

"To New Orleans," Nicholas replied and raised his glass. "And her name's sake."

"Her name's sake?" Lydia asked.

"Yes, I have decided to name the first steamboat to go down these western rivers to be named the New Orleans."

"To New Orleans," Andrew, Nicholas, and Lydia raised their glasses to their future venture.

Nicholas still had not talked to him about the wreck on the Mississippi.

During the next few days, Andrew showed them around New Orleans.

They walked to the edge of Lake Pontchartrain.

"Lake Pontchartrain was named after Louis Phelypeaux, Count Pontchartrain, minister and chancellor of France. Lake Maurepas was named after Jean-Frédéric Phelypeaux, Count Maurepas, minister and secretary of state. A third body of water, Lake Borgne, was originally a land-locked inlet of the sea; its name referred to its incomplete or defective character."

"How do you know all this, Andrew?" Lydia asked.

Andrew shrugged. "I like to talk to the old timers. Actually, they like to talk, and I like to listen. Then I remember the stuff they tell me."

"I have seen a lot that is French here in New Orleans," Susanna said, "but I see a lot that is not French. Spanish, isn't it?"

"Yes, that's right," Andrew answered. "Let me see if I can explain it to you. Despite Britain's victory in 1763 in the Seven Years' War, the French colony west of the Mississippi River—including New Orleans—was ceded to the Spanish Empire as a secret provision of the 1762 Treaty of Fontainebleau. This fact was confirmed the following year in the Treaty of Paris. This compensated Spain for losing Florida to the British, who also took the remainder of the formerly French territory east of the Mississippi River."

"So why does so much of New Orleans remain French-looking if Spain took over the city?"

"Fortunately for the French, no Spanish governor came to take control until 1766. French and German settlers, hoping to restore New Orleans to French control, forced the Spanish governor to flee to Spain in the bloodless Rebellion of 1768. A year later, the Spanish reasserted control. They executed five ringleaders and sent five plotters to a prison in Cuba and formally instituted Spanish law. Other participants of the rebellion were forgiven because they pledged loyalty to Spain. Although a

Spanish governor was in New Orleans, it was under the jurisdiction of the Spanish garrison in Cuba."

"I understand that there were several fires here in New Orleans during the Spanish period," Nicholas replied.

"That's right. Two massive fires burned most of the city's buildings. The Great New Orleans Fire of 1788 destroyed 856 buildings on Good Friday, March 21 of that year. In December 1794, another fire destroyed 212 more buildings. After the fires, the city was rebuilt with bricks. These buildings you see here now replace the simpler wooden buildings constructed in the early colonial period."

"Let's go to the French Quarter, as it's called. I'd like you to see some of the most beautiful sites."

They went to the center of the city.

Here, the fine metal grate-work of the handsome town and fine overall appearance were all Spanish in origin. The streets were straight. The houses were surrounded by canals, communicating with each other.

"The city reminded me of what I have read that Venice, Italy, must be like," Nicholas replied. "Perhaps the city should have been named New Venice rather than New Orleans.

They walked down St. Peter Street (rue Saint-Pierre) on the upriver boundary and St. Ann Street on the downriver boundary. They then strolled past the Cabildo.

"This building was originally called Casa Capitular. For many years, this was the seat of the Spanish colonial city," Andrew continued. "The original Cabildo was destroyed in the Great New Orleans Fire in 1788. The building was rebuilt between 1795 and 1799 as the home of the Spanish municipal government in New Orleans. The Spanish coat of arms still hung on the façade pediment. The building took its name from the governing body that met there—the "Illustrious Cabildo," or city council in English. The Cabildo was the site of the Louisiana Purchase transfer ceremonies late in 1803 and continued to be used by the New Orleans city council."

As they strolled around the building, they saw that the building's main hall, the Sala Capitular or "meeting room", was used as a courtroom.

"The Spanish used the courtroom from 1799 to 1803, and since 1803, this hall has been used by the Louisiana Territorial Superior Court," Andrew explained.

They continued exploring the French Quarter. Immediately beyond the Cabildo was the St. Louis Cathedral. This church was located next to Jackson Square and faced the Mississippi River in the heart of New Orleans.

"I learned from the old timers that the first church had been a crude wooden structure in the early days of the French colony. Because the French were Catholic, their church was prominently located in the town square. The construction of a larger brick and timber church was begun in 1725 and was completed in 1727. Like the Cabildo, that second church was destroyed in the Great New Orleans Fire on Good Friday, March 21, 1788. The cornerstone of this new building was laid in 1789, and the building was completed in 1794 when the Spanish ruled Louisiana. In 1793, Saint Louis Church was elevated to cathedral rank."

They moved on. Beyond the Cathedral was on the northeastern side of Jackson Square, between St. Ann Street and the cathedral, was the Presbytere. This two-story brick building had a flat roof with a balustrade topped by urns. Its ground floor had a nine-bay open arcade of elliptical arches, with white columns in the corners. The upper level also had arched openings, all articulated with columns and multi-pane windows. The center three bays on both levels have engaged columns and are topped as a group by a gabled pediment.

"The Presbytere was designed in 1791 by the French-born Gilberto Guillemard to match the Cabildo on the other side of St. Louis Cathedral. By 1798, only the first floor was completed, and its second floor remained unfinished as Andrew escorted the other two through the city. Originally called the Casa Curial 'Ecclesiastical House', its name derives from the fact that it was built on the former site of the residence of the Capuchin friars and presbytery.

"While it had been intended to house clergy, it was never used as a religious residence. The building is currently used for commercial purposes," Andrew replied.

"So, how did New Orleans become part of the United States?" Susanna asked.

I know this part," Nicholas replied. "On October 27, 1795, Pinckney's Treaty was signed on October 27, 1795. In this treaty, Spain granted the United States the "Right of Deposit" in New Orleans, allowing Americans to use the city's port facilities. Then, in 1800, Spain and France signed the secret Treaty of San Ildefonso, stipulating that Spain give Louisiana back to France, although it had to remain under Spanish control until the French transferred power. There was another relevant treaty in 1801, the Treaty of Aranjuez, and later a royal bill issued by King Charles IV of Spain in 1802; these confirmed and finalized the retrocession of Spanish Louisiana to France."

Andrew continued, "I first visited New Orleans shortly after, in April 1803, Napoleon sold Louisiana to the U.S. in the Louisiana Purchase. A French prefect, Pierre Clément de Laussat, who had only arrived in New Orleans on March 23, 1803, formally took control of Louisiana for France on November 30, only to hand it over to the U.S. on December 20, 1803. In the meantime, he created New Orleans' first city council and abolished the Spanish cabildo."

"I have never seen so many different types of people anywhere as I have here in New Orleans," Lydia replied. "Not even New York compares."

"The population is diverse. During the 1791 to 1804, the Haitian Revolution in the former French colony of Saint-Domingue established the second republic in the Western Hemisphere, the first led by blacks. Refugees, both white and free people of color, arrived in New Orleans, many bringing slaves with them. While Governor Claiborne and other officials wanted to keep out additional free black men, French Creoles wanted to increase the French-speaking population. As more refugees were allowed into the Territory of Orleans, Haitian émigrés who had gone to Cuba also arrived. Nearly 90 percent of the new immigrants settled in New Orleans."

Andrew enjoyed showing Nicholas, Lydia, and Susanna around the city. He especially felt connected to Susanna. Sadly, the day came when they had to leave to board the ship that would take them back to New York.

Andrew went with them to see them off. When the time came for Andrew to leave them, they stood on the dock as they prepared to board the ship,

Nicholas shook hands with Andrew. He placed his left hand over Andrew's right that he held in his own right hand. "Thanks for piloting for us. I couldn't have done what I did without you."

Andrew looked down and, like a kid, kicked a clump of dirt at his feet.

"I'm sorry about your boat."

"Look, I know that was a freak storm. I don't think that anyone could have done any better than you did. Your quick thinking kept all of us safe, and you got us here in one piece. I wouldn't have asked any more of anyone else."

"I don't know if I could have forgiven myself if something had happened to you or the ladies.

"Well, you did tell me not to bring the women along."

"That's not what I meant. The women handled themselves well. I wouldn't have expected any more from an all-male crew or male passengers."

"I'm glad to hear that. I want you to know how valuable this trip has been, even though the boat didn't make it. By using the data we gathered on this trip, I don't see any reason we wouldn't be able to get a steamboat down the Ohio and, consequently, the Mississippi. I believe the partners will not have any problems helping me secure the financing for building a steamboat and bringing it down to Natchez. You, of course, will pilot the boat, won't you?"

"Me? You want me to pilot for you even after what happened to your flatboat?" Andrew asked.

"Like I said, you can't be blamed for that gale we ran into," Nicholas replied. "I know you did the best you could, and you didn't let any of us perish in the storm. It was all I could expect."

"Thank you, Nicholas, I appreciate your confidence in me," Andrew replied.

"In us, Andrew, in us," Nicholas replied. "You will pilot our steamboat, won't you?"

Andrew nodded. "Of course I will. I would be honored."

Andrew stood there and watched the Roosevelts and Susanna join the other passengers on the gangplank. They then stood at the railing of the sailing ship and waved down at Andrew.

Andrew waved back. He suddenly felt lost. He suddenly felt like a piece of driftwood abandoned on a river's shore. He turned around and went to the hotel where he and PJ had stayed.

"Are you ready to go out on the town?" PJ asked. PJ was dressed in new clothes that he had purchased that week.

Andrew shook his head. "I think I'll just go for a walk. We can leave in the morning."

"Suit yourself," PJ said, leaving Andrew to his own devices.

Andrew didn't know why he felt he needed to walk around New Orleans. The city seemed to have lost its magic. Andrew had been to the city many times and had seen many of its changes during the past few years. From the early days, the city was noted for its cosmopolitan polyglot population and mixture of cultures. It had rapidly, with influxes of Americans, Africans, French, Creole French, and Creoles of mixed European and African ancestry. Many of these latter two groups fled from the violent revolution in Haiti.

The city's enchantment was now lost on Andrew. He never felt as alone as he now did. He walked around the city aimlessly and passed the same sites he had seen with the Roosevelts and Susanna. He kept remembering Susanna's reaction to the city. He remembered her sighs whenever they came to something that seemed even remotely French. He knew she missed the country of her birth, and for some reason, he, too, could feel her pain.

He had to admit that he missed her French charm, and this city didn't do much to relieve his loneliness.

Andrew tried to forget the French influence of the city and Susanna. He tried to imagine what the New Orleans area had been like before the French built the city. He could hardly believe that this city had once been as wild as the rest of the country, but along the river still was. He had heard from old-timers that French explorers, fur trappers, and traders arrived in the area by the 1690s. Some made settlements amid the Native American village of thatched huts along the bayou. By the beginning of the 1700s, the French had made an encampment called "Port Bayou St. Jean" near the head of the bayou. This would later be known as the Faubourg St. John neighborhood. The French also built a small fort, "St. Jean," known to later generations of New Orleanians as "Old Spanish Fort," at the mouth of the bayou in 1701. They used the fort as a base for a large Native American shell midden dating back to the Marksville culture. In 1708, French settlers from Mobile received land grants along the Bayou. Most of these settlers left within the next two years because they could not grow wheat there. These early European settlements were now within New Orleans's city limits, though they predate the city's official founding.

New Orleans was officially founded in early 1718 by the French as La Nouvelle-Orléans, under the direction of Louisiana governor Jean-Baptiste Le Moyne de Bienville. After considering several alternatives, the city was set on high ground, along a sharp bend of the flood-prone Mississippi River. This created a natural levee. It was adjacent to the trading route and portage between the Mississippi and Lake Pontchartrain via Bayou St. John and offered access to Biloxi, a Gulf of Mexico port, without going downriver 100 miles. The city's location was far from Spanish and English colonial settlements, ensuring the city's safety from invasion. This gave France control of the entire Mississippi River Valley and control of trade along the Mississippi.

For this reason, the French intended New Orleans to be an important colonial city. The city was named in honor of the regent of France, Philip II, Duke of Orléans. The regent allowed Scottish economist John Law to create a private bank and a financing scheme that increased the colonial population of New Orleans and other areas of Louisiana. The scheme, however, caused an investment bubble that burst at the end of 1720. Law's Mississippi Company collapsed. The flow of investment money to New Orleans stopped. Nonetheless, in 1722, New Orleans replaced Biloxi as the capital of French Louisiana.

In September 1722, a hurricane struck the city, blowing most of the structures down. After this, the administrators enforced the grid pattern dictated by Bienville but had previously been ignored by the colonists.

Much of the colonial population had been wild. Deported galley slaves, trappers, and gold-hunters caused the colonial governors to write letters full of complaints regarding the riffraff. Soldiers were sent to keep the peace. Shortly after the city's founding, slaves were forced to build the public works of the city for thirty days after they had harvested the crops.

The city was vastly different now than it had been back in those days. Andrew sighed. He looked up and saw that the sun was setting. It was time to get back to his room at the hotel.

The following day, Andrew, PJ, Jerrold, and Marcus all purchased horses and supplies for their long trip back up the river. He didn't realize it then, but this would be the last time Andrew would ever take any flatboat down the river, and he would never again have to find land transportation for his trip north to Pittsburgh.

Chapter 7

Andrew returned to his parents' home in late winter. The weather hadn't been too bad in the south, but in the north, the weather was colder and snowier than he had seen in many years. At Pittsburgh, he sold the horse to a man planning to travel west in the spring by overland route.

He wasn't certain when Roosevelt was planning to return, so he didn't book any other trips during 1810. Instead, he helped others build their boats at the shipyard. There wasn't much money in it, but the work kept him busy.

As spring waned into summer, the boat-building spree ended as Andrew watched the last loaded flatboats head down the Ohio.

"I got a letter from Nicholas Roosevelt today," his father told him. "He says he will arrive here with his steamboat next spring."

Andrew sighed. "Next spring? I wasted a whole year waiting for him."

"You can't rush a perfectionist like Roosevelt," Jonathan explained. "You just have to be patient."

"I waited all year, and now he says he won't be here until spring!"

"He says it has to do with having to arrange to get his mechanics and equipment out here to assemble the engine."

"What am I going to do all fall and winter?" Andrew asked.

"I'm certain you'll find some way to spend your time," Jonathan replied.

If he were like many men, he would have spent his time at the saloon drinking, but he wasn't like most men. Instead, he helped prepare the boatyard as well as he could to build the largest barge he could imagine.

In late fall, Roosevelt sent a letter asking Jonathan Mayford to arrange to harvest the tallest trees in the area for the boat building. He gave him the dimensions for the lumber that he would need for the steamboat.

Now, Andrew had a productive way of spending his time. He offered to take over the operation. Jonathan gladly allowed him to find the loggers to cut the trees and helped his son locate the sawyers to work in the sawpit to saw all the lumber and planks for the steamboat.

The work in the sawpit was tedious. A long, narrow trench was dug that was deep enough for a man to stand up inside. A log was rolled onto the pit, and then two men worked together using a two-man saw. One man stood in the pit, while the other straddled the log and the trench. They worked together to square up the log, cut beams, and trim off the boards from each log they cut.

Occasionally, Andrew took his turn in the saw pit. Even though he didn't let the men dally in their work, his men respected him because he was not afraid to do the hard work alongside them.

Andrew and the men finished cutting the lumber that Roosevelt had ordered. That wood was drying so they could use it for the steamboat in the spring.

The muddy days of late winter had come. He was usually preparing for a trip downriver, but here he sat for the second straight year. He had prepared the boatyard to the best of his ability, and the lumber was in the first drying stages. He had run out of things to do. He was bored and anxious to get started. He had put off all his usual trips downriver, and here he waited for Roosevelt to begin his work on the steamboat if the man ever arrived in Pittsburgh. He spent the rest of the winter with his family in Pittsburgh, waiting for Roosevelt to finally arrive.

The first daffodils of spring had opened their yellow petals when one day early in the spring of 1811, Andrew was sitting in his father's parlor reading a book when they heard a horse whinny out front. Charles Mayford rushed to the parlor window.

"They're here!" he exclaimed.

The entire Mayford family rose from what they were doing and went to the door.

Nicholas Roosevelt finally arrived by coach with Lydia, Susanna, and another older, homelier maid. In Lydia's arms was Roosevelt's sleeping child.

Lowri Mayford rushed out to Lydia.

"May I hold her?" Lowri asked.

"Of course," Lydia replied and allowed Lowri to take the child into her arms.

Lowri pulled the baby's blanket to reveal the tiny face. "Oh, what a beautiful baby girl. What's her name?"

"Rozetta," Lydia touched the child in Lowri's arms.

Lowri looked down at the child, who was now starting to squirm from her nap. Andrew imagined that the little girl had to be about a year old by now. Andrew's mother had always loved babies, and Andrew felt that it was more than likely that Lowri wished she had access to her grandchildren. Her daughter Lacey and son-in-law Matthew's children lived in Boston. Andrew also knew that she hoped that he would one day marry and have children of his own. His wanderlust did not seem to offer any hope that he would ever settle down. The river was his mistress, and he didn't have time to settle down.

It would be a few years before Charles would be old enough to marry. Andrew's brother would no doubt marry a woman whom his parents approved of. She would be a woman from a good family, probably a local girl from a prominent family in town.

Andrew moved forward and held out his hand. Nicholas took it into his own right hand and heartily shook it.

"It's good to see you again, Nicholas. How were things after we parted ways in New Orleans?"

They talked as they strolled toward the house.

"I wonder if it might not have been easier to have gone overland with you," Nicholas replied. "It was a disastrous trip. Our captain got sick almost immediately after we left port. Not long after that, some of the passengers fell ill with yellow fever. General Wilkinson's nephew, who was onboard, died of it. "

"It was horrible," Lydia replied. Rozetta was squirming and asking for her mother. Lydia took the child and hitched her little girl high on her hip. "Nicholas insisted that we be taken from the ship by a pilot boat. We landed at Old Point Comfort, where we traveled by stage to New York. We arrived sometime in the middle of January in 1810."

"It was the fifteenth, love," he said.

"Well, I was quite preoccupied," she looked down and ruffled the hair of her young daughter.

Lydia Roosevelt had given birth to their daughter, Rosetta Mark Roosevelt, shortly after returning to New York City.

"I have some promising information to share with you, Jonathan," Nicholas said.

"Shall we discuss this in my office?" Jonathan asked.

"By all means," Nicholas replied. Nicholas and Andrew followed Jonathan into the office. Andrew closed the door between them and the women cooing over young Rozetta.

Nicholas took some papers from the tube that he carried and laid them out across Jonathan's desk.

"I'm sure that you're aware from your father that Fulton and Livingston were impressed with the information I shared our findings with them concerning the suitability of the river. They have offered their full support for this project, including the money in their belts."

Over the winter, Roosevelt sent his report to Fulton, Livingston, and Mayford. While Andrew was cooling his heels at the family home and helping with the sawyer work, Jonathan Mayford took a coach to New York, where he determined he would aid Roosevelt in the enterprise. Chancellor Livingston was the same Chancellor Livingston who administered the oath of office to George Washington when first inaugurated as president of the United States on April 30, 1789. He was also a friend of Napoleon Bonaparte while an envoy from his own country to France. Chancellor Livingston furnished the greater part of the funds for the enterprise, and Jonathan Mayford added a small portion of the costs, including the boat-building location.

"That's wonderful news."

Jonathan added, "As you know, I will help you with anything you need that I can offer. I want you to know you have access to everything you need from my resources."

"Most of what I'll need from your end, in addition to the location, we'll need workmen to build the steamboat's shell."

Thanks to Andrew and his crew, we have all the lumber you requested cut to specification for the steamboat hull," Jonathan replied.

"Splendid, and I have already arranged for some mechanics from my business back in New York to handle the boat's engine work," Nicholas replied. "The boatmen can start building the hull while I look into securing some of the other aspects of building this boat."

"It sounds like you're well on your way to making this steamboat a reality," Jonathan replied. "Andrew tells me that during your trip downriver, you not only verified that the rivers were deep enough, but you also located supplies and coal deposits that could be mined and brought later to the western rivers to fuel steam-powered boats. I'm impressed."

"Don't forget, you also asked me to pilot the steamboat," Andrew replied.

"As I said before we left New Orleans, I wouldn't want anyone else piloting my steamboat," Nicolas replied. "Next on the agenda is setting up our shipyard."

Now that he knew that a steamboat could make the journey, he had the financial backing for the project and was supplied with enough materials to get started on the project. Nicholas Roosevelt began supervising construction in Pittsburgh at Jonathan Mayford's Monongahela River dock.

Although the steamboat's size and plan had been determined in New York, the keel would be laid in Pittsburgh. Pittsburgh seemed an insignificant place to build the first western steamboat. However, the city was already the logistical center. It was located next to the head of the Ohio River and close enough that Roosevelt could get the metal works from New York that were not readily available this far west.

Andrew was happy that this steamboat was finally being built and hoped that their downstream expedition would soon begin.

Now that he had gone down the Mississippi with the Roosevelts, Andrew knew that making this natural highway system accessible by steamboat would be key to opening the western territories. If the New Orleans was successful, it would bring about the advent of reliable steam power, which would open the door to commerce on America's rivers.

The question remained. Would this steamboat or any steamboat ever actually run on the western rivers?

Once Roosevelt had inspected all of Jonathan and Andrew's preparations, he brought shipbuilders and mechanics from New York to build the steamboat on the banks of the Monongahela River, at Jonathan's dock, a short distance from its junction at "The Point" with the Allegheny River.

Jonathan and Andrew knew the boat's carpenters. These men were accustomed to constructing the barges of that day and were easily found in Pittsburgh. However, the shipbuilder and the mechanics required in the machinery department had to be brought from New York. Most of the boat's machinery was made in New York and hauled overland to Pittsburgh because Pittsburgh did not yet have a local manufacturer with sufficient capacity to do the work. The boat's single-cylinder, low-pressure steeple engine was based on James Watt and Matthew Boulton's design. Its copper boiler was assembled by engineers William Robinson and Nicholas D. Baker and placed in its hold.

Under these circumstances, Mr. Roosevelt began the work.

One of the first troubles that annoyed him was a rise in the Monongahela when the waters backed into his shipyard and set all his buoyant materials afloat. This happened again and again, and on one occasion, it seemed unlikely that the steamboat would be lifted from its ways and launched on schedule.

As the days passed, the steamboat took shape. The New Orleans was a side-wheeler. The lumber that Andrew's team had cut was used to form the steamboat's hull. The pine wood to be used for planking, Jonathan Mayford arranged to be cut in nearby forests and sent down the Monongahela River. Like other Fulton-designed steamboats, New Orleans also carried a mast, spars, and two sails as a backup if the steam engine failed or fuel ran short.

Finally, the day came when Nicholas finished the steamboat. he stood back and admired the beauty of the vessel. Jonathan and Andrew joined him as he inspected the vessel.

"It's beautiful," Jonathan exclaimed.

"I have never seen anything like it." Andrew touched the smooth, ornate woodwork. "This is as nice as any of the finest homes in Pittsburgh."

"Finer, I'd say," Jonathan exclaimed. "When your mother sees this, she'll want to use this design in her own home."

"All difficulties were overcome by steady perseverance," Nicholas exclaimed. "Next on the agenda is to get this boat launched."

Everyone for miles around came to watch the boat slide into the water.

"I can't believe how big that thing is," Andrew heard a man in the crowd say.

It was a sight to behold. The New Orleans was larger than any barge that had ever come out of Pittsburgh. It was the largest craft on the rivers. Rarely were there barges that exceeded 100 feet long. The size and plan of this steamboat had been based on those built in New York, and Mr. Fulton had furnished that plan. The boat was 116 feet long with a twenty-foot beam. The engine was to have a 34-inch cylinder, and the boiler and other parts of the machine were to be in proportion to that cylinder.

Finally, the moment came for the launch. Dressed in their finest clothes, Nicholas and Lydia stood at the bow of the steamboat. P. J. threw a mooring rope down to Andrew, and Andrew tied it to one of the pilings. Nicholas broke a wine bottle on the boat's hull, and Andrew cut the rope that held the boat in the launch bay. The boat's aft slid back into the water, and the bow followed it into the river with a splash. The boat remained buoyant. The crowd cheered. The launch was a success.

"It looks like we're ready," Nicholas said. "Are you ready to pilot this thing, Andrew?"

"I'm as ready as I'll ever be," Andrew exclaimed.

Nicholas, Lydia, and Andrew joined the rest of the crew on the steamboat. Andrew piloted the boat, and Nicholas acted as captain on this, their trial voyage. If everything worked out well, they would be able to immediately begin their journey.

The ice was barely off the river when they launched The New Orleans in March 1811.

The engineer, Nick Baker, along with PJ and a couple of other men, ignited the fire in the boiler, and soon there was enough steam to get the paddlewheels moving.

"Here goes nothing," Nicholas said. A man on the dock untied the moorings. They started the paddlewheel in reverse until they could get the boat away from the dock. Nicholas then shut down the wheel and allowed the front of the boat to get ahead of the back end, and the boat floated down the Monongahela under the river's powerful current toward the headwaters of the Ohio River.

As the boat floated, Nicholas reignited the paddle wheels. This time, the paddle wheels moved forward.

They reached the location in the river where the Monongahela and the Allegheny met to form the Ohio. They turned to go up the Allegheny.

"Let's see how fast she goes!" Nicholas exclaimed and yelled to the boiler crew to load the firebox with more wood.

The paddlewheel moved faster. Its powerful blades cut into the water like a knife, propelling the boat forward. The boat moved upstream faster than a man could walk on the road beside the river. It was a true miracle.

Suddenly, the boat lurched.

"What the. . ." Nicholas yelled.

"Something is wrong with the boiler. It stalled!" one of the mechanics exclaimed. "A gear axle broke."

Nicholas cursed.

The heavy current of the Allegheny River pulled the New Orleans downstream, and it edged closer to shore. If something wasn't done soon, the boat would ground out against the shore. The damage that would occur would be catastrophic.

"Drop the anchor!" Andrew exclaimed.

P. J. lowered the anchor at the steamboat's aft. The current whipped the front of the boat to face downstream, but the boat wasn't going anywhere. The boat was dead in the Allegheny's current.

Once the anchor stopped the boat, Andrew unhitched one of the lifeboats from the side of the steamboat and rowed it to shore. There, he got several men to get ropes and wenches to draw The New Orleans toward a nearby pier.

Upon inspection, they found that the boat's structure had not been damaged, but Nicholas found that the engine was not powerful enough to maintain the paddlewheel against the current of these western waters.

"Is it over?" Andrew asked. "Have we failed?"

Exacerbated, Nicholas raised his hands to his head and grabbed his hair. "No, it just means that we have to make those components of the gearing apparatus stronger."

"How do you propose to do that?" Andrew asked.

"I don't know yet," Nicholas shook his head.

Over the next several weeks, Nicholas sat in his office in the house he rented and contemplated how to retool the mechanics of the boat. He spent time debating with his mechanics on their best course of action.

Lydia spent much of her time visiting with Lowri Mayford and her friends at the Mayford house. Lydia was pregnant again and was already starting to show. Roosevelt's little girl toddled around the house, and Lowri doted on the child as though Rozella were her own grandchild.

Because he had nothing else to do, Andrew returned to helping the men who were building flatboats and barges. He helped load barges with goods to take downstream and then watched others go downriver. He even saw some who went downriver early in the season return. Still, he was stuck in Pittsburgh, waiting for the steamboat to be finished.

One evening in September, while the family and the Roosevelts were having dinner together, Andrew came out to the garden and found Susanna staring up at the night sky.

Susanna turned and motioned for him to sit down beside her.

"The newspapers say that there's a blazing star, like a comet," Susanna pointed up toward the Big Dipper. "It's right there."

Andrew followed where Susanna's finger pointed to the northern night sky. There, a bright star circled the north star like the pointers in the bear.

"Lucky star. At least that star can travel," Andrew complained. "We've wasted a whole summer, and for what? I could have gone down the river twice in the time that I've waited for Nicholas's steamboat to be built. Instead, I have been sitting here, cooling my heels, waiting for this blasted steamboat to be finished. If it ever will."

"Mr. Roosevelt knows what he's doing."

Andrew then turned on Susanna. His lips pressed into a firm line. "Doesn't anything ever bother you?"

"Well," Susanna replied. "Getting angry and throwing a fit never helped anyone. I always found that letting God handle the outcome is much better than worrying and complaining."

Andrew raised his hands in frustration and walked down the path toward the river. He kicked a clump of dirt along the path. What did that woman know about anything? Susanna and her God were more than he could take.

Her God had let her not only lose her home but also lose the members of her family as well. What kind of loving God allows bad things like that to happen? He knew better than to leave things in the hands of a God who either didn't care or wasn't even there.

He understood flatboats and the river currents, but he didn't understand women. He certainly didn't understand God. At this point, he doubted whether Roosevelt would ever deliver a working steamboat that could navigate upstream on the Ohio and the Mississippi. He had wasted two seasons because of Nicholas Roosevelt's delusion of steamboat travel on the western rivers.

Chapter 8

Finally, on October 14, Nicholas inspected the redesigned engine. He got up from examining the engine. He pursed his lips tightly together and nodded.

"Looks like we can give it another go. Let's take her out for a spin on the waterwheel tomorrow."

Andrew and the other men picked up wood from around the area where they had been repairing the boat so they could use it for fuel for this next trial run.

They ran the boat from where it had grounded after the ill-fated run earlier. This time, the steamboat went down the Allegheny and up the Monongahela. It then returned to the original landing, where they stockpiled supplies to load for the trip down the Ohio and Mississippi Rivers.

The trip was successful. They moored the boat, shut the engine down, and immediately began to load for their long trip.

On the evening before their planned departure, Lowri Mayford approached her son. She held a small wooden box in her hand.

"Andrew, I'd like to see you in your father's office," she said and motioned him toward its open door.

What is Mother up to, he wondered. Any time she called him into his father's office, she had some feminine idea that she wanted from him. *What was it this time?*

"Yes, Mother?"

I have something for you. I think it's time you started to think about getting married," Lowri said. "I contacted your cousin Isaac and asked that he send the family locket here for you. It came by mail today."

The family locket had been worn by most of the brides in the family for a long time before he was born. It had been a gift to his paternal great-grandmother from her second husband, and passing it from bride to bride on her wedding day had become a family tradition. Now, his mother was foisting the locket onto him.

Andrew shook his head. "But there isn't anyone I am interested in."

"Take it," Lowri said. "You never know when you might need it."

Andrew sighed. "Alright. I'll take it with me to appease you, but you know I'm not likely to marry anyone anytime soon."

He took and thrust the old wooden box into his pocket.

"Be careful with that," Lowri replied. "It's an old family heirloom, you know."

Andrew did know. He smiled as he thought about what it would be like when he returned from the river and gave the locket back to her, not having married at all. That would fix her ideas about matchmaking!

There were two cabins in the boat, one aft for ladies and one forward for gentlemen. In the ladies' cabin were four berths. One was specifically set up for a makeshift toddler bed. The crew consisted of the engineer, Nicholas Baker, the pilot, Andrew Mayford; six hands including PJ who had previously gone down the Mississippi with them. Susanna and another two other female servants accompanied Mrs. Roosevelt and Rozetta. There was also a waiter, a cook, and a Newfoundland dog named Tiger.

Andrew wasn't sure that he liked the idea of having a pet on board, but, like having women onboard the boat during their previous trip, it wasn't his decision to make. Lydia Roosevelt chose the dog because she liked the brown, 30-inch tall, 150-pound dog's friendly nature and the fact that he immediately took a liking to Rozella.

Nicholas liked the dog because of the dog's massive stature. Its large muscles gave it the power it needed to take on rough river currents. The dog had a huge lung capacity for swimming large distances. The dog's thick, oily, and waterproof double coat would protect him from chilly waters. Plus, the dog would be protection for Lydia and Rozetta if they needed it. He had not forgotten that Indian incident during their last trip downriver. His wife and daughter's safety were paramount.

The dog would likely scare away any natives trying to obtain whiskey from the stores aboard his boat. Andrew doubted it would be necessary, but he could understand Nicholas's protective nature. He not only had a wife to think about, but he had a daughter as well. Plus, there was also another child on the way.

Andrew understood Nicholas's concerns. Andrew felt the same about the passengers he carried on the boats that he piloted. However, he decided that in this case, they had nothing to worry about from the Indians. If the roar of the steamboat engine wasn't enough to scare away Indians, he doubted that a dog could. Andrew didn't say anything about this. He would let Nicholas keep his illusion of the dog, creating safety for his family.

Lydia Roosevelt had made many new friends during her summer in Pittsburgh, and most of those friends were also Lowri Mayford's friends. Lowri Mayford. On the day of their sendoff, several of her high-society friends stood at the foot of the gangplank as Lydia was about to get aboard the boat. Susanna was holding Rosetta's hand and was helping her onto the boat.

"Lydia, you don't have to go on this trip. Are you certain you won't change your mind?" Lowri asked. "You know you can stay here while your husband takes the boat downriver."

Lydia shook her head. "No, I want to go with my husband."

"But surely, you see that your journey may be too dangerous for your little daughter, and you with child to boot. You need to be sensible."

"I will be fine," Lydia replied. "I'm going with my husband."

"Now, Lydia, your baby is due any day now," Mrs. Fitz, the May-fords' next-door neighbor, replied.

"I can handle this. I assure you. I had no problems giving birth to Rosetta, and everyone says a second child is usually easier than the first. I am interested in this business my husband is in, and I plan to report back to my father everything I can about this trip."

The New Orleans finally steamed for New Orleans on Sunday, October 20, 1811, with Roosevelt as the captain. His pregnant wife, their young daughter, and their staff were the only passengers because no one else would take passage on the steamboat's maiden voyage. Not that Andrew blamed them. A trip like this one, at this time of the year, was considered foolhardy by anyone with any common sense.

As the passengers made their way onboard the boat, people of all ethnic backgrounds, age groups, and economic statuses showed up at the pier at Monongahela Landing to witness the commencement of the voyage.

Women with young children, elderly couples, immigrant families, dock workers, women dressed in fine dresses and carrying parasols, and men in fancy suits all gathered to watch the steamboat that they had seen just a few days earlier travel around their city take its final exit from the region.

The steamboat crew busily cleared the boat of the docks, but the passengers stood at the steamboat's railing and waved at the crowd below.

Susanna held onto Rozetta's right hand while Lydia grasped her other. Both women used their free hands to wave at the growing crowd below.

As they moved downstream, the figures of the crowd grew smaller and soon disappeared around a river bend. Not far beyond the outskirts of Pittsburgh, the terrain became more wooded. The shores everywhere after leaving Pittsburgh were covered with the virgin forest down to the water's edge.

All day, they traveled under the rhythm of the engine's mechanical system and the paddlewheel. Mr. and Mrs. Roosevelt sat up most of the first day of the voyage, watching the boat's paddlewheel as it progressed downstream.

About an hour before dark, Andrew put them into a deep cove where he tied the boat to a nearby tree. The men went out to the woods to cut and bring in wood to run the steamboat the next day.

Nick Baker disengaged the heat of the firebox from going into the boiler and banked the fire for the evening. He didn't want the fire to go out completely because it would take too long to get the fire going again in the morning.

Darkness fell upon the steamboat that night, and as they finished their evening meal, Andrew sat at the table with the Roosevelts. Susana was in the women's berthing area getting Rozetta ready for bed.

"Now that you've seen the New Orleans at work, have you reconsidered your apprehension of steamboats on the Ohio?"

"I concede to your opinion, Nicholas. When the New Orleans completes her journey from Pittsburgh to New Orleans, it will be a turning point in transportation west of Appalachia. Once the New Orleans demonstrates that steamboats can travel on these western waters, mark my words, steamboats will proliferate on the Ohio and the Mississippi and their tributaries. Steamboat traffic will create a national economy, opening markets for farm goods and drawing people and commerce to cities all along these rivers."

Nicholas nodded. "We will get this boat onto the Mississippi, and we will open all those markets. It's just a matter of getting this boat down to New Orleans."

Andrew heard the excitement in Nicholas Roosevelt's voice. Here they were on the first day of their journey, and already he was talking about events that probably wouldn't happen for years.

Andrew saw Susanna standing at the boat's rail. She was looking up at the great expanse above them. The stars in the sky were bright, and the Great Comet could be seen with the naked eye.

That's quite a sight, isn't it?" Andrew asked as he stood beside Susanna at the rail.

"There's a change in the air," Susanna exclaimed. I can't explain it, but I can feel it."

Perhaps it's your God trying to tell you something," Andrew said drily.

"Perhaps it is," Susanna said and left Andrew alone at the rail.

The next day, Mr. Roosevelt and Lydia spent most of it on deck and watched the shore, covered with an almost unbroken forest. Roosevelt decided to see how fast the steamboat could travel. Nick Baker, the engineer, stoked the fire and revved the engine full out. They traveled reach after reach and bend after bend at a speed of eight to ten miles an hour.

The regular working of the engine and the ample supply of steam proved the steamboat successful.

As the hours passed, Andrew was further reassured about the chances of success by the boat's ease of steering and uniformly quick speed. Nicholas Roosevelt knew everything about this steamboat. After all, he had designed and supervised every aspect of its construction.

Andrew said. "How did you get into learning about steam power?"

"I started manufacturing copper and steam engines at the Soho Works on the Passaic River at Belleville, New Jersey, one of the best foundries in the nation. I then worked on a stern-wheel steamboat for Livingston from 1798 to 1800, but stopped when I lost my government contracts for supplying copper for warships."

"Fortunately, that quasi-war with France didn't amount to anything, but sorry to hear that you lost your contract."

Nicholas shrugged. "It taught me that it's never a good idea to depend on government contracts if I want to make my fortune. I've learned that working in private enterprises is the best practice."

"Did you go to work with Livingston immediately?"

Nicholas shook his head. "No, in 1798, I tried to convince Livingston to use my side wheels in his designs, but Livingston was dead set on using a stern wheel. However, after exhausting all other options, Fulton and Livingston eventually used my sidewheels on the Clermont. The two men were in my debt because I trained and employed many of Fulton's highly skilled workmen. Fortunately, he let me employ Nick Baker as our engineer for this trip."

"Nick seems to be a good man."

Nicholas nodded. "Yes, he does."

"Are you planning to build more boats on the Mississippi?"

Nicholas smiled grimly. "I probably won't have to. As soon as people start seeing what this steamboat can do, every mechanic along the Ohio and Mississippi will be copying the New Orleans. I'm guessing Nick Barker will be one of them."

When they tied the steamboat up for the night, Nick Barker took out a long cylinder and set it up along the steamboat's rail.

"What do you have there?" Susanna asked.

"It's a telescope," Nick replied.

"What does it do?"

"I'll show you. Just give me a minute while I set it up." He unfolded a stand and put the telescope on it. He then looked through one end and made some adjustments by turning at the other end.

"There, take a look," he said. Susanna looked where he indicated. There, she saw the Great Comet bigger than she could see with her naked eye. Not only could she see the tail, but she saw the front of the comet's body as it flamed in front of her eyes.

"How fascinating!" she exclaimed. She looked through it again. "I have never seen anything like it!"

She took her eyes away from the scope and smiled at Nick.

At that moment, Andrew came on deck. He saw Nick and Susanna standing close together, their eyes fixed on each other and smiling.

They didn't seem to notice that he was nearby.

Andrew felt anger bubbling up in his stomach. Was he jealous of Nick Baker? What was he thinking? He had no claims on Susanna. She was just a passenger on the steamboat. She was Lydia's servant. She meant nothing to him. Did she?

Andrew cleared his throat.

Susanna stepped away from Nick and took a couple of steps toward Andrew. She didn't even have the decency to blush.

"You should see this, Andrew! With this thing," she looked at Nick. "What did you call it?"

"Telescope," he replied.

"With this telescope, you can see the comet as if it were right at the top of the trees."

"By all means," Nick replied. He seemed put off that Susanna had invited Andrew to look into his telescope. "Steamboat mechanics isn't all I'm adept at. I am also fascinated by the wonders of the space beyond our world. I use every opportunity to add to my stock of astronomical knowledge by ascertaining the elements of the orbit of The Great Comet of 1811, as the papers are now calling it. I have studied this aerial visitor and made other observations and calculations of its appearance and its short stay within my view for as long as possible."

Andrew looked through the telescope and saw what Susanna and Nick had already seen. By now, the Roosevelts and other crew members had joined them.

The comet was no longer in the part of the sky where Andrew and Susanna had originally seen it. It was now five degrees higher above the horizon.

Andrew stepped away from the telescope, and Lydia took a turn at looking into the scope.

Nick continued to speak. "Its apparent smallness and the haziness of the atmosphere had prevented it from being seen for several evenings. However, this evening is favorable for viewing it. Its location was a little south of the west, about twenty-five degrees above the horizon. It was surrounded by a small portion of the atmosphere, for which most bodies of this kind are so remarkable- yet its tail was perceivable some distance from the body."

The others were asking Nick questions about the telescope and what he knew about the comet.

Andrew couldn't help his feeling of being put out by the steamboat engineer. He left and continued his mission to make sure everything was in order with their moorings.

The last thing Andrew heard was Nick saying to the fascinated crew members and passengers of the New Orleans was. "It had passed the point in its orbit where it was closest to the sun and was receding from it."

"Show off," Andrew mumbled under his breath. "If that's the kind of man Susanna wants, then she can have him."

Andrew felt the pang of jealousy again. He shook his head. He refused to be jealous. He had no claims on Susanna. It was freedom to do what he wanted with his life that he wanted most, and he would not let some woman get in the way of that. Instead, he turned his attention to the New Orleans. Knowing the many things that could go wrong with the steamboat, he had to admit that the boat's uniform speed quieted his nervous apprehension.

The following morning, Nicholas offered to let Andrew handle the steamboat's helm.

Andrew was delighted with the way the vessel steered and with its speed. With the patience of a schoolmaster, Nicholas had taught him how to manage the giant beast. Though he was not accustomed to piloting something so large and so fast, he learned quickly. His apprehension of the steamboat ceased, and he relaxed. Nicholas appeared more pleased than ever with the likely success of the voyage's beginning.

This steamboat would be a game changer. Andrew imagined how northern and southern travel would change here in the West. Once steamboat travel became commonplace, the days of walking or riding back to Pittsburgh from Natchez and the fear of river bandits attacking travelers on the Natchez Trace would be obsolete. Towns would grow because the nearby farmers would deliver their crops to these towns on the rivers to be delivered to ports like New Orleans, where their produce could go anywhere in the world.

PJ. was also coming around to the excitement of this type of travel. Even though PJ had worked to build the boat's hull, he had never been convinced that the steamboat could run down the river any better than the flatboats he had built. That changed after a day and night on the river. He now heartily embraced steamboat travel. It had changed the minds of all the crew.

The following morning, the New Orleans reached a long reach in the river. Here, villagers who had heard and then seen the boat approaching lined up along the shore and greeted the boat as she sped by. The Roosevelt entourage and all hands, except Andrew, who was at the helm, assembled on deck to wave. The Roosevelts and the crew called out to the villagers of the small villages, who cheered them on.

They captured the excitement of the journey. As they passed these small towns, the figures waved from the shore, and at nearly every small town, at least one person ran alongside, appearing to try to catch up to the boat. The passengers and crew alike waved back, unfazed by the black smoke billowing from the stack overhead.

The Beaver, Pennsylvania, villagers cheered as the strange, noisy boat passed their homes along the river. They had seen and heard the boat approaching down a straight stretch of the river.

"We're celebrities," Lydia said as she waved down to the crowd on the beach.

"This is the biggest thing that has probably happened to them all year," Andrew replied.

Later that day, they made their first stop at Wheeling on Virginia's northwestern point.

Here, Nicholas stopped to fill up on wood and some fresh food. He also talked with the village leadership about developing a port for future steamboat traffic. He welcomed crowds aboard the ship and charged them twenty-five cents for the opportunity to tour the novelty vessel. They made enough at Wheeling to pay for the supplies they secured there.

For several days after they left Wheeling, the passengers and crew, except Andrew, spent their evenings watching the comet in the northwestern sky. They were able to view it after dinner in the evening and in the northeast before sunrise in the morning.

The comet was better seen in the middle of October than at any other time before. The tail was forked, and the light was very strong on either side of the tail but very faint toward the middle. The area outside of the comet between the head and the two points of the tail was dark. The forks tapered to a point, making this a bifurcated comet, which meant that it was more pointed or angular.

The comet had become more luminous than when first discovered and had a tail that measured about 8 degrees.

When viewed through Nick's telescope, it appears to be surrounded by a dense atmosphere, which prevented the nucleus from being distinguished. The comet was most intense in the center.

Andrew had a sense that the steamboat and the comet were somewhat connected. Both were lights in a darkened world. Both created excitement just because they existed. The future looked bright. What could go wrong when you had a comet for a river escort?

Chapter 9

On October 27, the boat anchored offshore at Cincinnati, Ohio, because the water wasn't deep enough near the pier. The New Orleans rounded a curve in the river, Nick shut down the engines, and PJ dropped the anchor. All the town's citizens crowded at the river's dock to see the giant barge that billowed smoke from its smokestack.

If Cincinnati wanted steamboats to dock there in the future, they would have to dredge their portage deeper.

Many of the men whom Nicholas had met during his first time through the area came out in rowboats to congratulate him on his success.

"I see you made it," James Findlay replied. He had been the first mayor of Cincinnati after Ohio became a state. He served from 1804 to 1806. He was also the and who in 1806 and 1807 had helped quash the Burr conspiracy that required him to confront his partner Smith, an alleged conspirator. This conspiracy made him lose the next election, but he was re-elected in 1810 and still held the office.

"I would never have guessed that you would make it this far with that contraption, but I still don't think you'll ever go upstream with this boat." This time it was Martin Baum who spoke.

He had been elected mayor in 1807 and was already favored to be re-elected in 1812. Baum was active in Cincinnati civil affairs and business even before becoming mayor the first time. Through his agents in Baltimore, New Orleans, and Philadelphia, Baum attracted many German immigrants to work in his various enterprises.

"If you want steamboats to dock here in the future, you'll have to dredge your portage deeper," Nicholas told Baum as the rowboat carried Cincinnati leadership to the New Orleans.

"We'll probably do that if your steamboat can move upstream as you claim it can," Baum replied.

Andrew saw that the man had his doubts, but Baum seemed the most interested in knowing more about the steamboat during the steamboat tour. He asked Nicholas and Andrew about the various aspects of the boat's paddle wheel and its mechanics.

Once he seemed satisfied with what he knew about how the New Orleans worked, he expressed numerous other ideas about adding commerce to Cincinnati as well. He told Andrew he wanted to build a sugar refinery and a foundry.

"Do you think that you will be able to do all that you want to do and get involved in steamboat building as well?" Nicholas asked him.

"Why, of course," Baum said. "I'll do all of it.

"No doubt he will," answered James Findlay. "He's already founded the Western Museum, and he helped start the first public library here in 1802. He's also a deacon of the First Presbyterian Church. It's always good to have God on your side, wouldn't you agree?"

"Certainly," Nicholas replied.

"I don't think I could have done it without either God or my wonderful wife. Anna and I were married in 1804, and she has been the backbone of all my operations ever since. I have been thinking about building her a new house, and exactly as she would like it."

"I heard that there's a 9-acre property available at Pike Street that would be a beautiful place to build a home," Nicholas said. "It hasn't been sold yet, has it?"

"No," Baum said. "How do you know about that?"

"I came through here last winter and did some research. That's when I heard about it."

"Is that a fact? For someone not from here, you certainly seem to know the area," Baum said and turned toward Lydia, who was standing next to her husband. "I understand that you're Henry Latrobe's daughter. I also heard that he was the architect of the United States Capitol building. Perhaps he would be willing to design our home."

"Of course, my father might be interested in such a prospect. Perhaps you should contact him about it. If you buy that property, that is,"

Andrew listened to the conversation and imagined that Lydia probably heard those types of requests all the time, but he doubted that any of them ever carried out the request.

A stately man shook Nicholas's hand. He had already known many of the men in Cincinnati, but Andrew had not met him before. "Hello, I'm Daniel Symmes."

"Oh, I have heard of you," Andrew said. "You're one of the US. Senators from Ohio."

"That's right," Symmes replied.

"He's also been an Ohio State Senator and an Ohio Supreme Court Judge," Baum replied.

Andrew knew that Symmes was an important man. He had heard his father talk about Daniel Symmes. Daniel Symmes was a nephew of the pioneer land speculator of southwest Ohio, John Cleves Symmes. He had been educated at Princeton College and came west with his family, among the first settlers in the Miami Purchase.

Symmes married Elizabeth Oliver on April 10, 1796, in North Bend, Ohio. Symmes then set up his law practice in Cincinnati, and, in June 1803, he was elected to the first Board of Directors of the first bank established in Ohio as well as the Miami Exporting Company of Cincinnati. That same year he was appointed Prosecuting Attorney for several counties.

Just after statehood, Symmes was elected to represent Hamilton County in the Ohio Senate for the first through third General Assemblies, 1803–1805. In 1805 the Ohio Legislature appointed him as judge of the Ohio Supreme Court, to fill the vacancy created when Return Jonathan Meigs, Jr. resigned.

In 1808–1809, Symmes served as President of the Cincinnati Council which was the same as being the mayor of the town. After James Findlay was elected as mayor, President Jefferson appointed Symmes as register of the Cincinnati Land Office. Symmes resigned from the court and served as land register.

"Well, you are as good as your word. You have visited us in a steamboat," he said. "But we are not likely to see you again in this vessel. Your boat may go down the river, but, as to coming back upstream, the very idea is an absurd one."

Andrew had to leave the party to get the supplies loaded for their continued journey. While on shore, getting supplies, Andrew talked with some keelboat men.

"I hear that your boat's captain believes that steamboat of yours will move upstream in the same manner that it goes upstream."

"He does," Andrew answered.

"I have seen you come down our river before by flatboat," said another man. "Do you think that steamboat will be able to fight the current of the Ohio."

"I do. We traveled upstream around Pittsburgh on the Monongahela, the Allegheny, and the Ohio. I see no reason we can't manage the Ohio and the Mississippi as well."

"Oh, but you know that the currents around Pittsburgh aren't as strong as they are here at Cincinnati! Why my shoulders hardened as they pressed their poles for many a weary mile against that current. He shook his head. Other keelboat men crowded around the strange visitor and bandied river wit with Andrew and the rest of the crew that had been selected from their calling for this first voyage.

A flatboat pulled up to the dock. The men stood on the deck and stared at the New Orleans.

"What the heck is that monster craft?" one of the men asked.

"You like?" Andrew asked. By the looks on their faces, these men were not pleased with their experience with the massive boat.

"Like? That boat almost capsized us upriver!"

"The pilot of that boat seems to think that it can go upstream as well as down."

The newcomer nodded. "I wouldn't doubt it! I can't believe the power that machine has."

"So, you think that it could go upstream?"

"Oh, yes. I should think that your steamboat could tow us back upstream and save my aching back!"

"I'll tell you what," said one of the dock workers. "I'll bet you one hundred to one that that boat or any steamboat will ever be able to fight the current here!"

The challenge was on, and a bet was made. The local banker secured the bets. Because the odds were so high, Andrew himself bet a gold dollar that the boat or one like it would come back upstream within the next two years. As they were placing their wagers, Nicholas came ashore with some of the city officials. When they heard about the bet, they too wagered sizable amounts of cash.

The New Orleans' crew didn't have much time to entertain the dockworkers. They only stopped at Cincinnati long enough to take in a supply of wood. Andrew and the three deckhands filled it with enough firewood to get them to Louisville. Within a couple of hours, they continued down the Ohio River.

The water's depth started worrying Andrew. It wasn't as deep as he would have liked, and he was concerned. The problem they had with the engine back in Pittsburgh had taken way longer than they had anticipated. Everyone aboard The New Orleans knew they had to get as far south as possible when winter came to the area above the Falls of the Ohio River.

"I have some bad news," Andrew said to Roosevelt as they stood in the wheelhouse as the steamboat got underway.

"What is it, Andrew?" Nicholas asked.

"The keel men told me that they believe that the river on this side of the falls is considerably lower than the last time we traveled down the Ohio River. Based on what they say, I have serious doubts that we can make it over the falls with this steamboat if the water is as low as I think that it might be."

Jovial Nicholas Roosevelt became a more serious version of himself. A crease developed between his eyebrows that Andrew had never seen before. Even when the engine failed, Nicholas hadn't appeared this worried.

Just beyond Louisville, the series of dangerous rapids, the Falls of the Ohio, would likely be their biggest obstacle to completing this trip. Relatively flat-bottom boats were the only boats that could travel over the falls, except during high water.

"The weather is one thing that I can't control," Nicholas said that evening. "I know that I can fix an engine, but the weather is not something I can fix. I hope we didn't arrive too late in the season to take the boat over the falls."

"Well, we could wait until spring rains," Andrew replied.

Nicholas sighed. "Because there's a chance that the river could freeze over. I don't know if that is a viable option for us. The sooner we arrive in Louisville, the better our odds of getting over the falls sooner rather than later."

Andrew nodded, but still, he couldn't help wondering if they weren't too late in the season to tackle the falls.

Chapter 10

"Shouldn't we stop for the night?" Lydia asked Andrew as the sun was setting the following evening.

"No, we're almost to Louisville. The sky is clear, and the moon is full tonight. I discussed it with your husband, and he agrees we should continue so that we can dock at Louisville tonight. It may take a few hours in the dark, but I know the river well enough, and the moon is bright enough, so I don't think we'll have any problems navigating these waters."

"He's worried about the falls. Isn't he?"

Andrew nodded. "The sooner we arrive at Louisville, the sooner we'll be able to know the situation at the falls."

Lydia nodded.

No one on board retired that evening, including Rosetta. The child sensed the adults' excitement and wanted to be on deck with the crew. Only Nicholas Baker was absent because he manned the fires in the boiler room.

With the Great Comet of 1811 flashing across the sky above them, the Roosevelts, their toddler daughter, their house servants, and the crew steamed into Louisville late on October 28, their fourth day on the Ohio. It was after midnight as the New Orleans approached the village. The sky was clear, and the moon was full.

With their arrival at Louisville, the New Orleans crew got another taste of how their new technology was received by those less familiar with the sights and sounds of a large steam-powered engine. The roar of the boat's engine proved so unsettling and novel that crowds rushed down to the wharf to see what was happening.

As the New Orleans approached the village, the noise of the escaping steam and the wheel's revolution was heard for the first time in the tiny hamlet. The steamboat's echoes roused the entire population in an unwanted uproar. Even though it was after midnight, crowds came rushing to the bank of the river to learn the cause of the unwanted uproar that they had never heard before. They were certain that something terrible was happening. Men haphazardly dressed in inside-out pants and coats over shirtless chests were common. Women dressed in nightdresses dragged protesting children, still in their nightclothes, to the shore.

The New Orleans dropped anchor opposite the town. The brilliant moon was almost as bright as day.

"I guess we should tell them everything is fine," Nicholas chuckled. "Let's row the rowboat to shore and reintroduce ourselves."

Nicholas, Lydia, and Andrew went onshore and greeted the citizens of Louisville.

"That glorified barge of yours woke me and my wife up. We thought that the Great Comet had fallen into the Ohio River."

"Durn pretty boat you got here," said another. "Too bad it ain't gonna go back upriver."

Nicholas Roosevelt chuckled and slapped his friend on the back," We'll see. We'll see."

"Congratulations on having descended the river," other people said without exception. "Too bad this is the first and last time this or any steamboat will be seen above the falls of the Ohio."

"I don't know about that," Andrew said. "My father is already gearing up to have some more steamboats built at Pittsburgh. This boat may not come back, but it won't be long before more steamboats will be heading your way."

"How are the accommodations on the boat, Mrs. Roosevelt?" one of the women asked.

"It's as beautiful on the inside as it is on the outside," Lydia replied. "It's almost as nice as the home where we stayed in Pittsburgh."

"Is that a fact?" one of the women replied.

"It certainly is," Nicholas replied.

The next morning, Nicholas's friends in Louisville came aboard and told him the same things that the leadership of Cincinnati had told him. They assured him this trip was not just the first but would also be the last trip this steamboat or any steamboat that went downstream would ever make to Louisville.

However, all the leaders in the town agreed that the steamboat would likely be stuck in Louisville for some time.

One man shook his head. "I've been down to the river lately, and from what I can tell, the river is too low for this boat to navigate without tearing up its bottom. You might be stuck here until the spring rains."

Nicholas's forehead furrowed, and he nodded. "Andrew and I will check it out later today."

Nicholas explained that the boat was intended to carry goods between Natchez and New Orleans and was built for that purpose, but they had to get through this part of the river to make that possible. If the water at Louisville was not of sufficient depth to go over the falls, they wouldn't be able to go anywhere until it was navigable again.

The Falls were the biggest obstacle on the Ohio River. This series of ridges was caused by the Ohio River dropping 26 feet over a rise in the limestone bedrock. Andrew and Nicholas borrowed a canoe and traveled down to the area where the rapids of the falls began. They pulled the canoe up on the bank, and they walked down the road beside the rapids. Along the river, they took periodic water levels.

At the first few locations where Nicholas measured the water depth, he was hopeful. "What do you think, Andrew?"

"We might be able to get through this if we're careful." Andrew acknowledged.

Nicholas nodded. "If we're careful, we might."

At one specific location, Nicholas stood up, brushed the dust from his knees, and shook his head. He didn't have to ask Andrews's opinion. "There's no way that we will ever be able to get through this area. We're going to have to wait for some rain upstream."

Andrew nodded. There was nothing to do now but wait.

They found a driver with a wagon and paid him to return them and their canoe to the landing across from where the steamboat was moored at Louisville.

Susanna had been taking Rozella for a walk around the deck as the wagon rolled up to the dock. She saw that they were in the wagon and waved. She picked up the little girl and watched the men as they rowed to the boat and came aboard. She carried the child to where the men climbed the boat's ladder.

"Well?" She hiked the little girl up on her hip.

Andrew shook his head. "There's no way we'll be able to go over the falls right now with the steamboat without wrecking it on the rocks."

"I was afraid you'd say that." Susanna lowered her lashes. Andrew felt something inside himself as she did. He thought about the locket that his mother had given him and shook his head. He would not let his mother have the satisfaction.

Rozella held out her hands to Nicholas, and he took her in his arms. "How's my little pumpkin doing?"

Rozella nuzzled her father. "Good, Papa."

"How's Lydia doing?" Nicholas asked as his daughter hugged him.

"She's a bit uncomfortable," Susanna replied. "She's resting right now. I took Rozella out for this walk around the deck so that Lydia could rest."

"Thank you, Susanna, I'm glad that you are watching out for her. Sometimes Lydia doesn't know the phrase 'take it slow'".

Susanna chuckled. "Isn't that the truth?"

Do you think you should have left Lydia back in Pittsburgh?" Andrew asked.

"You should know by now that she would never do that. Once Lydia makes up her mind, there's no holding her back. I'm guessing that Rozella here will be no different."

Later that morning, a messenger came by boat to the New Orleans. The town's leadership invited the Roosevelts and the crew the next day to honor them at a public supper.

"What a wonderful gesture on their part," Lydia replied. "I think that Andrew here should escort Susanna to the supper."

"Who's going to keep an eye on Rozella?" Susanna asked.

"She'll be in bed by the time we leave, so I'm sure that P. J., who will be on watch, will be able to keep an eye on her for a couple of hours."

"I'd love to watch the little urchin," P.J. said.

Lydia lent Susanna one of her dresses for the occasion.

It was as grand an affair as any in this frontier region. The lady of the house, Mrs. William Faith, used her finest China and crystal for the Roosevelt family, who sat at the head of the table. She had an African American servant who cooked the meal and two others who served the meal at the table.

At the event, Andrew saw a man with long, thin, dark hair. His face was bare of any whiskers. His ears stuck out from his face. His face and body were long and lanky, and he wore western buckskin, unlike most of the other men in the room who were trying to make an impression on the captain of the New Orleans.

"Well, if it isn't John Audubon!" Andrew exclaimed.

"Well, if it isn't, Andrew Mayford!" he said. "May I introduce you to my wife, Lucy Bakewell Audubon?"

"So, John here got hitched," Andrew said.

"Are you married, Andrew?" Lucy asked.

"No, I have not yet found any woman who would have me," Andrew replied.

"Perhaps this young lady?" Lucy exclaimed. This caused Susanna to blush.

Andrew shook his head. "No, Lydia Roosevelt wanted Susanna here to enjoy the party, and she asked me to be her escort."

"Don't tell me that you are part of the crew of this monstrous and noisy boat," Lucy said.

Andrew shrugged. "Guilty as charged. Nicholas Roosevelt needed a pilot, and my father volunteered me."

John Audubon laughed. "How is your old man?"

"Father is doing fine. He is making money hand over fist as always. I'm just glad he has Charles, who enjoys that kind of thing." Andrew looked over toward Nicholas, who was talking with Richard Chenoweth and his wife. Nicholas nodded at something that Chenoweth was saying, but he looked like he needed rescuing.

"How would you like to meet Mr. Roosevelt?"

Audubon looked at his wife, and she nodded.

"We would love to," Audubon replied.

Andrew and Susanna led the Audubon couple to where Nicholas and Lydia were listening to Richard Chenoweth talking about his race-horses.

Andrew introduced Nicholas and Lydia to John James and Lucy Audubon.

"I've heard of you, Audubon," Lydia said. "My father speaks of you quite often."

"Your father?"

"My father is Henry Latrobe."

"Oh, yes, we met in New York a few years back."

"What are you doing for work, Mr. Audubon?" Nicholas asked

"I'm an ornithologist, naturalist, and painter."

"You're a what?"

"An ornithologist." Audubon saw that she didn't know what an "ornithologist" was, so he explained. "I study birds."

"What brings you to this area?"

"I am drawing photos of birds, animals, and plants in the area," Audubon replied. "Some people believe that I'm crazy. I would be more concerned about how that monster vehicle of yours will affect the wildlife on the river, but that's just me."

"So far, I have not seen a single bird or salamander harmed by the steamboat," Nicholas replied.

"Good to know," Audubon replied.

"So, why are you here specifically in Kentucky?"

"Well, I guess it was providence. I moved here in 1808 to Kentucky, which was rapidly being settled. Almost immediately, I met my beloved Lucy, and six months later, we were married. We traveled up to Fatland Ford, Pennsylvania, to her family's estate for the wedding. We went back to Kentucky the next day."

"So, do you share James's fascination with wild animals?" Susanna asked Lucy.

Lucy replied. "We probably wouldn't get along as well as we do if we didn't share many common interests. I also love exploring the natural world around us. Though our finances are often tenuous, our Audubon family is still growing. We have a son, Victor Gifford. He's back home. A friend of ours is watching him."

"So, you're here with just your wife?" Lydia asked Audubon.

"Oh, no. I had a partner until recently. I had a merchant business partnership with Jean Ferdinand Rozier, but we recently dissolved that partnership. I'm in the process of moving west to Saint Genevieve, Missouri, a former French colonial settlement west of the Mississippi River and south of St. Louis. We will be leaving in the next day or two."

"Until recently, Rozier and I had a general store here. Unfortunately, Louisville has increasingly become an important slave market, and slavery just doesn't sit well with me."

Andrew expected the two of them to discuss the woes of slavery, but Nicholas took the conversation in another direction.

"But Louisville is the most important port between Pittsburgh and New Orleans," Nicholas replied.

"Yes, but I can't help feeling that there's something wrong with holding another man as property, so we're moving to someplace with fewer slaves."

"I believe that what another man does is between him and God," Nicholas said. "If he feels that slavery is wrong, then he shouldn't have any slaves."

"I suppose. I would much rather study my birds than debate slavery."

"Yes, Lucy replied. "When I saw how much John loved his birds and wanted to return to drawing bird specimens again, we thought it was best to go west. He regularly burns his earlier efforts to force continuous improvement. He was also making detailed field notes to document his drawings."

"I would love to see them sometime," Nicholas replied.

"I would love to show you the good ones sometime, Mr. Roosevelt."

"Call me Nicholas. All my friends call me Nicholas."

"Truth be told, due to rising tensions with the British, President Jefferson ordered an embargo on British trade in 1808. The embargo hurt my trading business."

"How do you make ends meet without your business?" Lydia asked.

"My family and I are taking over an abandoned log cabin that I found earlier in the summer over by St. Genevieve. In the fields and forests, I can wear typical frontier clothes and moccasins, and carry my ball pouch, a buffalo horn filled with gunpowder, a butcher knife, and a tomahawk on my belt".

Lucy continued. "Like everyone else in this part of the country, he frequently turns to hunting and fishing to feed us, considering business is so slow. On a prospecting trip down the Ohio River with a load of goods, John had joined up with Shawnee and Osage hunting parties, learning their methods. He drew specimens by the bonfire, and when he parted ways with them. It was as if he were part of their tribe."

John Audubon then said. "I have great respect for the Indians. Whenever I meet Indians, I feel the greatness of our Creator in all its splendor, for there I see the man naked from His hand and yet free from acquired sorrow."

Andrew nodded. "My experience with Indians has been good too. Like anyone else, there are good people and bad people in every culture."

Lucy seemed to pick right up where John Audubon left off.

"People admire John's skill with Kentucky riflemen and the 'regulators', citizen lawmen who created a kind of justice on the Kentucky frontier," Lucy said with pride.

"Do you do a lot of traveling downriver to find specimens to draw?" Nicholas asked.

"I made a trip upriver on the Missouri this summer when I was looking for a place for us to settle," John Audubon replied. "I met the infamous Daniel Boone, who now lives near the mouth of the Missouri River."

Andrew nodded. "My cousin Isaac and his wife Rebecca live near them."

"You don't say."

"What's his last name? I might have met him."

"His name is Isaac Thorton."

"Thorton is your cousin? Yes, I met him. Nice fellow."

Other local citizens joined the festivities at the dance after supper. The farmers brought in jugs of whiskey from their farms, and the liquor flowed freely. Several men took out their musical instruments, and soon, everyone in the village was dancing to the music.

"You have a beautiful boat there," William Faith, the homeowner, said. "Too bad we'll never see it again."

"Of course, you won't see this boat this side of the falls again, but I can assure you, there will be more riverboats than you can count along these western rivers sooner than you can say 'going upstream'".

"So how is it that your steamboat can steam upriver without the aid of a pole, paddle, Cordell rope, or sail?"

Andrew saw Roosevelt's smile and the wrinkles around his eyes he got every time he was asked that question. Roosevelt happily explained the workings of the steam boiler, how the amount of steam it could produce, how it moved the gears that turned the paddle wheel that propelled the boat up or downstream.

William Faith shook his head. "That might work on eastern rivers, but I would imagine the currents here on the Ohio River and down on the Mississippi River, the currents are a lot swifter and have a lot more snags that can wreck any vessel, even a fancy one like yours."

Nicholas looked over at Andrew and smiled. "I thought about the risk of snags. That's why I chose to hire one of the best pilots on the river."

William nodded. "I would have to agree with you, my friend. I have heard a lot of good things about young Andrew Mayford here."

Nicholas then further explained how the mechanics of the boiler, gears, and paddlewheel worked. Andrew, who barely understood how the concept worked, could see by their glazed eyes that none of these men understood what Nicholas was talking about. Nicholas also saw that their companions didn't understand anything he said.

"I'll tell you what," Nicholas said to the leaders in the community. "Because you have been such fine hosts, I would like to return the hospitality of this invitation. I would love for you to come dine with us tomorrow evening aboard the New Orleans."

The Faith couple agreed. Lydia also invited several other couples to attend the dinner that the servants of the New Orleans would produce and serve.

The following day, the couples came at noon, and Nicholas showed them through the boiler room, where he explained the same information as he had told them at the previous day's meal. He showed them the boiler room, then the gears that moved the paddlewheel. This time, they seemed more interested because he had shared a point of reference.

The husband shook his head. "I see how all this will move the paddlewheel, but what makes you think that this will move the boat upstream?"

Andrew wanted to tell them that he had seen the paddlewheel go upstream at Pittsburgh, but he said nothing. Like he learned from experience, these people would have to see the steamboat in action themselves.

Nicholas motioned his guests to go to the upper deck to the gentlemen's cabin while he stayed back.

"Go on in, folks. I'll be right in. I need to speak with my crew for a moment. Andrew and Nick Baker stayed back while Nicholas gave them instructions. Nicholas and Andrew joined the couples who were in the gentlemen's cabin. Nick Baker excused himself.

As they entered the cabin, Nicholas said to Andrew. "Let's see how this goes."

At the dinner, Nicholas opened a bottle of the finest wine that he had reserved for occasions like this. Several complimentary toasts were drunk.

"To the New Orleans," William Faith exclaimed. "May the boat make it safely to its destination."

Nicholas would not be outdone. "And may it prove valuable in bringing supplies upstream as well as down."

"I'd like to see that!" William exclaimed.

"Perhaps you might!" Nicholas had a gleam in his eye that Andrew had seen before. He had a surprise planned for the guests.

Nicholas nodded at Andrew, and Andrew nodded back.

"Excuse me," Andrew said and stood up. "I need to check on something in the front cabin."

He left. He suddenly felt excited about what he was about to do. The crew, passengers, and their guests were about to go on an adventure they would not forget.

Susanna was serving dessert to the guests when she saw Andrew leaving.

"What have you and Mr. Roosevelt got cooked up?" she asked.

"You'll see," Andrew smiled back and exited the room.

Andrew met Nick outside the ladder that led down to the boiler room. "Are you ready?"

Nick smiled and nodded. "Yes, we're ready."

Andrew went to the wheelhouse. As he passed the gentlemen's cabin, he heard Nicholas giving a speech to his guests.

Andrew started the paddle wheel. The entire boat began to shake.

This will get them, he thought.

Andrew imagined the guests' reactions as they heard the rumblings and groanings from the lower deck and realized that the boat was in motion.

The boat lurched. That would get them.

Back in the gentlemen's cabin, Susanna watched the guests' reactions. She had guessed what was happening and was amused by those reactions.

The company had but one idea. They were horror-struck.

"The boat has escaped from her anchor and is drifting towards the falls!"

"We're all going to die!" Mrs. Faith screamed.

They were horror-struck.

A few minutes later, the guests heard a loud clatter and felt the boat lurch.

"Oh, my Lord, the boat has slipped its moorings!" Mrs. Faith screamed. She clutched her husband's arm.

Susanna looked at Nicholas, he saw that he seemed unscathed. Susanna nodded. She continued cutting the pie made of dried apples that she was serving.

"No, she's dragging her anchor!" Richard Chenoweth exclaimed.

"We're going to go over the falls!" yelled William Faith.

The guests instantly and simultaneously rushed to the upper deck. Their expressions turned from horror to confusion.

Instead of drifting towards the Falls of the Ohio, the New Orleans was making good headway up the river and would soon leave Louisville downstream in the distance.

"Why, we're not going downriver, we're going upriver!" Mrs. Faith exclaimed.

As the engine warmed up to its work and the steam blew off at the safety valve. The engine worked its magic as the steamboat increased speed.

"So, the boat really can move upstream!" Richard Chenoweth's wife exclaimed. "I am so relieved."

Yes, as I said, the boat can navigate upstream as well as downstream under her own power," Nicholas replied. "Just relax, folks, and enjoy your coffee and dessert."

But that wasn't happening. They weren't ready to just sit back to enjoy dessert in a cabin where they couldn't watch the landscape pass by them as the steamboat moved upstream.

They waved at the equally enthusiastic crowd of people from the settlement who saw the event unfold. The guests waved at the townsfolk as some of them ran toward the boat, excited to see this moment when the business owners and leaders of the community gazed over the bow.

They watched the people of the crowd on the riverbank grow smaller and listened to the rhythmic turn of the paddlewheel as they moved upstream.

"How far are we going upstream?" Mrs. Chenoweth asked Nicholas.

"I think we'll go all the way up to Cincinnati. I have a bet to win up there."

Mrs. Faith looked alarmed. "We can't leave our business that long!"

Nicholas held out his hand and lowered it. "Now, don't worry. We'll have you back to Louisville this evening around dark."

They all stood at the boat's railing and watched as the trees and river grass passed by.

"This is amazing," Richard said. "I have never seen anything like this. Is it safe?"

"As near as it can be. Although I suppose the boiler could explode," Nicholas smiled slyly.

The startled looks came as Andrew knew Nicholas had expected.

"Not to worry. I built the boiler to be as solid as possible. There's no danger of that."

Andrew didn't know if what he was saying was true or not. What he did know was that Nicholas wanted the New Orleans to put on a good show for his guests, and so far, it had succeeded.

"Can you imagine what this means for us in the future?" William Faith asked. "Soon, there will be no more poling upstream to get our goods to Cincinnati to sell them."

"That's right," Nicholas exclaimed.

When they arrived in the waters outside Cincinnati, Nicholas blew the steamboat's steam-powered horn to let the villagers of Cincinnati know that the steamboat had returned.

Not that they hadn't heard the boat when it was still miles away, Andrew thought drily.

He put a small rowboat into the river, and Andrew rowed the boat to the shore where an astonished crowd stood, including the men who had bet against the steamboat ever returning to Cincinnati. Nicholas and Andrew collected their bets and returned to the New Orleans.

Though the citizens of Cincinnati wanted Nicholas to stay, he had little time to spend there. He had to get his kidnapped passengers back to Louisville.

Upon return to the boat, Nicholas announced. "Reverse engines!"

Nick Baker and reversed the engines to return to Louisville

This expedition satisfied the croakers in Cincinnati and Louisville that the boat could go upstream. The New Orleans returned to her anchorage.

Andrew knew that moving the boat upstream had served primarily as a symbolic gesture. He knew that this trip down the Ohio River and soon, the Mississippi River, would make the old technology obsolete. Flatboats and barges would soon be replaced with steamboat travel in these western waters, as they were in the process of doing in the East.

When the boat returned to Louisville, she was greeted with an enthusiasm that exceeded, even, what was displayed on her original descent into Louisville. The business owners were now enthusiastic about the prospect of what they would gain when steamboats regularly traveled up and down the river from Pittsburgh.

Nicholas' quick thinking the day before, when he demonstrated the steamboat's ability to go upstream as well as downstream, had been genius. He had convinced the incredulous Cincinnatians and citizens of Louisville of what the New Orleans could do with one short trip upriver. Mr. Roosevelt had provided this mode of convincing his incredulous guests, and their surprise and delight may readily be imagined.

"You handled that beautifully yesterday," Andrew told him the next morning.

Nicholas smirked. "I had to prove to both cities that the New Orleans could indeed go upriver, as I always knew that she could."

"I think you just wanted to collect on those bets," Andrew laughed.

"Well, the money will come in handy to buy the supplies we need while we wait here for the river to rise so we can traverse the falls."

"That's true."

"Besides, let it be a lesson to you. Never bet against the man who owns the deck."

I'll try to remember that." Andrew smiled.

"Especially the man who owns the deck of a steamboat! Speaking as the man who owns the deck, how about if we head downriver and see what changes the river has in store for us?"

This time, it wasn't a man who held the cards. The weather and the river were the house in this case. Andrew doubted any positive change would occur that day, and he was right.

Chapter 11

Again, they had to wait. This time, it was because of the weather. Andrew had grown used to waiting. He knew that Nicholas had hoped to leave Pittsburgh and proceed as rapidly as possible to New Orleans to begin its planned route between Natchez and that city. He had intended for his wife to deliver their second child in New Orleans. However, that was not in the cards. He had already been delayed in Pittsburgh with the engine issues and was now delayed in Louisville.

The morning after the river ascent, Andrew and Nicholas again measured the river at the falls. This time, the river was lower than it had been the day before.

Nicholas shook his head. "It looks like we're in for a long wait."

Andrew shook his head. He had spent so much of his time over the past two years since they went down the Ohio River that first time. Waiting was something he was getting good at doing.

Susanna met them on shore when they returned from measuring the river again. She had come ashore using the canoe.

"Any progress?" she asked.

Andrew shook his head. "It was just as we had suspected. The water level did not rise. It's not as though we thought it would rise, but we didn't expect that it would drop another inch."

Susanna shrugged. I guess it's just as well because Lydia is in labor."

"In labor?" Nicholas rushed past Susanna and ran toward the rowboat that would carry him to the steamboat.

"You don't seem as though you're in a hurry, Susanna," Andrew said as he quickened his pace to reach the rowboat before Nicholas rowed it to the bigger vessel.

Susanna put her hand on his arm.

"You don't have to hurry," Susanna laughed. "It'll be a few hours before the babe makes his appearance. Lydia told me to take a break and to leave Rozella with her for now."

Nicholas had already launched the rowboat and was fighting the waves to get back to the New Orleans.

Andrew nodded. "I'm guessing you'll let me ride back with you on the canoe."

"Of course," she replied.

Andrew chuckled.

"We don't have to hurry," Susanna said. "Why don't we go for a walk?"

"Do you think that Nick will like the fact that you're on a walk with another man?"

"Nick? Why would he care?"

"I thought that you..."

"Nick and I? No, don't be silly. Nick and I are both just interested in the stars. I don't have any interest in him as a beau or anything."

Andrew felt his heart jump in his chest. Susanna wasn't interested in Nick Baker after all.

"I would love to take a walk with you," Andrew replied.

As they walked along the shore, they talked.

"How are you feeling about the possibility of being stuck here in Louisville until spring?" Susanna asked.

"It's the way of everything that we've had to face on this adventure."

"Do you think that maybe God has been trying to tell you to learn to let things work themselves out?" Susanna asked.

"Is that what you believe? Do you believe that God is trying to teach me something?"

"I do. I've seen you stress out, but I have also seen how you've become more patient with the situation. I do think that you need to give God a little more credit," she replied.

Andrew shrugged. "I don't know. How can I believe in God when there is so much pain in the world? It seems like God's just out there making fun of our pain."

Susanna shook her head. "I don't know what to tell you. I can't just wave a magic wand and make you believe. It's something that you have to work out for yourself. All I can tell you is that the God who put that comet out there cares about you."

They continued debating God's virtues. Susanna was not able to convince Andrew of what she knew about God. Andrew would have to discover his own path to God, but she was relieved that he was willing to discuss it with her.

Before they knew it, the sun was no longer rising in the east but was beginning to lower toward the west.

"It's after noon," Andrew said. "We'd better get back."

"Yes, Lydia probably needs me," Susanna replied.

They rowed back to the steamboat.

By the time they returned, Lydia's labor was further along than even she had expected. Nicholas was holding Rozella while at the same time holding Lydia's hand.

"Would you take, Rozella?" Susanna asked Andrew. "I need to assist Lydia."

"You sound like you know what you're doing."

"I did help her with Rozella's birth, you know."

"I didn't," Andrew replied. "I can see that you're a woman with many talents."

"I do what I have to," Susanna replied. As much as she loved talking with Andrew, she had work to do. "Can I trust you to keep an eye on Rozella?"

"I can do that," Andrew said.

"Out on deck, please?"

"Of course."

He took Rozella's hand and led her out on the deck, where the two of them played with Tiger. A little while later, Nicholas joined them. Nicholas picked up the stick that Andrew had been tossing for the dog and tossed it himself.

"Lydia told me to get out of the room," Nicholas replied.

"Why did she do that?" Andrew asked.

"She said I wasn't helping and just making the labor more difficult."

"You seem competent to me," Andrew replied.

"Well, apparently I'm not competent when it comes to assisting women who are in labor."

Two hours later, Susanna stepped onto the deck.

Nicholas stood up. "Is my wife okay?"

Susanna smiled and nodded. "Your wife and son are doing well."

"Son? I have a son?" he asked and then turned toward Andrew. Nicholas took a firm grasp of Nicholas's hand and pumped it. "I have a son!"

"A healthy baby boy," Susanna grinned.

Nicholas took Rozella into the room to see her mother and new baby brother. Susanna followed him back into the room. He left Andrew to continue throwing the stick for the dog to chase.

Susanna stood by Lydia's bed and was clearing out the mess made during the delivery while Nicholas cooed over Lydia and their son.

"What shall we name him?" Nicholas asked.

"I was thinking we should name him after my father," Lydia answered

Nicholas pressed his lips together. "I think it's as good a name as any. I think your father would be proud."

Lydia smiled. "That's what I thought."

In many ways, Susanna was relieved that Lydia had been able to give birth to the couple's second child while they were waiting in Louisville. It was good to know that experienced midwives were nearby if Susanna ever needed help. There were so many things that could have gone wrong. As they say, timing is everything. Fortunately, nothing had gone perfectly. Lydia was now the mother of a son as well as a daughter. They were the perfect family: father, mother, daughter, son.

Susanna felt a sudden loss. She thought about the home she left behind in France. They owned a beautiful home just outside the gardens at Versailles. Her mother would come out to the garden and have tea parties with her. Sometimes, others would join them. Other women and little girls often shared the backyard of their estate.

She sighed. She had just witnessed something she might never have the privilege of having herself. She ached to have a family of her own. She wanted a husband who loved her. She imagined living on an estate where she could have tea parties with her daughters. Life was not fair.

Her mind went to Andrew. She wished he would be able to see her as someone other than a Roosevelt servant. She shook her head. It would do her no good to think about something that would never happen. He was one of them. He might like to spend time with the average working person, but Susanna would not be fooled. She was not and was not likely to ever be one of them again.

After the excitement of the trip upstream to Cincinnati and Henry's birth, the great interest of all on board the New Orleans centered on watching the rise in the Ohio River's depth. Rain in the upper country was needed for them to continue, but fate seemed to be resisting the inevitable. Day after day, Andrew or Nicholas went to the falls to measure the water depth. Some days, the water was lower. On other days, the water was as high as it was the first time they measured the river's depths. However, the water never rose above that level. There seemed little promise that the Ohio River tributaries would ever oblige.

Over the next several weeks, Lydia and Susanna spent much of their time caring for the children, but for Nicholas and Andrew, it remained just a waiting game.

Rain in the upper country was what was wanted, but there seemed to be no clouds forming in the northern sky. There was nothing in the aspect of the heavens here in Kentucky that indicated it. On the contrary, a dull, misty sky without a cloud hung over them. Its heavy, leaden atmosphere weighed upon the spirits would have been better understood at Naples under the shadow of Vesuvius than on the banks of the Ohio. The sun, when it rose, looked like a globe of red, hot iron, whose color brightened at noon to resume the same look when it sank below the horizon. All day long, Andrew gazed at it with unflinching eyes. The air remained still and heated. He felt weary as the hours and then days ticked by.

The river had risen, but not enough for them to safely navigate the falls.

The air was oppressively warm for that time of the year. A sense of weariness wore on them as the hours wore slowly by. Nervous impatience affected everyone on board. While they remained in Louisville waiting for the river to rise, the townspeople shared rumors about Tenskwatawa and Tecumseh and of the Kentucky men who left Louisville to join William Henry Harrison's men in a show of force against them. Indian-white hostility finally erupted with the Battle of Tippecanoe on November 7, 1811. The Roosevelts and crew got news of the battle about two weeks later while still in Louisville.

One day, a pilot of one of the flatboats out of Cincinnati brought them a copy of the Cincinnati Western Sky, the newspaper out of their nearest other town.

"Hey, look here, there are a couple of articles about us," Nicholas read one of the articles aloud:

Western Spy (Cincinnati,)26 Oct 1811

Mr. Roosevelt, it is stated, is building a steamboat, to run on the Ohio and Mississippi, of upwards of 400 tons burthen, which it is supposed will traverse that stream against the current, at the rate of 35 miles a day, which will require six weeks to navigate from New Orleans to Pittsburgh.

"Here's another little piece," Nicholas stated.

Western Spy Cincinnati 26 Oct 1811

With pleasure, we announce that the steamboat lately built at this place by Mr. Roosevelt (from an experiment made on Tuesday last) fully answers the most sanguine expectations that were formed of her sailing.

She is 150 feet keel, 450 tons burthen, and built with the best materials and in the most substantial manner. — Her cabin is elegant, and the accommodation for passengers is not surpassed.

We are told that she is intended as a regular packet between Natchez & New Orleans.

"Ooo, here's some news that doesn't look good," Nicholas's forehead furrowed as he read the following article.

News of the Indian uprising, November 15, 1811

We're stopping the press to announce the following important intelligence brought by Doctor John M. Scott, who arrived this evening directly from Vincennes. This gentleman has politely favored us with the following particulars of a battle between the troops under Governor Harrison and the Indians. Captain Dubois of Vincennes arrived at that place express from the Governor - - states, that on the seventh the Indian prophet Tenskwatawa and his party consisting of about 190 Indians after professing friendship on the sixth in the evening, that they would the next morning come into the camp of Governor Harrison, with a white flag, and take him by the hand in friendship; made an attack on his army about 4 a.m. of the seventh, and continued the Battle until six that morning, when they were put to flight. There were left dead on the ground about fifty or sixty Indians, with some wounded. It is supposed they suffered considerably in their wounded, but the number is not known, as the Indians are in the habit of carrying them off together with as many of their dead as possible.

"Indians are attacking soldiers in the territory?" Lydia was sitting in her chair. A blanket covered the baby nursing at her breast. She refused to stay in bed as any midwife would have recommended. Susanna had tried to keep her in bed, but Lydia said she wasn't an invalid and wouldn't be treated like one.

"Will this affect our trip the rest of the way down the Ohio and on the upper Mississippi?" Nicholas asked.

Andrew shook his head. "I guess it depends on how many tribes Tenskwatawa can convince to join him."

Nicholas shook his head. "If those Indians we encountered last time we went down the river join him, we're in deep trouble."

Andrew shook his head again. "I have always known the Chickasaw to be aloof from the politics of those other tribes."

Nicholas nodded. "I hope you're right. As long as we have the fuel, I'm certain that the New Orleans can outrun any Indian."

Nicholas returned to reading the article.

The Governor sustained an injury, as his report says, of about one hundred and twenty. Some say there were 160 or 70 killed and wounded.

"Governor Harrison was injured? I wonder how bad," PJ said.

The governor, in a letter to Doctor Scott, states. . .

"Well, I guess he can't be too badly injured if he can send a letter to Doctor Scott, whoever he is." PJ shrugged.

Nicholas went back to reading.

. . that among the killed were Col. A. Owen, of Shelby County, Kentucky, aid to the governor, Colonel Joseph H. Daviess, of Lexington. Colonel Isham White, formerly the United States' agent at the Saline Saltworks. Captain S. Spencer of Corydon and his two subalterns, Captain Warrick Thomas Randolph, esq., and Mr. Mahon of Vincennes. - - That the prophet's town was burnt on the morning of the eighth. The corn crop, amounting as was supposed to 5000 bushels, was taken or destroyed. He expected to commence his march on the ninth to Vincennes, but it would be slow on account of the wounded and the precautions necessary to prevent annoyance from the enemy. Captain Dubois reports that Captain Berry was also killed in the engagement and that the troops under the governor's command behaved with great bravery. Too much cannot be said in favor of Colonel Boyd's regiment of regulars and Major Floyd's detachment, who sustained the heat of the action and acquitted themselves like heroes. Indeed, the whole army did wonders, considering the disadvantages under which they labored. An attack was not contemplated by the troops generally after the professions made by the Indian Chiefs on the sixth. That

Colonel Daviess lived nine hours after the action, and that Captain Bane of the regular troops was not dead, but expected to die every moment, from his wounds, that the governor received a shot through his hat which scratched the skin on the side of his head, and his horse was wounded.

"It sounds as though General Harrison's not too bad off if he can continue to give orders," PJ remarked. Nicholas continued.

Judge Taylor, of Jeffersonville, by the side of the governor, had his horse killed, which fell on him, and he remained in that situation until relieved by a person pulling the horse off him.

It will be particularly noticed that the troops under Gov. Harrison did not exceed the number of the Indians at the time of the engagement, he having been obliged to leave troops at the different forts on his way up.

"I guess they needed those forts well-guarded, but if he'd had a full contingency..."

Mars and Somerville are killed, along with many others. The number of wounded is very great. Geiger and Captain Hunter are slightly wounded. Most of our men from Kentucky are safe or not badly wounded.

"I'm guessing the Indians could learn a thing or two about fighting from those Kentuckians," PJ continued his commentary. "Why, I knew a trapper from Kentucky who..."

"Can we just listen to the rest of the article?" Nick Baker asked.

"Oh, all right," PJ threw up his hands.

Andrew knew that PJ might have argued more and maybe even started a fistfight with Nick Baker, but with the ladies present, Andrew knew that his friend would restrain his temper.

The rascals have got all our beef and many of our horses. Such a battle has never been fought. We have killed many of their Warriors—the most that we have found are old men; they were all through our camp. An old woman was left in the Town, who says that we have killed many of them and wounded many more. We are all in high spirits.

Another letter, received in a later post, states that the army was on the watch—that they were momentarily expecting another attack. From the situation and circumstances of the army, we think another attack by the Indians is very probable.

Will our government act, or will they always sleep? Surely, this is enough to arouse them from lethargy. In our next post, we will be able to give our readers a more particular statement about the battle, together with what may have happened subsequently.

Nicholas put the article aside. "Well, that's the end of that. Time to find something to do."

Everyone drifted away.

There wasn't anything to do but wait. One morning, Nicholas and Andrew would announce that there had been a significant rise in the river during the night. When would that be? When they finally did go, would an Indian attack stop their trip down the river?

Andrew looked at Susanna, Lydia, and the children. Were they wise to bring them along when there was an Indian uprising in the territory?

He didn't need to ask because he knew the answer. No matter what may be in store for them, these women would not back down and seek the safety of a fort or town.

Morning after morning, the rise in the river during the night was recorded. Finally, in the last week of November, they discovered that the water's depth was increasing. The morning finally came when in the shallowest portion of the Falls, exceeded by five inches the draught of the boat. It was a narrow margin. The next day, the water level was the same. The rise had ceased. They either left now, or they would have to stay in Louisville until after the spring rains.

Chapter 12

In the last week of November, storm clouds formed in the northern sky, and the river depth rose. The good news came when Andrew measured the shallowest portion of the Falls as exceeding the draught of the boat by five inches.

"It's not much. It is a narrow margin, but the river has ceased to rise. It may be now or never," Nicholas said as he and Andrew threw their equipment into the boat.

Andrew was certain that Nicholas was trying to reassure Andrew and perhaps even himself of the condition of the Falls.

"Perhaps we should wait longer."

"No, let's do it." Nicholas slammed his fist down on a rotten nearby stump. "As you're my witness, I will take full responsibility for the results to go over the falls whether we can or not."

They hurried back to the steamboat with the news.

"If we're going to do this, we'll need to lighten the boat's load," Andrew said.

"Yes, we'll need to unload our supplies to lighten the boat," Nicholas told the crew. "PJ, you know the area. Go hire a supply wagon and hire someone to take it to the dock in Shippingport. We'll be able to reload there. I don't want anything to happen to my family, so Andrew, I want you to let the pilot we hired know that we're ready to launch the steamboat. I also want you to hire a coach to take Lydia and the children overland."

"I will not ride around the falls like a child." Lydia had been listening from the women's quarters to Nicholas talking with the crew because she stalked out of her quarters' door and stood before him with her hands on her hips.

"Lydia, I just want to keep you and the children safe," Nicholas retorted. "It will be much more dangerous than when we went over the falls in the flatboat."

"I know you are just trying to keep me safe, but I'll have none of it. If something happens to you and the boat, I don't think I could live without you."

"Now, Lydia. . ."

"I made my mind up," Lydia said. "I won't be swayed into not going with you on the boat over those falls. I have been over those falls before, and you know I'm up to the task. Plus, you need as many eyes as you can to watch for obstacles in the river. I can keep watch as well as any man."

Nicholas rolled his eyes. "I refuse to allow the children to accompany us over the falls. Insist that the children go around by land."

"I agree," Lydia answered. "That's why I think Susanna should take the children around the falls by coach."

Susanna was standing beside Lydia and heard every word. "I would be happy to do that."

"Then it's settled," Lydia replied. "I will help us maneuver the steamboat over the falls, and Susanna will take the children to Shippingport overland."

"We'll pick up when we stop to get the supplies in Shippingport.

PJ did as Nicholas instructed and hired a wagoner company to help load and carry the heaviest supplies overland to Shippingport. Andrew went to get a coach to take Susanna and the children overland.

The coach would arrive later in the afternoon. The driver agreed that he would be able to have Susanna and the children at Shippingport by nightfall.

To increase their odds of making it safely over the falls, they took everything off the steamboat they could. They removed their supplies from the boat and loaded them onto wagons to be carried to Shipping-port, where those same items would be reloaded. The work was tedious but necessary.

The men worked feverishly to unload as many of the supplies as possible. Even Nicholas rolled up his sleeves and offloaded bags of flour from the steamboat. It took three wagons to carry all the supplies they would need to reach New Orleans. This included any excess firewood that they still had on the boat. ould carry little more than what they had to carry over the falls.

"That's probably close to a ton of goods removed from the boat," Andrew said. He wiped his sweaty face on his sleeve. Even though this was November, he had worked up a sweat.

Right on time, in the early afternoon, the coach arrived to carry Susanna and the children downstream by land.

When the coach arrived, Susanna carried Henry and held Rozella's hand at the same time. The Roosevelts and Andrew went to the coach to see them off.

Lydia kissed her daughter and then her son. Nicholas did the same.

Susanna smiled at the two of them. "I'm sure everything will work out fine. We'll see you on the other side of the falls."

Andrew suddenly felt a huge lump in his throat that wouldn't clear. He realized that he might never see Susanna again. He might not live long if the boat suddenly crashed on the giant rocks along the falls' path.

"I plan to be at the port when you arrive, Susanna, but if something happens to me, promise me you'll immediately take them to stay with my parents." Lydia sounded so certain of that as a fact, but her face was pale. She may have been brave, but she was still afraid. She wasn't as foolhardy as she sometimes sounded.

Susanna's eyes grew wide. "I promise. I'll see you on the other side of the falls."

Andrew's eyes met Susanna's. Their eyes locked for what seemed like an eternity. Time seemed to stand still as only a few seconds had passed. She turned away first.

Nicholas lifted Rozella into the coach. Lydia held Henry while Andrew helped Susanna into the coach.

"Nothing is going to happen to you," Susanna then asked for Lydia's reassurance. "Promise me."

Lydia said. "I promise."

Susanna then spoke directly to Andrew. Her voice was barely above a whisper.

"You make sure everyone safely makes it to the other side. These children will need their parents."

"I'll make sure they make it," Andrew swallowed hard. His mouth was dry, and the seriousness of the situation hung heavily in his chest. He had been over the falls many times with flatboats, but he never piloted anything as big or heavy as this steamboat. They had very little wiggle room and no room for any errors.

He wanted to say more, but the lump in his throat wouldn't let him get the words out.

Nicholas closed the door to the coach and knocked on the coach's side, signaling to the driver that he could leave. Nicholas laid his arm over Lydia's shoulders, and the three of them silently watched the dust trail of the coach rolling down the road.

Nicholas broke the silence. "Well, let's get our steamboat moving."

At the boat, he asked Nick Baker. "Do you have enough wood to get us to the other side of the falls?" Nicholas asked.

"Yes, sir," he replied.

"Not too much, though?" Nicholas asked. We need this boat to be as light as possible."

"We'll have just enough wood to get us to your pile of coal," Nick replied.

"That's good to hear," Nicholas replied. "Let's get a head of steam going and see how this boat can move."

All hands were on deck except Nick Baker, who had gone below to pile wood into the boiler's firebox. Lydia, whom her husband would have willingly left behind, joined him near the stern.

Andrew and the hired pilot took their places at the bow. The second pilot had been hired as an extra pair of eyes to help guide the passage over the falls.

The anchor weighed. The boat ran on the Indiana side rather than the Kentucky side of the river. To get into the Indiana side of the channel, which was the best, a wide and deep circuit, Nicholas navigated the boat into position and brought the steamboats head upstream. Once in position, the New Orleans began the descent.

Nick Baker put on all the steam the New Orleans could produce. Nicholas Roosevelt steered the craft and watched Andrew's instructions from the boat's bow.

Steerage's way depended upon her speed exceeding that of the current. The faster she went, the easier it was to guide her. All the steam the boiler would bear was put upon her. The safety valve shrieked. The wheels revolved faster than they had ever done before.

Crowds collected on the shore to watch their departure from Louisville. The vessel flew past the crowds.

Andrew thought about that crowd for a moment. He contemplated that the crowd gathered on the shore was cheering as much to see the steamboat wreck as they did to bid farewell to the Roosevelts and their crew. It was a morbid thought, but no doubt true.

"They won't get their wish if I do my job." Andrew had not forgotten about the incident the previous year when the flatboat had grounded during that storm. Fortunately, there was no storm today, but there were boulders to avoid at all costs.

Andrew glanced over at the other pilot. His eyebrows furrowed. His mouth pressed in a line. His gaze was fixed on the water below. Andrew imagined that he was thinking that joining them on the New Orleans had been a mistake.

Instinctively, each one on board now grasped the nearest object that was firmly attached to the boat. With bated breath they awaited the result. The black rock ledges appeared and then disappeared as the New Orleans flashed by them.

The waters whirled and eddied. Waves tossed spray upon the deck as a more rapid descent caused the vessel to pitch forward to what at times seemed inevitable destruction.

Not a word was spoken by any of the crew. They all focused on the job at hand.

With hand motions, the pilots directed Nicholas, who was at the helm. Even, Tiger, the great Newfoundland dog, seemed affected by the apprehension of danger and came and crouched at Lydia's feet with his paws covering his eyes.

Andrew didn't know how he handled the stress he felt in his mind and body. He felt his heart pounding in his chest and wondered if at any moment it would burst. He couldn't imagine having to sustain this degree of stress for long. He looked forward to the moment when the danger had passed.

Then, almost as quickly as the turbulence started, the river smoothed like glass. The Shippingport dock came into view.

The paddlewheel slowed and then stopped as the New Orleans neared the dock.

"We did it!" Lydia exclaimed and hugged her husband.

"We did it!" Nicholas exclaimed. He hugged her back, picked her up, and swung her around.

The entire crew joined the celebration. Andrew and the extra pilot hugged one another. Nick Baker came up from the boiler room and joined the rest.

"Thank God!" Lydia exclaimed. "I can hardly believe that we are safely below the falls!"

With profound gratitude to the Almighty, Nicholas Roosevelt, his wife, and the whole crew aboard the New Orleans actively thanked God that they had arrived safely below the Falls.

They stopped at Shippingport in front of the pile of coal at the side of the river. There, they would wait for the supplies, Susanna, and the children.

"Let's start loading the coal onto the boat," Nicholas said. "We've wasted enough time on the Ohio River. I'm ready to travel down the Mississippi."

Everyone on board agreed wholeheartedly. They all said goodbye to the extra pilot who had helped them get over the falls.

"Let's get this coal loaded," Nicholas said.

As they loaded the last of the coal onto the boat, he said to Andrew. "This should last us several days."

Andrew nodded. He now saw the value of the coal. The coal would not only burn longer, but it would burn hotter. It also had a higher flash point, so having a pile of it near the boiler was not as dangerous as having wood nearby.

When they ran out of coal, the crew of the New Orleans would have to load up the boiler room with wood every other day. The wood that they would have to scrounge also could not be too dry or too green. The task would be more difficult along the Mississippi River than it had been on the Ohio. There were not enough towns along the river in which to purchase a wood supply.

Now that they had succeeded and maneuvered the falls, they had to be more concerned about the Indian uprising and potential attacks. The fact that Indians had boarded the flatboat on their previous trip downriver left Nicholas especially anxious to get past the Chickasaw Bluffs. While the crew of the New Orleans was more amused than alarmed at this incident of the voyage, Nicholas, who had not forgotten the visit to the flatboat on the preliminary exploration.

Andrew knew that Nicholas felt especially anxious about that part of the trip because he could not forget those Indians who boarded the flatboat when they had been in the area two years earlier.

After reaching the Mississippi, the boat would be tied up each afternoon while the crew planned to go ashore to cut and bring in wood for the next day's consumption.

They had sat so long in Louisville that everyone was ready to put the miles between themselves and Louisville. No one complained that

Nicholas asked them to load the coal on the bank. Even Lydia helped by operating the rope on the pulley to bring the coal onto the deck and into the fuel bin.

They were still loading the coal when the wagon with the supplies and the coach that carried Susanna and the children arrived.

The coach stopped at the end of the pier while the supply wagons came down to the deep-water pier to where the steamboat was moored. The crew began unloading the supply wagon while the Roosevelts went to the end of the pier to retrieve their children. The parents gathered their children in their arms.

Susanna ran ahead toward Andrew.

"Thank God, you're okay." Susanna stopped dead in her tracks.

Andrew was amused. At the same time, he felt his stomach make a flip-flop.

"You were worried about me?" Andrew asked.

"Of course," Susanna answered.

"I'm glad," Andrew said. He saw her blush. Could it be that she felt about him the same way that he was beginning to feel about her?

Susanna moved closer to him but then stopped herself.

"I'd hug you, but you're covered with coal dust," Susanna replied.

Andrew shrugged.

'Enough lollygagging," Nicholas replied. "We're almost finished loading the coal, and we've still got all those supply wagons to unload."

"Yes, sir," Andrew replied and then turned back toward Susanna. "Duty calls!"

Nicholas and Andrew replaced the men on the ship who loaded the coal into the bin.

"I wish they had mined more coal," Nicholas replied. "This won't last more than a couple of days."

Andrew shrugged. "Well, there is plenty of firewood along the Mississippi."

Once the coal, supplies, and Susanna and the children were collected at Shippingport, the New Orleans was finally able to continue her voyage downriver.

There was still the same leaden sky -- the same dim sun during the day -- the same starless night. However, the great difficulty had been overcome. They were finally over the falls, and nothing had happened to them. Andrew believed that there would now be nothing but smooth sailing to New Orleans, their port of destination.

Surely the worst was over, he thought.

Chapter 13

The New Orleans steamed on down the Ohio River and onto the Mississippi River. The coal lasted longer than the wood usually did, but what little they had lasted only a couple more days, just as Andrew had predicted.

By the night of the fifteenth, the last of the coal was shoveled into the firebox of the boiler, which meant that they would have to return to gathering wood daily onshore in the evening of the third day.

The men loaded as much firewood as they could into the fuel bin and then put as much as possible by the cookstove set up in the kitchen.

"We have a little extra that won't fit in the hold," one of the men told Susanna. "Where do you want us to put the rest of what we've cut?"

"Go ahead and put it in the kitchen by the stove," Susanna replied. "I'm sure the cook will be able to use it. Just don't put it too close to the firebox."

"Very well," the man said.

"Susanna, can you come help me with the children?" Lydia called from the women's cabin.

"I have to go," Susanna said. "Just close the door when you're done."

Most of the crew went to bed that night, but Andrew was on watch when he smelled a familiar acidic smell.

Smoke.

He looked out onto the shoreline along both sides of the river but didn't see any signs of any campfires. He thought the smoke would likely be coming from the boiler room, but when he went to the hatch to the fuel bin, he realized that the smoke wasn't coming from below.

"Where could it be from?" he asked out loud and then answered himself. "It's the kitchen!"

The kitchen was beside the women's quarters. Susanna, Lydia, and the children were in danger.

He ran past the women's quarters to the kitchen. The smoke rolled out from under the door. He pulled the door open, and flames lit up near the cookstove.

He took a deep breath and ran into the room. He held his breath so that the smoke would not overcome him. Logs on the woodpile had ignited and were on fire.

He saw a shadowy figure moving about in the orange glow of the room. That person was coughing and at the same time swatting something at the flames. He saw the flames come and go each time whoever it was struck the flames with what he could only assume was a gunny sack.

He focused his eyes on that person's face. In the flicker of the fire, that person's face became apparent.

It was Susannah. She was striking the fire with a gummy sack. Still wearing her nightgown, her slim form was accentuated under the white fabric. Her hair was loose around her shoulders. He didn't have time to feel embarrassed about seeing her in this state.

"Get out of here!" Andrew yelled. He then called out to alert the rest of the crew and the Roosevelts. "Fire!"

"No!" Susanna shook her head. The woman was as stubborn as Lydia was.

Still coughing, she continued beating the fire. Her face was covered with black soot. Muddy-looking sweat dripped down her face.

Andrew grabbed another gummy sack and soaked it in the water barrel at the corner of the room. The gunny sacks and the flames sizzled every time they struck the fire. The flames soon diminished into smoke. Andrew grabbed the water dipper from the water barrel and doused individual smoking logs. Susanna took a pan off the wall and collected water to dump on the fire. The logs sizzled. The room became dark as they extinguished the flames. Soon, the fire was completely out.

Andrew was shaking. Not because he had been scared for himself or the rest of the steamboat crew. He was shaking because he was afraid for Susanna. If he hadn't shown up when he did, she might have. . . He didn't want to think about what might have been.

"Why didn't you call out for someone to help?" Andrew asked. "You could have been killed!"

He had been afraid for Susanna. The thought was crystal clear. At that moment, it was crystal clear that he loved her in a way that he had never loved anyone.

By now, the other crew members were running out of the men's quarters and onto the deck and toward the kitchen. With the idea of Indians still predominant, Nicholas had seized his sword—the only weapon at hand and rushed from the cabin to join the battle.

"I'll save us from those Indians!" Nicholas exclaimed. He must have thought that they were fighting the Chickasaws.

"The kitchen is on fire!" PJ exclaimed.

Lydia came running out of the women's quarters. She was still in her nightgown, but unlike Susanna, had wrapped a blanket over her shoulders to cover her nakedness. She carried a crying Henry and held the hand of a whining Rozella. Andrew guessed they had been asleep when their mother dragged them from their warm beds.

"Everything is fine, folks," Andrew exclaimed. "We got the fire out. Go back to bed. Some firewood was just too close to the stove."

The group groaned and murmured to themselves.

The crew member, the one Susanna had talked to in the kitchen before bedtime, looked at one of the other crew members. "You brought wood in after me! Why weren't you more careful when you brought in the wood?"

"I didn't put wood near the stove! I put it on the far right! You must have put the wood next to the stove!"

They continued blaming each other for who put the wood so close to the fire.

"It's all over, gentlemen," Nicholas exclaimed. "It's all under the bridge now. Like Andrew said, it's all over. Go on back to bed."

Only Rozella and Henry's eyes were closed for the rest of the night. The accident didn't tranquilize the nerves of the travelers.

"Are you sure you don't need any help?" Nicholas asked.

"No, I'll just toss the scorched pieces over the railing and then clean up. No need for anyone else to get their hands dirty."

Nicholas nodded. "Are you certain that you don't want any help?"

"I'll help you," Susanna replied. "I'm sooty too."

"You don't need to do that." Andrew objected. He didn't feel comfortable being alone with Susanna.

Nicholas was the last one to go back to the men's cabin. Because they weren't certain that there weren't any live embers still in some of the scorched logs, Andrew and Susanna removed any logs that contained any scorch marks.

"Do you think we should throw them overboard?" Susanna asked.

No, there aren't very many of these. Let's just put a few of them directly into the cookstove here, and the rest we'll take down and put in the boiler's firebox. No point in wasting the wood. Just be careful not to burn yourself. There might be some live embers in those logs."

Susanna nodded.

"You take them from the kitchen to the hatch, and I'll go below and put them in the firebox," Andrew said.

She nodded again.

The job didn't take long. Soon, the scorched wood was safely stowed in the kitchen stove and in the boiler's firebox.

What about the scorched woodwork?" Susanna asked.

Andrew let out a long, deep breath. "I guess we'll need to wet it down to make sure that it doesn't catch back on fire."

Susanna took a bowl from the cupboard and splashed water on the wood behind the stove and up the wall where the wood was scorched. In some areas, the wood sizzled, indicating live embers.

Andrew then grabbed a coffee cup from the cupboard and helped Susanna soak down the woodwork. It took longer than either of them had expected.

Susanna wished that they had not told the rest of the crew to go to bed, but at the same time, she was glad that she could spend time alone with Andrew. She felt safe when he was around.

Soon, the sizzling stopped. A pool of water had formed along the baseboards of the woodwork.

Susanna grabbed a ragged towel from the pile of dish towels.

"Here, let me," Andrew said. He took the rag and sopped up the water along the wall. At the same time he touched the wainscoting to ensure that the wood was cold and would not reignite after they went to bed.

"Thank you. I guess we need to wash ourselves up and get back to bed," Susanna exclaimed.

Andrew looked at her as if for the first time. Her nightgown was smudged with soot. Andrew went to the water bucket in the corner. He took his handkerchief from his pocket and dipped it into the water. He then squeezed the excess water from the cloth. He went back to where Susanna stood.

"What are you doing?" Susanna asked.

"Let me wipe the soot from your face," Andrew replied. He gently patted a sooty smudge with his damp handkerchief.

He could see her slim body under her gown. She had a burnt hole in the skirt of her nightgown.

He moved the cloth to the side of her head and cupped her face in his hands. He lowered his lips to hers.

Susanna suddenly realized her state of undress and pushed him away. "I don't."

She looked him in the eyes, but she wasn't angry. She was just questioning his motives.

"I won't hurt you," Andrew said. He liked the taste of her lips.

He bent and kissed her again. He felt her submit to his kiss. He deepened the kiss. He felt as though the boat was moving under his feet. He had never felt like this before.

"Did you feel that?" Lydia came out of the women's quarters.

Andrew stepped back from Susanna. She crossed her hands in front of herself.

"Something was rocking the boat," Lydia said as she approached the two of them.

Indeed, something was rocking the boat. The fowls of the air, which were usually sleeping in their roosts at this time, were flying up into the air and squawking angrily about being shaken from their slumbers. The waves on the river were higher than usual. Susanna wasn't the only one to rock his world. Something was literally rocking the boat.

She felt every fiber that moved suddenly stopped. It wasn't just her nerves that were affected, though. The boat shook and trembled.

"Earthquake?" Andrew asked.

They heard the door to the men's quarters open. The men aboard stormed out of the berthing area. P. J ran and vomited over the side of the boat. "I feel sick," one of the men said. The others complained too that they felt nauseated, as if they were seasick from being tossed during an ocean storm.

"I feel fine," Susanna replied. She felt confused about all that was happening. First, Andrew's kiss, and now the earthquake tied her stomach all in knots.

At that moment, Nicholas Roosevelt ran from the men's quarters.

"What was that?" Nicholas asked. He had a gun in his sword in his hand, the only weapon he owned. "All hands-on deck! We're being attacked!"

For the second time that night, all the members of the crew were on the deck.

Andrew shook his head and laughed. "No, we're not! I think it was a little earthquake."

"What makes you think we are being attacked by Indians?" Nick Baker asked. "That's the second time tonight."

"We're almost to the place where we were boarded by Indians, and I was alarmed that they were boarding the New Orleans like they did on our preliminary voyage."

In the morning, they examined the damage to the kitchen. The joiners' work close by had caught, and the entire cabin would have soon been in flames. The entire steamboat may have met its end before it ever made it to its destination, had Susanna, half suffocated, not rushed into the kitchen, and Andrew not been alarmed.

By dint of Andrew and Susanna's great exertion, the fire, which had been making rapid headway, was extinguished. However, the interior woodwork had been severely destroyed and defaced. They would have to replace it once they reached New Orleans if they could find workmen worthy of the task.

The fire and now the earthquake did nothing to tranquilize the traveler's nerves concerning the Indian threat. There was no way for them to know if the Chickasaw would join the other Indian nations in their push to retain their lands. Would the Indians determine that this earthquake was somehow an omen to do that?

Chapter 14

Andrew noticed that a diminished current speed indicated a rise in the Mississippi several miles into the mouth of the Ohio. The boat continued traveling downriver and soon entered the Mississippi. Water this high was unusual for this time of the year.

The boat had finally entered the Mississippi. Andrew planned to tie her up at night to the shore, but the shore caved so often from the earthquake that the plan was abandoned, and the boat was anchored at the foot of an island. They continued to feel aftershocks from the earthquake throughout the day as they moved down the Mississippi. Fortunately, the impact of the quake was gentled by the wave action of the paddlewheels at the New Orleans' flanks. Andrew could tell when an earthquake or an aftershock occurred by the movements of trees and birds that he saw on shore.

On the night of the fifteenth, they came to anchor on a sand bar, about ten miles above Little Prairie. Three barges and two keels had been moored along the shore, and all were affected the same way. An aftershock occurred, and then a second shock occurred fifteen minutes after the first. The second was much stronger than the first.

"Another full-blown earthquake. Look at the trees," P.J. said. The crew unanimously agreed that by the sway of their craft, it was a big one.

Susanna couldn't get rid of the rising panic she felt in the pit of her stomach. It was almost as bad as how she felt when she and her grandmother escaped France when she was a child. Would they survive this series of quakes and aftershocks?

Andrew weighed the anchor early in the morning, and in a few minutes after they started, more seismic activity occurred in quick succession, two other shocks, more violent than any of the former.

It was daylight, so Susanna immediately saw its effect on shore. The bank of the river had collapsed in all directions and came tumbling into the water. The trees were more agitated than ever before, except when she saw them in the severest weather. Many of them bent so much from the shock that they broke off near the ground. Others lay uprooted as though someone had pulled it out from the bank like a weed. Susanna felt more secure on the water, but the danger of grounding on new sandbars heightened the danger. What she feared most was that Andrew and the others had to go ashore to gather firewood for the next day's journey downriver.

Andrew was working in the wheelhouse. He and Susanna had not talked since the first earthquake had hit.

Susanna decided to go to the wheelhouse.

Andrew was looking at one of the gauges and writing information down in his logbook.

Susanna was not certain whether he heard her or felt her presence, but he looked up when she came to the door.

"I'm sorry. I see you're busy," Susanna turned to leave.

"No, don't leave, Susanna," Andrew said. "I can use a little company."

Susanna nodded. She went into the area where Andrew worked. Just being near him made her heart beat harder in her chest.

"How are you holding up?" he asked.

"I'm scared," she said.

Andrew nodded. "I'm not going to tell you there's nothing to fear because there is. I'm traveling blind here."

Andrew took her into his arms, not in a romantic way, but more like a father comforts a child.

"I want you to know that I'm doing everything in my power to get us out of this situation. Even if we lose the boat like we did two years ago, I promise you that I won't let anything happen to you or Lydia, or the children, or anyone else on the boat."

"Do you think that something will happen to the boat?" she asked.

Andrew placed his hand under her chin and turned her to face him. "I will do everything in my power to keep this boat afloat, but I have to admit that if you think your prayers can do anything to protect us, I want you to pray as hard as you can."

Susanna nodded. "I'll pray and God will protect us."

Andrew stroked her lips with his thumb and started to lower his mouth to hers when Lydia called for Susanna. She took a deep breath and stepped away from him.

"I have to go," Susanna replied.

"Yes," Andrew said.

Susanna went to the door and looked back for one last look at Andrew. This could be the last time she ever saw him. Another earthquake could slam them against shore, or it could get smashed on another sandbar. He could be killed, and she would never be able to tell him that she loved him. Sadly, now was not the time. She had a job to do.

"I'll see you later," Andrew said.

"Later," she called back and hurried to the women's quarters.

That afternoon, they arrived at the small village of Little Prairie on the Missouri Territory side of the river. They stopped there to resupply wood for fuel.

While the members of the crew were still ashore, a distraught man rushed toward the New Orleans. His body was soaked from the waist down.

"What's wrong?" Susanna asked the distraught man from the deck of the steamboat. "

"I watched from the shore, up at Plum Point, two boats, laden with port wine, were destroyed. Just like that! Waves came up out of the river like a sea serpent. One was smashed into pieces and the other capsized. Mr. Atwell will be devastated!"

"Mr. Atwell?"

"Yes, the man who hired the crew to haul the wine!"

"What about the crew?" Susanna asked

"I helped them to shore," the man said. "They all survived. But Mr. Atwell has lost everything. How devastating for such a worthy, industrious man to be deprived of his wealth."

Susanna frowned. She wondered what this man's connection was with Mr. Atwell, and she knew it was none of her business. In her mind, however, she wondered why two boatloads of port wine were more important to this man than the crew's lives. She said nothing to the man about this, who continued into the village of Little Prairie.

A few minutes later, the crew from the New Orleans returned with the firewood.

Susanna helped the cook bring wood from the rowboat to the kitchen while the rest of the crew put the wood below the deck near the boiler. The two of them made sure that the wood was safely stowed away from the stove.

"A man told me that the earthquakes capsized a boat upstream," Susanna told Cook.

Cook nodded. "Yes, we saw him. He was looking for Joseph Atwell to tell him of his loss. Last I heard, he went to find someone who could tell him where Atwell was. The man went off looking for someone, anyone to help him."

"How are the people in Little Prairie faring? Were any of them injured?"

"I had not heard if anyone was injured or if any lives were lost, or if an accident of consequence had occurred, because we found no one to ask. The town's inhabitants and the nearby settlers had all deserted their homes. They must have escaped into the hills or maybe the swamps and away from the trees that were falling.. Fortunately, I didn't see much damage in that town. All I saw was that tremors demolished a single brick chimney in Little Prairie."

At that moment, Andrew came into the kitchen carrying an armload of wood. He dropped the wood on the pile beside the stove.

"Did you see anyone in town?" Susanna asked. She stacked the wood that he brought onto the neat stack that she and the cook had made.

"I did. I finally found one man to talk with," he said. "He couldn't tell us exactly when the tremors started because everyone was still in bed. He said that the shock lasted several agonizing minutes, accompanied by a noise like that of an approaching storm, as heard in a forest, and was so violent that it shook the houses and awakened all who were sound asleep in their beds."

"About the time that we experienced that first quaking," Susanna replied. She then remembered that she had been kissing Andrew at the time. She felt the heat rising into her face. She looked shyly at Andrew, who was smiling at her intently. He was no doubt remembering the same thing, and realizing that, she blushed even more.

Mercifully, Cook continued the conversation. He seemed oblivious to the exchange between the other two.

"That was when I joined you, Andrew. The man said that the second shock, more violent than the first. He said he ran down to the river while the others ran for the hills. He said that the river current was three times its former velocity. The water, he said, had risen six feet. That was at seven-thirty this morning."

"Which is why the current slowed when we were still on the Ohio River," Andrew replied. "Well, it looks like we'll survive another day," Andrew had returned to his usual worried self. "I need to get some more wood."

As he started to leave the kitchen, another shock began. All three of them ran out of the kitchen and onto the deck. This shock threw sand and logs from the riverbed. Rocks and other debris tumbled down large portions of the Mississippi's banks. Logs that had probably lain prostrate for ages beneath the river's bed were instantly bolted upright. One log end was firmly fixed into the muddy river bottom, and another appeared from below and rose above the water.

As the tremors subsided, some hunters hailed them from the eastern shore of the Mississippi.

"Are any of you injured?" Andrew asked.

"Hey there. No, we're fine right now," one of the men called to them. "It's terrible out here. I've never seen anything like it. The Earth has been cleft in hundreds of places on the Bayou River. I swear, the fissures are deep enough to swallow up a man. The weird thing about the fissures is, the only way I can describe it is, that they are vomiting up torrents of water from the very bowels of the earth. An island, located a short distance above the river, was most violently agitated and cut in every direction with gaping chasms."

This dreadful visitor was wholly unexpected. The rest of the crew, except Nick Baker, joined them at the railing. The Roosevelts were not there. Susanna left to see if they needed any help calming the children.

"I'm glad we missed that one," PJ said. "This situation is becoming more unsafe with every tremor. The ground is cracked and torn to pieces. I wouldn't be surprised if some of the islands we passed by yesterday disappeared. One of them must have been about two hundred acres! Can you imagine it completely sunk!"

Andrew and Cook nodded. This once-friendly part of the Mississippi had now grown inhospitable. They needed to remain on their toes if they were to get out of this situation with their lives.

Nicholas blew the steamboat's horn. It was time to continue downriver. The crew and passengers of The New Orleans felt no tremors for the rest of the day.

On that first night beyond Little Prairie, the steamboat stopped for the night. Andrew secured her tightly to a tree along the riverbank. However, as he did, he saw trees swaying. Some that were standing for one minute, toppled and fell the next. The ground beneath them had shaken and given way.

Andrew untied the rope and threw it up to Nicholas.

"I think it's safest if we stop at the foot of that island overnight tonight rather than try to secure the boat to vegetation on the shore. Plus, the foot of the island will serve as a breakwater if there is another quake tonight."

"That sounds like as good a plan as any," Nicholas replied when Andrew suggested.

On the island, Andrew wanted to ensure there were no trees that were too close to the boat. He didn't want one to topple onto the boat if another tremor occurred. They settled in for the night.

"I'm glad that's over," Lydia said to Susanna that evening as they readied the children for bed. "I anticipate a quiet rest after all of that excitement."

"I agree," Susanna replied.

They laid down to rest, they might have been asleep for a couple of hours when something woke them. The steamboat shook, not rhythmically like wave movement during a storm, instead the shaking created a jarring sensation.

"What is that?" Lydia, half asleep, asked.

A noise continued. Hard objects grated against the planking outside the boat. Both women sat up in their beds.

"I'm sure it's just driftwood slamming against the boat," Lydia said. A continuous scratching mingled with the gurgling sound of the water. "Yes, we've heard that before. I'm certain that it must just be driftwood from upstream striking the boat."

The true explanation came in the morning. After Susanna had dressed and was changing Henry when Andrew gave a sharp yell.

Hastily, Susanna pulled the gown over Henry's head, wrapped him in a blanket, and took him out with her to see what all the fuss was about.

"The island has disappeared!" Andrew exclaimed.

It was true. The island had disintegrated into fragments of dirt and plant debris. It had swept down the river. The remnants of the island trees were striking the vessel and still creating the noises that had awakened Susanna and Lydia during the night.

"The boat has come loose of its moorings and been borne along by the current!" Nicholas said. He joined them at the bow of the boat.

Andrew shook his head and pointed at the landmarks on the banks. "See that. It's the same landmarks we had last night. We're in the same place we stopped. We haven't gone downstream! The island has disintegrated beneath us!"

It was true. The island had disappeared into pieces and floated downriver, while the steamboat ropes had kept their place. Where the island had been, there was now a broad reach of the river.

PJ had also joined them and asked. "What are we going to do?"

"There's only one thing we can do. Otherwise, it will be impossible to free the vessel," Andrew exclaimed. "PJ, cut the anchor."

Andrew looked out onto the water. He felt a sudden panic fall over him concerning their situation. He was utterly at a loss as to which way to steer. He wasn't sure how to proceed. He knew now that the New Orleans was in trouble. The Mississippi was no longer the river that he knew and loved. It was now an alien world to him. It had changed in so many ways that he had no way of knowing any of the landmarks. Known islands had disintegrated into mud and debris. Fallen trees clogged known river channels. Would this cause the New Orleans to fall prey to the same fate that Roosevelt's flatboat had two years earlier?

Andrew looked across the river to where several river flatboats were moored.

"Hey? What do you think we should do?" Andrew called out to them about what to do.

"I guess the thing we'll need to do is to use our long oars to keep where the current is strongest," one of the boatmen called back. "Otherwise, I don't know what else to tell you."

Andrew nodded. This was, evidently, the best plan for the New Orleans, too. Only he would maneuver the steamboat using the paddlewheel. It was not without risk, however. At the bends in the river, where the rushing river struck the shore, it could whirl around the curve and glance off to form a bend in an opposite direction. The deepest water was usually immediately under the bank. However, was that still true? Here, the trees, undermined by the current, could be seen at times, sinking into the stream, often erect until the waters covered their topmost twigs -- sometimes falling against each other, interlacing their great branches, struggling for life when drowning. Sometimes, they fell outward into the water, and then woe to the vessel that happened to be near them in the bend. Fortunately, the steamboat could power through these types of danger and avoid the trees.

The voyage was resumed. The weather was calm and cloudy. A drizzly mist fell. The temperature was a little above freezing. At about noon that day, they saw a familiar face riding a horse along the river. It was Audubon. He waved and they waved back. Nicholas dropped anchor and he and Andrew rowed to shore.

"I was wondering about you and your steamboat when the first earthquake struck," Audubon said. "It doesn't appear that you suffered any damage."

Nicholas shook his head. "No, Andrew here has kept us from hitting any debris in the river or channel changes. How about you?"

"I was out riding in the moonlight, looking for some night birds, when the earthquake struck. At first, I thought the distant rumbling was the sound of a tornado, but the horse that I rode knew better than I what was forthcoming, and instead of going faster, nearly stopped. He then pawed the ground with as much precaution as if walking on a smooth piece of ice."

"What do you mean 'the horse knew?'"

"Well, let me tell you what I observed, and you decide for yourself if the horse knew something I didn't. At first, I thought he had suddenly foundered, and speaking to him was on the point of dismounting and leading him when suddenly he fell, groaning piteously, hung his head, and spread out his forelegs. It was as if he was trying to save himself from falling. He then just stood still and continued groaning."

"The horse did that?"

"He did! I thought he was about to die, and I would have dismounted and shot him had a minute more elapsed, but at that instant, all the shrubs and trees began to move from their roots. The trees fell in successive furrows, like the ruffled water of a lake. It was then that I realized I was experiencing an earthquake. I never experienced anything like it before. If others hadn't experienced them and described one to me, I would not have known what it was. Now I know!"

Both Nicholas and Andrew nodded.

"First time for us, too," Nicholas replied.

"I can't describe the sensations which I experienced when I found myself rocking, as it were, upon my horse, and with him moving to and fro like a child in a cradle, with the most imminent danger around me. Finally, the shaking stopped, and I hurried home, but fortunately, there was no major damage. A couple of jugs fell off the mantle. The wife and children were shaken up, but they were fine. The aftershocks have been unnerving, though."

After talking for a few more minutes, Audubon went inland on the trail. Nicholas and Andrew secured some more wood and then rowed back to the New Orleans, and the steamboat continued downriver.

While underway, the jar of the steamboat machinery against river debris, the monotonous beating of the wheels, and the steady progress of the vessel prevented further earthquake tremors from being noticed. However, the steamboat passengers could see the destruction as it happened on shore. The passengers and crew were terrified.

Susanna counted twenty shocks that day with variable intervals between them. In the morning, the shocks were between 10 to 20 minutes apart. By afternoon, they were from 30 to 55 minutes apart. At nightfall, the shocks came less frequently, at one to two hours between tremors. She noticed that the lake waters forced their way out into the river. The birds, especially swans, geese, and ducks, could find no place whereon they dared to rest. They remained in flight most of the time, only settling long enough for a quick rest before they spread their wings and flew again.

The whole atmosphere was impregnated with a putrid smell that reminded her of rotten eggs.

The bottom lands on either shore were underwater. It was as though there had been a great flood, but these changes in the landscape were not caused by any flood. Canoes came and went among the boles of the trees. Sometimes, the Indians attempted to approach the steamboat but fled on its approach. The Chickasaws still occupied this part of Tennessee lying below the mouth of the Ohio.

In the afternoon, a large canoe, fully manned, came out of the woods abreast of the steamboat.

"Indians!" Nicholas exclaimed.

The Indians, outnumbering the crew of the vessel, paddled after it.

"They're coming after us!" Andrew yelled. "Tell Nick we need full power! They aren't going to catch us!"

A race between the steamboat and the Chickasaw warriors ensued. For a time, the contest was equal. The result, however, was exactly as Andrew anticipated. The steamboat had the advantage of endurance.

With wild defiant shouts, the Indians gave up the pursuit and turned into the forest from which they had emerged.

Still, Andrew found the river navigation extremely difficult. In many places, the snags were extremely thick, and he had to watch the river while Nicholas handled the steering.

As the days went on, the long continuance and frequency of these shocks wearied the crew.

Andrew began to wonder if these quakes would ever cease. He also wondered if the earthquakes were felt as far as New Orleans. What could be said about Natchez? Would they arrive at one of those cities and find them demolished? Would the city of New Orleans, so close to sea level, already be sunk into the sea, never to be seen again?

The next day, Nick Baker came running up to the bridge. "What is going on! The engine acted like it had to work like it was going upstream!"

"That's because it is! I have never seen anything like this!" Andrew exclaimed.
The Mississippi is running backward."

"What the...?" Nick Baker looked out at the river and saw that it indeed was moving backward.

Nicholas came to the vessel's bridge, and Andrew told him what was happening.

"You've never seen this before?" Nicholas asked.

"No, I have not."

The day continued as surreal things occurred. Two waterfalls briefly emerged in front of the New Orleans as the river's bed shifted to accommodate the tremors.

"Do you remember the last time we came down the Mississippi? At this spot, there was an island, and look up there! That one wasn't there before," Andrew exclaimed.

"Hold up here a minute. We need to turn this thing to the opposite shore," Andrew exclaimed. "The channel on the map is blocked by debris. The channel has moved to the other side of the river."

Susanna came out to the bridge and smiled at Andrew. She dropped her smile when she saw the look on his face. "What's wrong?"

"Everything is wrong," Andrew exclaimed. "Nothing's like it should be."

"What do you mean?"

"I mean, the earthquake has completely changed the course of the river, and I don't recognize the landmarks. The channels have completely changed."

Nicholas looked down at the navigation chart that he had used the first time they went down the Mississippi, "None of this is on the navigation chart!"

"This navigational chart is meaningless," Andrew wadded the chart and ceremoniously threw it into the rubbish can. "We're having to brave miles of utterly uncharted waters."

Tremors continued into the night. No one was able to sleep, even baby Henry slept fitfully. Susanna felt one tremor at two-thirty and then another at six in the morning. Another one occurred at eleven, just before the noon meal. It was immediately followed by a second shock that lasted eight seconds. She was glad to be on this big boat and not on shore while all this was going on. She tried to imagine what it was like for the people on shore, but the thought frightened her so much that she decided it was best for her to deal with her own fears.

The New Orleans moved into an area where the passengers and crew realized was the worst damage they had seen thus far. A continuous rain fell during the morning. That same day, they saw the longest tremor that they had experienced yet. It lasted for an entire minute.

Another violent shaking occurred several hours later. This time it lasted an entire three minutes. Smaller aftershocks occurred throughout the day, along with occasional bouts of light rain all through the afternoon. The evening grew chilly, and the wind's direction changed.

The following morning, the eighteenth, was winter cold and with snow flurries. Frequently, light shocks continued throughout the day. There were also six more significant ones. The wind blew from the northwest.

That day, they arrived at what they thought was once New Madrid.

"What happened to this place?" Nicholas called out from the railing of the steamboat. The pier at New Madrid was gone. Trees that lay toppled and submerged in the river. The log house that they had seen on their previous trips was destroyed. The roof had caved in, and the log walls lay in ruins. Too many of the landmarks that they knew were no longer available. What Nicholas had learned on their first trip down the Mississippi was almost worthless.

"Isn't it obvious?" The man who answered didn't sound too friendly.

The earthquakes had caused the ground to rise and fall, bending the trees until their branches intertwined and deep cracks opened in the ground. Deep-seated landslides occurred along the steeper bluffs and hillsides nearby. Large areas of land were permanently uplifted, and still larger areas sank and were covered with water that erupted through fissures or craterlets.

Nicholas ordered them to drop anchor in the deepest part of the river, and several of the crew, along with Nicholas, Lydia, and Andrew rowed the rowboat to the shore. Susanna stayed behind to care for the children.

"Come on, Tiger," Lydia called the dog. Tiger jumped into the rowboat and sat on the floor at Lydia's feet.

Nicholas looked questioningly at his wife.

"For protection, plus, I'm sure he wants to run around a little bit. Plus, if Audubon is right, he might let us know if there could be another earthquake."

As they neared the shore, Andrew noticed that people were fleeing the area and hiding behind the ruins that he remembered were homes when they were last at New Madrid

A man was fishing off the shore where the pier had been. He seemed unaffected by their arrival.

"Is this the result of the earthquake?" Nicholas asked.

The man spit on the ground and then motioned to his surroundings. "What do you think? People ran off because your boat made such a ruckus that they thought it was another earthquake."

"Is the Colonel around?" Nicholas asked one of the men near what had been the landing.

"Colonel? What Colonel?" the man asked, his eyes haunted, as if he had witnessed hell.

"Colonel George Morgan," Nicholas answered.

"Oh, Colonel George Morgan had died last year," the man said. "Say, do you have any food? I have a wife and six kids, and all the food we had stored was destroyed in the last quake."

Nicholas shook his head.

Some of the other boatmen shared the same distant, shell-shocked look on their faces. Nearby, several boats were smashed on the shore.

One of the boatmen stopped staring at one of the smashed boats and helped Nicholas drag the boat onto shore. Then Nicholas helped Lydia out of the rowboat. Though some people ran off, others surrounded the newcomers.

"I don't know what I am going to do," the boatman said. He glanced over at the destroyed hull. "I lost everything. My boat was heaved out of the water and crashed on the shore just before I could be tied up at the settlement."

"Huge waves on the Mississippi River not only destroyed my boat, but many boats and washed others high onto the shore. High banks caved and collapsed into the river; sand bars and points of islands gave way."

Nicholas nodded, "We saw a lot of the same things. Some land was raised and others sunken. That chaos makes it difficult to navigate. Someone will need to revise the navigational charts."

"A lot more damage can be seen on the land. There are fissures, sinks, sand blows, and large landslides," another man said.

"Even though many of our cabins were thrown down and most of our chimneys were toppled, we only lost one life, an elderly woman on the north side of town. We had a funeral for her this morning."

A woman with two children in tow, a boy and a girl, neither could have been older than four years old, came up to Lydia. Their clothes were torn and dirty. They looked like they were in shock. The boy had a wound on his forehead.

"Please, help us. We've got nowhere to turn. My husband is a boat-man who went downriver a week ago before the quake. Our food stores were ruined when the earthquake destroyed our home. We have nothing. We haven't eaten in two days."

Lydia looked over at her husband, but Nicholas shook his head. "I'm sorry. We can't. We barely have anything ourselves. I hoped we could get a few supplies here when we stopped. I can see that we won't be able to do that. We have barely enough food to take us as far as our destination. We don't have enough to share."

"Please, if you see my husband, let him know that we're hanging on," the woman replied.

"What's your husband's name?" Nicholas asked.

"His name is John Bradbury."

"Maybe we'll see him along the river," Lydia replied.

As the Roosevelts and the crew viewed what happened at New Madrid. The shocks have been uncommonly violent, throwing down chimneys and houses and compelling one-third of the inhabitants to remove from the place to the adjacent hills and the remainder to encamp in tents in open fields. The earth was so convulsed as to render it difficult for one to keep their perpendicular position — the motion being estimated at 12 inches to and fro. The shocks were accompanied by a partial darkness, tremendous noise, and the now familiar sulfurous smell. Sixty-seven shocks have been witnessed in all, which have split and cracked the earth in a hundred places in the neighborhood. During the violent shocks, the people yelled and shrieked. They discovered their extreme alarm, and upon one of those occasions, a lady had fainted and never recovered! The face of the country below Little Prairie has almost entirely changed — large lakes having been converted into dry land, and fields into lakes — the banks of the river fallen in — mills destroyed, and the earth cracked in every direction.

An inhabitant told Andrew about his experience. "About 2 o'clock this morning, we were awakened by a most tremendous noise, while the house danced about, and seemed as if it would fall on our heads. I soon conjectured the cause of our trouble, and cried out that it was an earthquake, and for my family to leave the house. They had difficulty doing that because the quake rolled and jostled them about. The shock was soon over, and no injury was sustained, except the loss of our chimney and my family's exposure to the cold of the night. At the time of this shock, the heavens were clear and serene, not a breath of air stirred. However, in five minutes it became very dark, and a vapor, which seemed to impregnate the atmosphere, had a disagreeable smell, and produced a difficulty in respiration. I knew not how to account for this at the time, but when I saw in the morning the situation of my neighbor's houses, I realized that all of them were injured in some way.

I attributed it to the dust and soot, and so on, that arose from their fall. The darkness continued till daybreak. During that time, we had eight more shocks, none of them so violent as the first."

That must have been terrifying for you and your family," Lydia exclaimed.

"It was. If we thought it was over, we were sadly mistaken. At half past six in the morning, it cleared up. Believing the danger over, I left home to see what injury my neighbors had sustained. A few minutes after my departure, another shock occurred. Extremely violent, it was. I hurried home as fast as I could, but the agitation of the earth was so great that it was with much difficulty that I kept my balance. The Earth's motion was about twelve inches side to side. I cannot give you an accurate description of this moment; the earth seemed to convulse. I watched the houses shake. Chimneys that had survived thus far fell in every direction. I can't stop the loud hoarse roaring of the earthquake, together with the cries, screams, and yells of the people from ringing in my ears."

"Do you think it's over?"

The man shrugged. "Who can tell? We have been having tremors several times every day for a week now. Fifteen minutes after seven o'clock, that same day, we had another shock. This was the most severe one we had yet. The darkness returned, and the noise was remarkably loud. The first motions of the earth were like the preceding shocks, but before it ceased, we rebounded up and down. The tremors were so bad, we could barely keep our seats. At this instant, I expected a dreadful catastrophe. I heard the uproar among my neighbors heightened the horror that has befallen us. I imagine that our screams and yells could be heard at a great distance."

"Does anyone have any ideas about what may have caused the quake?"

The local man continued. "One gentleman, who is quite educated, says that the convulsions from the earth are produced by the world and the comet coming in contact, and the frequent repetition of the shocks is owing to their rebounding. The closeness of the comet yesterday evening was so strong that the quake has leveled my chimneys. Another person with a very serious face told me that he was ousted from his bed, he was really afraid and thought the day of judgment had arrived until he reflected that the day of judgment could not come in the night."

"I wish there was more we could do."

Other people whose homes had been swallowed up in the earthquakes begged to be taken aboard the New Orleans. Others, frightened by the steamboat, took to the woods and hid. Already, plantations, stock of all kinds, cribs of corn, and smokehouses full of meat were offered for horses to help people leave the area. The misfortunes and privations were driving hundreds to acts of desperation.

Andrew knew that these people were in dire straits. Since 1808, cotton had been the staple crop of this part of the country. The average yield per acre was 1000 to 1200 pounds of cotton seed, but with these never-ending earthquakes and so much bottomland disappearing into the river, would they be able to plant when spring came? Would these people even be able to survive until spring?

Sadly, the crew returned to the steamboat with firewood, but not much else. Even hope was becoming questionable. If the situation was this bad here, could it be worse even further downriver?

Winter weather was setting in. The tremors and aftershocks continued day and night as the New Orleans steamed down the Mississippi. Fortunately, the steamboat avoided all the major debris the steamboat encountered.

The shocks have been uncommonly violent. When they stopped for wood that day, the men saw that a cabin's chimney had been thrown down, and the cabin was just a pile of logs. The cabin's inhabitants camped in tents in an open field.

"We didn't know what else to do but set up here in the field," the man said. "The trees are falling everywhere, and the only halfway safe place we could determine to set up was here in this field."

Nicholas nodded. "I've never seen anything like this."

The man introduced himself as Roger Campbell. His wife's name was Matty. His children's names were Janie, Pauly, and the baby's name was Ian. Ian wasn't much older than Henry.

The family looked haggard. The mother's dress was caked with mud, and the children looked like they hadn't bathed in months. The baby had a croopie cough.

Nicholas pulled out a package of coffee from his pocket. "I know this isn't much, but..."

"Land sakes, Mr. Roosevelt. I'd be happy to put some on the fire."

Matty readily took it and set a pot to boil.

As the crew was loading the last of the firewood onto the rowboat, Mattie came to them with her pot of coffee."

"The coffee is ready if you want some," she said. "I've got a squirrel soup cooking too if you'd like some."

Nicholas smiled sadly. These people had virtually nothing left, yet they were offering what little they had to the travelers.

He shook his head. "No, thank you. You enjoy what you have."

This family had not asked for anything and yet were willing to share what little they did have. They had not asked for passage downriver either. It seemed admirable, but at the same time, their situation seemed fatalistic.

As the crew got into the rowboat, the earth convulsed again. The motion rocked the waves beneath the rowboat, and they could barely keep the boat upright. Fortunately, the firewood was evenly distributed on the rowboat so that it didn't tip over, even though the waves were probably a foot high.

The shock was accompanied by a partial darkness, tremendous noise, and that same hellish sulfurous smell.

The tremors stopped, and mercifully, the rowboat did not capsize under the weight of the wood. All hands on the New Orleans quickly loaded the firewood. They survived another earthquake.

By the twentieth, the wind was calm. The bucket just outside the kitchen had a thick film of ice on it.

Susanna hoped today would be the day that they would no longer see the effects of the tremors that had become a daily part of their lives. She thought about what Andrew had told her about their outing the day before and the family who were living in that tent in the field.

All was calm, and then suddenly, the tremor arrived as though just thinking about it made that earth demon that caused the earth's movement to come to life. She looked out over the steamboat railing and saw that it was less violent than many they had experienced. She sighed. Weary of all this, she wondered if these constant earthquakes would ever stop.

Several more occurred before noon. That evening, around eight, Susanna looked into the sky. The comet was no longer visible, but even if it were in the night sky, she had lost her interest in that phenomenon. The night sky was clear except for a circle around the moon. She felt more aftershocks as she prepared for bed.

As she lay in bed, she felt yet more movement from the winter. She rolled over and wondered if these earthquakes would ever stop. How far south did the earthquakes affect the ground? Had the earthquakes gone as far south as New Orleans or even Natchez? Would they find everything gone? What would happen to them if they couldn't get more supplies? What would happen if they were the only people left on Earth?

As they passed more small settlements along the river, during the most violent shocks, Susanna heard the people yelling and shrieking above the din of the steamboat motor. They no longer stopped at these communities simply to help rescue people. Nicholas had decided their well-being had to be their utmost priority.

Later that day when they stopped for firewood, they learned of a woman who fainted and never recovered. The face of the country, below, about Little Prairie, has almost entirely changed. Large lakes became dry land, and fields were converted into lakes. The riverbanks had fallen in. Mills were destroyed, and the earth cracked in every direction.

Sadly, Andrew and Nicholas shook their heads. There wasn't much they could do to help these people.

As they continued down the Mississippi, the river was oppressive by its silence. The shores on either side were wilderness. The birds were eerily quiet. Wildlife was nowhere to be seen.

Again and again, tremors rippled waves on the Mississippi. Though not as intense as the original quake was, aftershocks continued to shake the landscape throughout the day.

Andrew constantly stood at the steamboat's bow to ensure they didn't run aground. He never felt so vulnerable. What if he made a mistake and drove the steamboat into an unseen sandbar?

Everyone was on edge.

"You're doing fine," he heard a voice behind him say.

It was Susanna.

Andrew shook his head. "What if I got it wrong? What if Nicholas made a mistake by not helping those people?"

Susanna put her hand on his shoulder. "I have faith in you and in Mr. Roosevelt."

Andrew felt electricity run through his body. *She had faith in him. It was the best thing he had heard all day.*

That night, Andrew tied up the steamboat at the foot of another island. During the night, another earthquake occurred while PJ was replacing Andrew for the last watch. At dawn, he discovered that the island had disappeared. Again, he had to cut the mooring rope to remove the boat from the submerged tree.

"It's as though this river wants to shake this steamboat out of the water," PJ said.

"Well, it hasn't done it yet," Andrew replied. "It won't either. I won't let this boat sink like the flatboat did. We have those children to think about."

Another large shock hit later that morning. Tiger howled and mourned and ran to Lydia for sympathy.

"It's okay, Tiger," Lydia said. "We're safe."

She crouched down and gave the dog an affectionate scruff of his hair. What she said next, she said in the same tone. The dog quieted and wagged his tail at her reassurance. "I sure wish I could reassure myself as easily as I have you."

A few more miles down the river, they met a flatboat moored on a small island.

At that moment, another tremor struck. When it ended, Andrew asked the man on the boat. "Everything okay?"

"No, it's terrible, but not equal to the first. Fortunately, my boat is still holding out. Say, did you pass by New Madrid?" He asked.

"We did," Andrew called out.

"You didn't happen to come across my wife and children, did you?"

"Perhaps," Andrew replied. "What's your name?"

"The name is Bradbury."

"John Bradbury?" Andrew asked to clarify.

"Yes! How did you know?" the man called back.

"Yes, when we saw your wife and children, they were alive."

"How are they?"

Andrew didn't know how Bradbury would take his answer. He pursed his lips and turned his head to the side. "They are hanging in there, but your home is destroyed. They wanted to let you know that they are hanging in there and that they miss you."

"Thank you!"

The New Orleans continued down the river and left John Bradbury and his crew to their own devices.

"Let's stop here for the night," Andrew exclaimed. As soon as he said it, there was another quake. The effect of this shock alarmed Andrew.

"Ignore the last!" Andrew exclaimed. "Full steam ahead!"

The steamboat lurched forward. Water rushed at the steamboat. Susanna expected the vessel to be grounded by the sudden tsunami that arose from the stream. The current increased to three times the velocity it had before the quake. The bow of a boat rose several feet. Due to the steamboat's speed, it was not overcome. Susanna watched in horror as they headed straight for a pile of debris. A sudden turn of the boat cleared the pile of uprooted trees.

They continued downriver for several more miles. They saw two flat-bottomed boats lying destroyed on the shore.

One was splintered into kindling, and the other overturned. The crew stood nearby. Another shock struck. Trees embedded in the mud at the bottom of the river suddenly had one end elevated to the surface, rendering the river almost impassable. Andrew found a channel and directed Nicholas as they cleared that area.

Again, they stopped to gather wood from another small river town. Again, the villagers begged to be taken aboard to escape the earthquake's desolation, but sadly, New Orleans lacked the provisions to feed the refugees and would have no more available until the boat reached Natchez, Mississippi, if that was if the town was still intact.

Other flatboat men on the river that they met and passed were similarly affected. They nodded as the steamboat passed, but they shared no jovial greetings.

Andrew saw one boatman. He recognized him as someone he had known most of his life on the river.

"Hey, Paul!"

"Hey, Andrew! Can you believe these earthquakes? I've never seen anything like it," the man exclaimed. These earthquakes have caved in so many of the banks, and made such changes in the river. I'm at a loss for how to maneuver on this river. How are you faring, Andrew?"

"We're just playing the river by ear," Andrew answered. "I have never seen anything like it either. Have you heard how things are further down the river?"

The man shook his head. "I can't tell you anything. I haven't heard anything about Baton Rouge, not to mention Natchez or New Orleans. All I know is that it's bad around here, extremely bad."

The New Orleans continued her journey. Andrew had to pilot the river like it was his first time down it. However, it was worse than that because, as Nicholas had discovered earlier, the navigation charts were now grossly inadequate to tell them anything about what they would encounter.

Tall trees that he used for navigation in the past had been swept into the river. Well-known islands had disappeared, and new ones appeared elsewhere. Cut-offs had been made where before there was forest. There was no place to stop and no way to learn the changes, and Andrew had to keep the steamboat on course.

Canoes came and went among the boles of the trees. Sometimes, the Indians attempted to approach the steamboat and, again, fled on its approach.

The banks of the Mississippi gave way in various directions – 10 to 15 acres of ground have sunk. Trees were prodigiously shaken, broken off, and torn up by the roots as is usual in the most violent storms. Nearly all the islands in the river, containing from one to two hundred acres, have sunk or splintered into smaller islands. The trees lay concealed in the river and threatened any craft that had the misfortune to float over them. As Andrew had seen many times, the trees had been raised erect several feet out of the water, as those shocks succeeded each other. The atmosphere continued to smell like rotten eggs.

Susanna and Lydia stood at the railing and looked out beyond one of the sandbars along the shore. They recognized changes in the shoreline compared to what it had been like during their previous trip down the river.

One day, as they stood there, they saw two great trees that had been growing along the shore for a hundred years sink and crash into the turbid waters.

Andrew came over to the rail and followed Susanna's and Lydia's gaze.

"That's exactly why I'm compelled to keep the boat away from the shores because I'm afraid trees will fall and damage the New Orleans. I'm even going to try to moor up to any islands until we're out of this mess."

An eerie silence came over the inhabitants during this stretch of the steamboat voyage. No one seemed disposed to talk, and when there was any conversation, it was carried on in whispers. Tiger seemed to be aware of the earthquake while the vessel was in motion. They knew when a tremor was shaking the earth because he paced the New Orleans' floor, moaned, and growled. Then he came and placed his head on Lydia Roosevelt's lap, it was a sure sign of a commotion of more than usual violence on shore.

Nicholas and Andrew gave orders in low tones. The usual cheerful "aye, aye, sir," of the crew was almost inaudible. Sleeplessness was another characteristic. Sound and continuous sleep had become unknown to the travelers on the steamboat.

Going ashore for wood during the evening every twenty-four hours was an event that the crew looked forward to, even though it involved heavy work. Still, Andrew noticed that the men did not toil sullenly, but silently. If the earth shook, as it often did, while they worked, the uplifted axe was suspended, or placed quietly on the log, and the men stared at each other until the earth's movement ceased.

This depression was not confined to the steamboat. The same occurred when they passed flatboats and barges. whose crews, instead of bantering with river wit, as they had done during the voyage from Pittsburgh to Louisville, now, keelboat men no longer gave any greetings as the New Orleans passed them.

Now, looking at each other, the crew and passengers on the New Orleans saw that they had started looking as haggard as everyone else.

Lydia said to Susanna, "I am living in constant fright. I am unable to sleep, sew, or read. I am afraid that at any moment, one of the trees will come crashing down and end our voyage and our very lives. Sometimes I wish I had accepted Lowri Mayford's advice and stayed in Pittsburgh. Not for my sake, mind you, I made this decision. However, I have my children to think about. What was I thinking? I should have listened to Lowri Mayford and stayed in Pittsburgh! What was I thinking?"

Susanna got down on her knees beside Lydia's chair and looked up into her eyes.

"We can't think about what we should have done or should not have done. Our situation is what it is. Your children will be fine. We'll be fine," she whispered. She didn't know if what she said was true or not. However, just saying it calmed Lydia's trembling.

Lydia took a deep breath. "I guess, like you say, things are what they are. I have to live with the decisions that I've made and do the best that I can with these circumstances. I want you to know, I am willing to die myself before I would let anything happen to one of my children."

Susanna nodded. "I know."

Early in the afternoon of each day, the steamer fastened to the bank, and the crew continued going ashore to cut the wood required. On some of these occasions, squatters begged to come on board with tales of their experience upon the land, which they insisted shook and trembled under their feet. Nicholas had talked about using the sail that he included on the boat, but Andrew argued that sailing would make river navigation more difficult.

One day, as the men were cutting their daily ration of firewood, some Indians joined the woodcutters. Nicholas stayed on the steamboat that day, and Andrew oversaw the operation.

"Good afternoon, "one of the Indians said in English to PJ. PJ jumped back and held his ax over his head as if he were going to strike the Indian.

The Indian raised his hand. "I mean you no harm. If we had, you would already be dead. We come in peace. In your language, my name is Indian Factor. I was once an agent with the American government for our people."

Andrew held out his hand in friendship, and Indian Factor and his companions shook hands with each of the men of the cutting crew.

"Are you men from the Penelore?" Indian Factor asked.

"Penelore? What's that?" Andrew asked.

"Penelore is Chickasaw for fire canoe." The Indian replied.

"We are," PJ answered. Andrew shot a stern glance at him. The Indian may have said they came in peace, but the crew of the New Orleans had to be careful with their responses. The man may have spoken English, but that didn't mean he and his companions weren't superstitious.

"Why do you call the steamboat a 'fire canoe"? Andrew asked.

"We call it that because the sparks from the boat's chimney are like the train of the celestial visitor. I believe you call it a comet."

"You think our boat has something to do with the comet?" Andrew asked.

"Yes, there are many in our tribe who believe that. They believe the rumblings of the earth are caused by your fire canoe's fast-revolving paddles and the beating of the river waters. We have never seen anything like your steamboat in our boundless forest that lined the riverbanks. Many feel that the coming of this "fire canoe" of yours is an omen of evil. The fire in the sky and the trembling of the ground are a warning that we, like many other tribes, will be removed from our ancient homes."

Andrew thought about this. He had seen native tribes removed from their homelands when he was a child growing up in Pittsburgh. The white man signed treaties with the red man. They told the Indians that the treaties gave the Indians certain rights, but in fact, instead only made demands of the tribal leaders. He had heard that often one Indian tribe would sign a treaty, signing land that belonged to another tribe over to the white men so that their tribal lands were left in peace. Andrew knew that a white man's treaty was never good for the Indians.

Andrew suddenly was afraid that the Chickasaw, with the assistance of their neighbors, would raise the long-buried tomahawk and attack the whites. However, these men were not dressed in war paint but remained in their regular winter clothing, so they weren't likely to attack the New Orleans' crew while they collected firewood.

Andrew saw that the former Indian agent, Indian Factor, was watching him intently.

"I see fear in your eyes," Indian Factor said. "As I said, we come in peace. I can tell you that the Prophet Tenskwatawa has sent messengers to our people. He said that he had spoken to the Great Spirit, and he found great displeasure in the white man's disobedience because they damaged the earth. He said that he predicted that the earth would be agitated and convulsed and threatened immediate dissolution for the Chickasaw disobedience for allowing the white man to cut down our trees and scrape our fields with their plows. Many believe in his magic. Especially now that the earth moves under our feet. Fortunately for you, our chief and our tribe's shaman are not so certain of this. Our women don't like having to mourn their warrior husbands' deaths, and they would rather our men not go to war. However, something great must be done to stop the Earth's movements."

This visit with Indian Factor left Andrew shaking. Would all the Indians along the Mississippi join the Indians in the north to crush the white man?

The delays back in Pittsburgh, then in Louisville, changes in the river, the comet overhead, and now the Indians all seemed to line up to prevent the New Orleans from being successful in her mission. Could all this somehow be a warning that taking a steamboat down these rivers was ill-advised?

Andrew squared his shoulders. He would not let the comet, river, Indians, or earthquake keep him from completing this mission. He would take the New Orleans safely to the city it was named for. He was up to the challenge, and he was determined to win this time.

That determination didn't change when New Orleans passed the Tennessee River. There, flatboat men warned them that three to four hundred Indians had embarked on Bear Creek, about thirty miles from Colbert's Ferry on the Tennessee River. They were stealing horses from many of the white families in the area.

Would the white man ever live in peace with his Indian neighbors, or would the white man crush their wills under their guns and heavy artillery? That was a question for another time. The crew of the New Orleans had a mission to accomplish.

Chapter 15

Although the trip on the Ohio River had been largely peaceful and easygoing, now they were apprehensive about what they faced, and it was not just because of the earthquake. The passage of the Mississippi River was fraught with danger and uncertainty. Nicholas was especially concerned about this part of the river because of what happened when they traveled this stretch two years ago. Now, Andrew too was on edge. The warning Indian Factor gave them had heightened Andrew's awareness of a potential attack.

As they continued through the Chickasaw country, Andrew and Nicholas watched the shoreline for any sign of Indians along the river. The banks had given way in various directions. Ten to fifteen acres of ground have sunk into the river. One of the Chickasaw bluffs had fallen in. The trees were prodigiously shaken, broken, and torn up by the roots. That was something that normally only happens in the most violent storms. Nearly all the islands in the river, containing from one to two hundred acres, have sunk or fragmented into smaller islands. The trees concealed in the river, raised erect several feet out of the water, as a series of shocks came one right after the other. The atmosphere was impregnated with a sulfurous smell. The entire stretch of the Mississippi was like traveling through hell.

Because they had received reports in Louisville about Indian uprisings, they had already felt apprehensive about traveling south through these areas that were controlled by these Native Americans, and now their fears heightened even more. Andrew was certain that some were hostile, and others were not, but how were they to know?. He knew that tensions between settlers and Native Americans continued to be high, and Nicholas was particularly nervous in this area along the Mississippi where the Chickasaw lived. They might have been peaceful when they left Louisville, but they could have decided to join the tribes in the north since then. They had no way of knowing.

From the conversation that Andrew had with that principal Chickasaw Indian, called the Indian Factor, from his having formerly been a kind of Agent for that nation, He was convinced that the Chickasaws with the assistance of their neighbors, intended to raise the long-buried tomahawk, and are meditating an energetic and destructive blow on the Whites.

As New Orleans passed the mouth of the Tennessee River, P.J., who was on the port side of the boat, gave a yell.

"Indians! Coming fast," he yelled.

Andrew ran to the railing on the left side of the boat. He saw what P.J. had been looking at. Five Chickasaw Indian warriors were loading into canoes. They were ready for battle because they wore a scalp lock with a roach headdress adorned with feathers. The most honored Chickasaw warriors among them wore a mantle of swan feathers. Their shirts were like the American frontier-style shirts and made of trade cloth. Their faces were painted with war paint. Were these warriors joining Tecumseh's fight in the north?

These Indians were no longer frightened of the monster of a barge with a giant wheel cutting into the river water. They no longer hid behind trees. They were ready to drive the monster from their lands.

Not that Andrew could blame them. The Chickasaw Bluffs belonged to the Chickasaw. Loud whoops sounded. More Indians carrying canoes flooded the shoreline. They placed their canoes in the water and began piling into them.

Now Nicholas was aware of the situation, "Indians!"

The crew grabbed their weapons and went to the railings.

"Don't shoot unless they are in the process of trying to board," Andrew yelled at the men. "We don't need the whole Chickasaw Nation against us!"

All had bows and arrows, but many also carried guns raised above their heads as they ran along the shoreline.

"Don't shoot or they'll swarm the boat!" Nicholas agreed.

"We can outrun them!" Andrew exclaimed.

"Why do you think they're chasing us?" Susanna asked.

"Get in the women's cabin with Lydia and the children!" Andrew exclaimed. He didn't want anything to happen to her.

"Why do you think they are chasing us?" Susanna ignored what he said and repeated her question.

"Some of them think the boat caused the earthquakes!" Andrew shouted.

"You don't have to shout," Susanna retorted.

"Get in the cabin with Lydia and the children," Nicholas said this time. He said it in his authoritative voice that no one on the boat would ever question.

"Yes, Mr. Roosevelt," Susanna said and did as he told her to do.

"What's going on between you and Susanna?" Nicholas asked as they watched the Indians on the land fall further and further behind the boat. None of the Indians had fired because the steamboat passed by them too fast for any of them to be able to get off a shot.

"What do you mean? There's nothing between us," Andrew replied.

"That's the biggest lie I've heard today," Nicholas replied. "Anyone can see that you and Susanna are in love."

"In love?" Was that how he felt for Susanna? He never thought to put it into words before. Could it be true? He had not been thinking about anything but getting this boat safely downstream and protecting the women and children onboard. Andrew had been thinking that he had included Susanna because she was one of those women.

He furrowed his forehead on the bridge between his two eyes. He remembered the kiss they shared when he and Susanna were on the bridge when the earthquakes first started. He had thought perhaps he felt something then, but the earthquake convinced him otherwise. He was so worried about getting through the earthquake zone that he could think of nothing else. He shook his head as though to clear his mind of that kind of thinking. No, he had to maintain his focus on getting them downriver to face whatever situation they found there. His feelings for Susanna had to wait.

Meanwhile, Susanna had entered the women's quarters. Lydia sat nursing Henry, and nearby, Rozella played with blocks on the floor.

Susanna knelt and handed the little girl a couple of blocks.

She sighed. "Oh, to be so oblivious to the problems of the world. I wish I could go back to when I was so innocent."

"What is going on out there, Susanna?" Lydia asked.

"Indians are chasing the steamboat," she answered. "I want to do something. I'm scared, but I can't do anything about it."

"Andrew knows the river and the people along it," Lydia replied. "I have faith in his ability to navigate us through this. Plus, the steamboat can travel faster than any barge ever could. We'll be fine."

"But some of those Indians have guns!" she exclaimed. "What if he gets shot?"

"Oh, now I get it. You're not afraid for you. You're afraid Andrew will get hurt."

"You're not afraid that Nicholas gets hurt?"

"All the time, he's my husband. Andrew isn't your husband, though."

"I.... .I.. ."

"You're in love with him. Anyone can see that," Lydia replied.

"But he barely knows that I'm alive!" Susanna moaned.

"I wouldn't say that," Lydia answered. "I think that he's very aware of you."

"He did try to kiss me the other day, but I thought he..."

Lydia chuckled. "Yes, men do have a way of using physical expression when they should use words."

"Do you really think he loves me?" Susanna asked.

Lydia smiled and shrugged. "Time will tell."

Susanna mirrored Lydia's shrug. How could she know what love was when she had never experienced the emotion? She couldn't remember her parents demonstrating their love for each other. She got more love from her nanny than she had from her parents. Maybe her parents were demonstrative when she wasn't around, but she had never seen it. The first time she saw the love of two adults toward one another was between Nicholas and Lydia. Even though Nicholas' age was almost twice that of Lydia, Susanna did not doubt that they loved each other.

How Susanna envied him. How she longed for what they had. What she felt for Andrew might have been love, but she didn't know if it was love. Back when her grandmother was alive, she had seen other girls her age who thought they were in love with every young man who gave them attention. She had never experienced that herself, and even then, she thought the whole idea of love was childish and something that could only be found in foolish stories. However, now she found herself thinking thoughts about Andrew that she had never experienced before.

"How can I be sure?" Susanna asked.

Lydia repeated. "Time will tell."

They felt the last earthquake at eleven o'clock on the twentieth. This last one, Andrew did not think was as severe as some of the former, but it lasted longer than any of the preceding; Andrew determined that it must have continued nearly a minute and a half. The presence of the shocks that were absorbed by the water, so he was only aware of the presence of ground movement and frequent rumblings in the distance, when they didn't feel the shocks. He was more inclined to believe these were shocks from having heard the same kind of rumbling with the shock that affected them. The navigation was still extremely difficult in many places because the snags caused by the earthquake were extremely thick.

Based on their long duration and frequency of the shocks, it is extremely uncertain when they cease, and if they have been as heavy at

New Orleans as we have felt them, the consequences had to be dreadful. Andrew was afraid of the possibility that when they arrived at Natchez, they would hear that the entire city of Orleans had been demolished and perhaps sunk into the sea.

They had passed the Indians at Chickasaw Bluff. More days passed. The earthquake activity along the shore appeared less noticeable. Soon, the tremors stopped rocking the steamboat altogether.

Obvious damage from the earthquakes also became less evident.

Andrew began to recognize landmarks, and that eased his concerns. The scenery became more recognizable, meaning that the earthquake's effects did not come this far south.

They were now beyond the earthquake region. Finally, they could rest at night. Andrew and Nicholas could use their navigation map to read the Mississippi River this far south. This also meant that Natchez and New Orleans had been spared the ravages of the earthquakes that did so much damage around New Madrid and the other smaller towns north of them.

That battle was done, but there was still something missing. The excitement of the trip down the Ohio and then the Mississippi was not as joyful as he would have liked.

He looked over at Susanna, who was supervising Rozella playing with blocks.

She must have felt his eyes on her because at that moment her eyes met his. She smiled, and this time, he turned away.

He now knew that he had to make her his wife. He now knew that he couldn't, or rather, he didn't want to live without her for the rest of his life. He only had to convince her of that.

Chapter 16

The New Orleans, constructed in Pittsburgh, Pennsylvania, long awaited in Natchez, finally steamed into the town safely on Monday evening, December thirtieth, after a remarkably short passage with its original passengers and baby Henry, who was born during the voyage.

Thousands assembled on the bluff and at the foot of the steamboat's intended landing. Men, women, and children, many dressed in their finest clothes, stood cheering as the steamboat drew up to the landing. Nicholas and Lydia stood at the boat's rail, waving to the crowd as Andrew piloted the boat to the landing.

"They must have known we were coming!" Andrew smiled at Susanna, who stood at his side. She smiled back.

Suddenly, the boat began drifting away from the landing and downstream.

"What's going on?" Susanna screamed.

Andrew didn't answer her, instead, he yelled. "Nick, we need more power!"

Expecting to remain here for a day or two, Nick Baker, the engineer, had allowed his fires to die down so that when the boat turned its head upstream, it lost headway altogether and was carried down by the current far below the intended landing.

"I'm on it," Nick replied. He had joined the rest of the crew on deck. He climbed down the ladder to the boiler room.

For a moment, it would have seemed that after all she had achieved, the New Orleans would be overcome by the Mighty Mississippi after all.

Fresh fuel was added to the fires, and the engine was stopped so that steam would accumulate. The boat continued to drift downstream. Finally, Nick lifted the safety valve. With a few turns of the wheels, the steamboat steadied. A few more gave her headway. She was now able to overcome the river. She arrived at the shore amid shouts of praise and applause from the crowd that gathered on the dock.

The following day, on New Year's Eve, Andrew purchased a copy of the local newspaper.

"Why did you purchase a paper?" Nicholas asked.

Andrew handed the newspaper to Nicholas.

"Because our trip has already been put into print here in Natchez. Check out the front-page headline."

Splashed across the front page was *The New Orleans Makes History.*

The passengers and crew gathered around Nicholas as he read.

The Steamboat the New Orleans arrives in Natchez. This steamboat is intended to be a regular packet from Natchez to New Orleans.

Nicholas Roosevelt from New York predicts that the New Orleans will be able to make a trip downriver to New Orleans and back again in five to seven days.

"You talked to them?" Andrew asked Nicholas.

"Not officially. A newspaper reporter was among the people in the crowd when we landed," Nicholas replied. "Read on, Andrew."

Andrew nodded. Nicholas continued reading:

"The Steamboat, The New Orleans has descended the Ohio and the Mississippi Rivers. It passed out of the region of the earthquake, and the principal inconvenience was the number of shoals, snags, and sawyers. These were all safely passed, and the vessel came in sight of Natchez yesterday evening. It foundered opposite the landing place.

The crew and passengers conversed with our journalist about the steamboat lately arrived here. Our papers have been informed that the earthquake, shocks of which were felt here a week or two since, has done great injury to the settlements on the Ohio and Mississippi, by throwing down houses, chimneys, etc. In several instances, islands in the Mississippi of considerable magnitude, had been sunk or destroyed. The river on both sides fell into a prodigious extent, and at one place about 300 acres caved in of a solid body. He also informs that the western side of the river was the most affected. The shocks lasted for about twelve days while they were on the Mississippi. The tremors occurred at intervals of fifteen or twenty minutes.

Mrs. Roosevelt and he were still discussing their adventure when they retired to rest. They had scarcely fallen asleep when they were aroused by shouts on deck and the trampling of many feet.

Because of a previous experience with the Indians and the idea of Indians was still predominant, Mr. Roosevelt sprang from his bed, and seizing a sword - the only weapon at hand - - hurried from the cabin to join the battle, as he thought with the Chickasaws. It was a more alarming enemy that he encountered. The New Orleans was on fire. Flames and smoke were issued from the forward cabin.

The servant who attended there had placed some green wood too close to the stove in anticipation of the next day's wants and discovered the cabin was on fire. The stove had overheated, and the wood had caught fire. The woodworking close by had caught, and the entire cabin would soon have been in flames, had not the servant, half suffocated, rushed on deck and given the alarm. By dint of great exertion, the fire, which, by this time, was making rapid headway, was extinguished; but not until the interior woodwork had been either destroyed or defaced. Few eyes were closed for the remainder of the night, nor did the accident tend to tranquilize the nerves of the travelers.

They reached Natchez in late December 1811.

Later that day, a man came to the New Orleans. He had to have been in his thirties. He was clean-shaven, but he was grizzled like an older man. He wore a broad-brimmed Quaker hat. His coat was an unadorned brown over gray knee-length trousers, and he wore simple old-fashioned shoes.

"Hello," He called up to the steamboat. "May I come aboard?"

"State your business!" P.J., who was on watch, called back. Andrew joined him.

Before the man could utter another word, he started coughing. The coughing sounded croupy. His face turned red, and his lips turned blue. Finally, he caught his breath and was able to speak again.

"I would like to interview your captain and crew if I may," the man said.

"I know you," Andrew replied. "You're Zadok Cramer. You had a print shop for several years along the Monongahela, not far from my father's boat yard."

"That's right," Zadok replied. "You must be Andrew."

"I am."

Zadok Cramer was an author, publisher, printer, and bookseller in Pittsburgh, Pennsylvania, United States. His book The Navigator was an influential guide for settlers and travelers on the Ohio and Mississippi Rivers in the first half of the nineteenth century.

"I read in the paper that you traveled through the earthquake region," Zadok said.

"That's right," Andrew replied. "Numerous changes have occurred, and I wouldn't be surprised if even more have occurred since we left there."

"Navigation maps are changing up that way then?" Zadok asked.

Andrew grimaced. "Very definitely."

"May I come aboard so you can tell me all about your experience?" Zadok asked.

By now, Nicholas had joined them on deck, and Andrew looked at him.

"I have other plans," Andrew replied. "I have some business I need to attend to."

Andrew didn't have any other business, but he did have something important that he wanted to do.

He had plans to take Susanna out on the town.

Andrew had made up his mind. He knew now that he could not stay on the Mississippi River as pilot of the New Orleans and let her go back to New York with the Roosevelts. He knew that he had to ask her to marry him.

"The wife and I have plans too," Nicholas replied. "We're meeting with city officials to discuss business-related issues concerning the steamboat."

"It would just take a few minutes," Zadok replied. "I'll talk to the two of you now, and after that, I'll get more information from the crew."

"I guess we can do that."

As promised, Zadok was quick but thorough with his questions. He was knowledgeable of what the river had been like as well as the towns along the Mississippi, so his questions were brief and on point.

As soon as he was done being interviewed, Andrew went to find Susanna.

"Come with me to dinner tonight," he said.

"Just you and me?"

"I want to take you to Mrs. Bower's restaurant. It's the nicest place in town."

"But what about the children?"

"I already talked to Lydia, and she intends to take the children with them to their meeting with the city leaders."

"I don't know that she can handle the children by herself," Susanna said.

"I have every assurance that if Lydia could handle everything we encountered on the Mississippi, I am sure she can handle her children without your help for a few hours."

"I suppose," Susanna replied.

"You act like you don't want to spend the day with me," Andrew exclaimed.

"That's not..." Susanna began and then said. "Of course, I want to spend the day with you."

I want to spend the rest of my life with you, Andrew thought, but he didn't say this yet. He wanted to save this for a more appropriate time. Andrew smiled his big, unnerving smile at her. "Believe me. You won't regret this outing. Now you go and get into your finest dress. I'll be waiting for you here on deck."

"I'll do that," Susanna replied.

Andrew started getting ready for his evening with Susanna. At the same time, all the other crewmen, except PJ, joined him to prepare to go ashore for the evening. PJ, who had been to Natchez numerous times, agreed to keep an eye on the boat.

Susanna dressed in the finest dress she had. It was a dress that had been Lydia's but had been made over for her. She wore her woven hat over her dust cap.

Lydia watched Susanna put on her hat. She shook her head. "No, that won't do for today. Here, wear one of mine."

Lydia removed her best bonnet and put on her second-best one, with a soft crown and stiff, close-fitting brim. She then tied it under her chin.

She handed her best one to Susanna. "Here, wear this."

The hat was made of silk pink taffeta with a tucked and ribbon-trimmed brim.

"I can't take that," Susanna replied.

"You can and you will," Lydia smiled. "I insist."

"What do you know that I don't?" Susanna asked.

"All I'm saying is 'don't disappoint me', Susanna." She then took the hat from her maid and placed it on Susanna's head. She then tied a neat ribbon bow under Susanna's chin.

"There, you look perfect," Lydia replied.

"If I didn't know you better, I'd say you know something I don't," Susanna exclaimed.

"Perhaps you don't know me at all," Lydia grinned. "Now, go. Don't keep the boy waiting."

Andrew was on deck when Susanna came out of the women's quarters. Lydia followed her so that she could get Andrew's reaction.

His jaw dropped.

"A regular lady, wouldn't you say?" Lydia was smiling ear to ear.

Andrew's intense gaze at Susanna made her nervous.

"A beautiful lady," His voice was low.

"You two enjoy your day. You both earned it."

Andrew took Susanna out for a meal at the best restaurant that Andrew knew in Natchez.

Andrew bought one of the restaurant's finest wines and raised his glass in a toast. "To the most beautiful woman I know."

Susanna blushed. "You are too kind. It must be the dress."

"I only tell it as I see it," Andrew replied. "Your beauty has always brightened my day."

The matron of the restaurant came and poured them a second glass of port.

"Are you and your missus enjoying your meal?" Mrs. Bowers asked.

"Oh, I'm not. . ." Susanna started and then stopped herself. It was then that she realized that she was out with Andrew alone. She wondered what her grandmother would have said to discover that she was out with a man and without a chaperone. She could hear her saying, "It isn't proper! Only women of ill repute are ever seen out with a man alone and unchaperoned.

Susanna didn't correct her, but she was surprised that Andrew didn't correct her, either. He thanked Mrs. Bowers, and she moved on to the other patrons at the restaurant.

"Let's go for a walk," Andrew replied. "I'd like to take you up on the finer part of the city. They walked up the stairs that threaded their way from the riverbank to the upper part of the town. From here, they had a beautiful view of the river. Someone had put up a railing along the outcropping above Natchez under the Hill.

Andrew took her hand.

"What are you doing?" Susanna asked.

"Susanna, the terrors of the river, the comet, the earthquake, nor even this fear I'm feeling in the pit of my stomach can prevent me from saying this. I can't imagine the rest of my life without you. Will you marry me?"

"Yes! Yes!" Susanna exclaimed.

Andrew pulled an old leather-covered box from his pocket and opened it to reveal the old family locket.

"This is the family heirloom locket that every bride is meant to wear on her wedding."

"How did you get this?"

Andrew chuckled. "My mother insisted that I bring this with me when I left Pittsburgh. She said that it was time that I got married."

Susanna took a step back. "Are you telling me you're marrying me to please your mother?"

"No, I had no idea when we left Pittsburgh that I felt this way. However, after the fire in the kitchen, I've been afraid of losing you."

"Why didn't you say something before?"

"Well, I was busy trying to keep the New Orleans afloat during the earthquakes. I wasn't going to let this boat sink like I did the flatboat."

"The flatboat sinking wasn't your fault," she said. "It could have happened to anyone."

"I know," Andrew nodded. "I just never lost a boat before."

"Perhaps, Mr. Roosevelt shouldn't have insisted on such a large monstrosity of a flatboat."

"I would never tell him that," Andrew chuckled.

Susanna looked down at the old locket in the old wooden box. She caressed it.

"It's such a fragile old piece."

Andrew took it from the box and laid it over Susanna's wrist.

"This locket has been in the family since my great-grandmother Drusilla received this locket from her second husband. This locket has been in the family for seventy years, and it has been a tradition that every bride in the family wears this locket. I will give it to you now."

Susanna picked up the crafted old piece of jewelry.

"It's beautiful," Susanna said, examining it more closely. "There seems to be a hinge on the side here."

She opened the locket, and inside was a piece of light brown hair. "Whose hair?"

"That belonged to my great-grandmother's second husband."

Andrew then proceeded to tell the story of Drusilla Codman and Kanter Thorton.

They looked out over the landscape. They watched the moon as it cleared the horizon and rose over the river. Its bright white light shimmered over the water. He took her hand and put it to his lips.

"You know that for the next few years, I will be piloting the New Orleans to New Orleans and back. I don't want to live in New Orleans, I'm much more familiar with this town, so I want to make this our home. Do you agree?"

Susanna nodded. "Yes, I agree."

Andrew nodded. "I'm glad."

"I would like to be a member of the crew on the steamboat with you."

"No, I won't have my wife working on my boat."

"You'll need staff on the steamboat. We can work together."

"I don't want my wife to work as a servant."

"I don't want to be stuck alone in a rented house while you're working on the river either. I want to be with you. I'm like Lydia Roosevelt, you know. I won't sit at home waiting for my man to return."

"I want you to be with me too," Andrew replied, "but…"

"Then it's settled. We won't have to rent a room. We can live on the steamboat until we start a family."

"You've been hanging around Lydia Roosevelt too much, Susanna."

"I have learned a few things from her, yes," Susanna smiled. "But I don't think I ever want to raise my children on a steamboat."

Andrew smiled back and kissed her on the nose.

Susanna nuzzled into Andrew's neck. "Do you want to wait to get married until your parents can come to be a part of the wedding?"

"No, your parents couldn't be here, so I don't think it would be fair to you to wait for mine."

"I wouldn't mind. Your parents are amazing people."

"That's one of the things I've always loved about you. You always think about other people. No, to tell you the truth, I can't wait until you're my wife. I want us to get married as soon as possible. We could get married right now if you want."

Susanna shook her head. "To tell you the truth, I would rather wait and get married in New Orleans so that we can be married by a priest."

"That's my girl. I can't agree more. I want nothing more than to grant you your wishes. We'll get married by a minister in New Orleans."

They turned in unison and looked out at the river. So much had happened, but they had made it through, and the experience had made them stronger, drawing them together. They now had a future together in this unique part of the country.

"We can work together for now, but someday I will build you a townhouse up here on this hill and have a plantation where we can raise our children, and you won't have to work."

Susanna laughed. "If you don't think I will work, you don't know what raising children is like."

"As I was the youngest child in my family for most of my childhood, you're right. My brother Charles was a pleasant surprise for my parents. It's a good thing I have someone like you who can show me how to be a proper parent."

Susanna and Andrew returned to the steamboat after Lydia had returned with the children.

When Susanna returned from her time with Andrew, Lydia had already put both children to bed. She was dressed in her nightclothes and was brushing her long, dark hair.

Susanna took off the old locket necklace and laid it on the lid of her traveling trunk.

"Did Andrew give you that locket?" Lydia asked.

Susanna blushed and nodded. "He asked me to marry him."

"Well, it's about time," Lydia replied. "I guess I will have to find a governess to care for the children."

"You don't mind? I forgot all about your family. I mean, I can stay with you and the children until you find someone."

"For heaven's sake, no," Lydia replied. "I'm sure I can manage."

"If you're certain," Susanna said.

"I'm certain."

They left the next day to continue their trip down to New Orleans.

As the paddlewheel pushed the New Orleans past Natchez, they came across the island where the remains of the damaged flatboat that they had lost two years earlier lay. The back half was on land, and the front lay in the water, half buried in mud. Some of the parts of the flatboat appeared to be scavenged by flatboat men who had traveled through the area during those two years. The lumber planks had been removed, and only the boat's hull remained.

They arrived in Baton Rouge, which had been part of Spanish West Florida. Since the Louisiana Purchase, it had been the only non-US-held military post on the Mississippi. However, several of the inhabitants of the Baton Rouge District had organized conventions to plan a rebellion, among them Fulwar Skipwith. At least one meeting was held in a private home.

On September 23, 1810, the rebels overcame the Spanish garrison at Fort San Carlos. They unfurled the flag of the new Republic of West Florida, known as the Bonnie Blue Flag. The West Florida Republic existed for almost ninety days, during which St. Francisville served as its capital.

Seizing the opportunity to claim the land, President James Madison ordered W. C. C. Claiborne to move in and seize the fledgling republic to annex the area into the Territory of Orleans. Madison used the premise that the territory had been a part of the US since 1803, citing the terms of the Louisiana Purchase, an explanation largely believed to be a deliberate error. The rebels provided no resistance to Claiborne's forces. With minor resentment, they watched the "Stars and Stripes" raised on December 10, 1810.

With Baton Rouge's annexation, rumors flew that Louisiana would soon become a state. There was talk that Baton Rouge could become the state capital.

The New Orleans didn't stay in Baton Rouge for long. They stayed just long enough to greet the crowd and take a couple of hours to show the village leaders around the boat. Everyone saw how this modern marvel would turn their small village into a major port on the largest river on the North American continent.

Susanna was glad they had wonderful accommodation on the New Orleans. She didn't want to face spending any more nights in the nasty hotel that they endured on their previous trip.

Lydia didn't attend this tour because she and Susanna were busy planning Susanna's wedding. She and Susanna searched in the women's dress design book Lydia had picked up back in Natchez.

"This design is pretty," Susanna said.

Lydia looked at it. "Yes, it is. When we were last down in New Orleans, I found a dressmaker who could design this exact dress for you."

Susanna shook her head. "You know I don't have money to get a dress designed for me. Besides, there's not enough time."

Lydia laid her hand on Susanna's. "There's time. This woman can do amazing work in a short time. She has a staff of seamstresses who could put the dress together in no time."

"But I still can't afford a new dress like that."

"Don't worry about the cost. Nicholas and I want to give it to you as a wedding gift."

"Does Mr. Roosevelt know about this?"

"Of course, we talked about it while you and Andrew were together in Natchez."

"You knew that Andrew was going to ask me to marry him then?"

"Yes, well, we didn't know exactly when, but I had a feeling you were. I have already talked it over with Nicholas, and he agreed that if Andrew did ask you to marry him, we would give you a new dress for a wedding gift."

"Thank you, Lydia, you're the best."

That evening, while Andrew was piloting the boat, Susanna sat beside him while he steered the boat.

"We'll be in New Orleans in a couple of days. Are you ready for this?"

Susanna nodded. "I can't wait to finish this voyage so we can be married and have our life together."

Andrew and Susanna looked at each other. Both grinned. It may have been the end of one journey, but they were about to enter another equally momentous journey.

Chapter 17

The New Orleans brought in the New Year during its journey between Baton Rouge and New Orleans. The steamboat steamed into New Orleans on January 10, 1812.

The crew, the Roosevelts, and Andrew and Susanna had done what no one thought they possible. They had faced and conquered everything that nature could throw at them, and yet they had succeeded. They had doubted their fate several times on this trip, but they persevered.

The crew of the New Orleans overcame unthinkable odds to reach its destination. They knew they would have their place in what everyone knew was a milestone in history. A steamboat had gone downriver and through all the devastation, and now triumphantly entered the city for which the steamboat was named.

However, was this just a fluke? Would this steamboat be the last one to go from Pittsburgh to New Orleans? Andrew wondered. There was still the issue of the Falls on the Ohio River. The chance that a steamboat could run aground or capsize was too great. It would be a much better solution to run one steamboat on the Ohio River above the falls and transfer whatever load or passengers they had to another boat below the falls at Shippingport, like many of the barges already did when going downriver.

"We did it!" Lydia exclaimed as they moored the New Orleans.

"We couldn't have done it without anyone here," Nicholas stated. "We all did it."

"We certainly did," Andrew replied. "We made it over the falls, through an earthquake zone, and past Indian territory. We beat them all."

"We certainly did," Lydia replied. "We got the two of you together in the process."

"Like you planned for us to fall in love," Susanna said.

Lydia grinned. "I'll bet you'd be surprised that Andrew's mother and I had all this planned before we left Pittsburgh."

"Knowing my mother, I wouldn't doubt it," Andrew said drily. He smiled at Susanna. "Not that I'm complaining."

"How long do you and Lydia plan to remain in New Orleans?" Andrew asked.

"We've already heard that there was a boat leaving by the end of the week for New York, and we plan to be on it," Lydia exclaimed.

"I see," said Susanna.

"That's why I made an appointment for Susanna tomorrow at the best dress shop here. If I'm leaving her here, Andrew, she must be properly married before I do."

With that, Susanna blushed. Andrew felt the heat in his face.

"Of course, we'll be married as soon as possible," Andrew said.

The rest of the week was spent in a flurry of activity. Andrew and Nicholas found a minister willing, on short notice, to marry the two in his tiny chapel in an alley just off Beale Street. He wasn't a Catholic priest, but they didn't have time to get Andrew converted. The Presbyterian minister they located would have to do.

Eight days later, Nicholas was handed newspapers from cities back East. These had come by ship via the ocean. One was from Pittsburgh. It was dated back in October. It contained the same news he had read before they left Louisville. The other was from Cincinnati, which he examined.

"You know, in the future, the newspapers won't have to go by ocean clipper to arrive at any of these ports on the Mississippi," Nicholas replied. "Mark my words, newspapers from all over the country will be seen in other parts of the country in weeks rather than months."

He picked up the Western Spy out of Cincinnati, dated a few days earlier, and read from it.

"The barge New Orleans arrived at the city of New Orleans on the tenth of December, having made one of the best trips ever known in such a season, and at such a stage of the water. She left Cincinnati on the 27th of October.

DeWitt Clinton and Governor Morris arrived at Washington City as agents to the commissioners and legislature of New York, who intend to petition Congress for aid in opening the great canal in that state."

Nicholas laid the paper down and addressed the listeners.

"Steamboats like this and canals like the one will change everything," he said. "They will open the country for settlement."

"It is a grand day for America," PJ said. He had already agreed to stay with Andrew to be part of his crew. Nick Baker had as well.

The women spent the next few days in town getting fitted for the gowns they would wear at the wedding. In the meantime, the men spent their time not running the errands that the women had them do in preparation for the wedding, but also to commission the first load that the New Orleans would haul back upriver to Natchez.

Two days later, a coach arrived at a small church on the outskirts of New Orleans. The coach door opened. A footman opened the coach door. Lydia Roosevelt exited the coach. She was dressed in her royal blue silk dress. After Lydia exited the coach, Susanna stepped out.

Andrew stood at the church door. He drew a sharp breath. Even though he had seen her every day for several months, she was the most beautiful woman he had ever seen, especially dressed in her wedding gown.

Andrew knew from his cousins' weddings over the years that it was common for brides to wear everyday colors such as blue, pink, green, dark brown, burgundy, and, yes, even black, rather than white and ivory. Susanna's gown, a gift from Lydia Roosevelt, was cotton white silk covered with lace and lined with white satin. Her high-waisted bust was embellished with intricate embroidery that Andrew knew had been re-purposed from a dress Lydia had worn back in Pittsburgh.

She didn't wear her usual maid's bonnet. Her fine hair was elegantly and yet simply arranged. Its beauty owed more to its natural, beautiful waves and ringlets draped her face than the hairdresser's skill. It was crowned with a superb wreath of dried greens and florals, forming rose-buds with their leaves.

What made her most beautiful to Andrew was not what the clothes she was wearing or her hairstyle. She wore on her countenance that tran-quil and chastened joy which a female so situated could not fail to ex-perience. He hoped he could keep her as happy and content as she was now for the rest of their lives together.

This was a magic moment for Susanna, too. She felt as though she was floating. This was a dream come true. Her heart swelled. She had gained the heart of him whom her heart had selected, and the man her friends approved. She felt at peace with where her life was now heading. All that she had lost in her past no longer haunted her. No longer was she just Lydia Roosevelt's maid. Within a few moments, she would be Mrs. Andrew Mayford. And what an honor it was. He would be part of this new, growing transportation network.

For now, they would start their married life on the steamboat. They would save money to buy land. Without a doubt, they would purchase property in Natchez. Andrew preferred Natchez to New Orleans. At least, that was what he told her the night before as they dreamed about their future.

"Are you ready?" Andrew asked.

Susanna nodded.

They were married in the small chapel and spent the night at one of the local hotels in a room across from the Roosevelts' room.

On the day after the wedding, Andrew and Susanna saw the Roo-sevelts off on the sailboat bound for New York.

"I'm going to miss you, Susanna," Lydia replied. "You were the best personal maid that I ever had. I don't know how I'll ever replace you as a maid."

"I'll miss you and the children too," Susanna said tearfully.

"My best to the two of you," Nicholas's voice broke as he spoke.

The bell on the boat signaled that it was time to go.

"So long, Mr. and Mrs. Mayford," Lydia smiled. She and her husband and their two children climbed onto the ship together.

18

Epilogue

Upon returning to New York, Roosevelt took up other entrepreneurial ventures and discontinued his partnership with Fulton and Livingston. After tying things up in New Orleans and seeing the Roosevelts off, Andrew took over the running of the New Orleans Steamboat. Soon, the New Orleans was making regular runs between New Orleans and Natchez.

To make a home for him and Susanna, Andrew sectioned off part of the kitchen as their sleeping area while he piloted the boat, and she ran the steamboat's kitchen.

Word came downriver that along the New Madrid region of the Mississippi, the earthquakes continued to rock the area into February. Fortunately, few people were injured, and most of the keelboat men knew no one who died from the earthquakes. The river's face had been entirely changed.

The fighting between the Americans and the Native Americans was another problem that stopped steamboat travel in some areas. The fighting continued north of the Ohio River through the War of 1812. However, the Chickasaw tribe, which the New Orleans had encountered, remained peaceful allies of the Americans and declined to join forces with the great warrior and chief, Tecumseh.

By April, Andrew ran the New Orleans on an established regular passage from New Orleans to Natchez. The New Orleans provided considerable profit for its owners and for Andrew and Susanna. Andrew kept his gold coins in the steamboat safe.

In June, Andrew received a letter from Nicholas. Andrew glanced through the letter and stuffed the document into his pocket.

Does he say anything about Lydia and the children?" Susanna asked.

"No, I'm afraid not," Andrew replied. "He's all business. He just wanted to tell me about some expenses that still need to be paid on the steamboat's furnishings."

Susanna was disappointed, but she understood that this was a business letter.

The next day, Andrew received another post. This time, the letter was from Pittsburgh.

"Mother sent us a package," Andrew said. He held the small package. "I think it's just paper."

"Well, open it and find out," Susanna said.

He opened the small package. A letter and a newspaper clipping fluttered to the floor. Susanna picked them up and handed the letter to Andrew.

"What does it say?" Susanna asked.

Andrew read, *"Andrew and Susanna, congratulations on your nuptials. Your father and I forgive you for not waiting for us to join you on your wedding day. We're just glad I had the forethought to give the locket to you so you could share that part of the family tradition.*

This article was mailed to me, and I thought you would like to have it for posterity.

Your loving mother,

Lowri Mayford

Susanna held out the article, and Andrew took it from her hand.

"Why, it's from New Orleans!" Andrew said. "Someone sent it to my parents, and they sent it back to me!"

Susanna took the article back and began reading it in the Louisiana Gazette:

Steamboat

This vessel set out for Natchez on Thursday last, the 23rd of January, for her first time, more for experiment than emolument. From a gentle-

man passenger, of correct information, who is enabled to state that she can steam the upriver current at upwards of three miles an hour, she went from this city to the Homas. She traveled 75 miles in 24 hours.

As Nicholas Roosevelt had predicted, the arrival of New Orleans signaled the beginning of significant economic change along the inland rivers. Fulton and Livingston intended to have six boats running between the "Falls of the Ohio" and New Orleans and five between the Falls and Pittsburgh. However, because of the War of 1812, their dreams would have to wait.

The New Orleans hauled cotton from Natchez. Cotton was now growing into the South's cash crop thanks to the invention of the cotton gin a few years earlier and the ability to quickly send cotton downstream to New Orleans. On the return trip from New Orleans, the steamboat carried boatmen to Natchez so that they could make the trek up the Natchez Trace. In addition to passengers, the boat carried more manufactured goods from back east to the settlers along the rivers. These goods were more easily and more quickly moved upstream.

Natchez under the Hill, along the river, became even more rowdy as men from flatboats and barges were dumped in that town with money in their pockets. These men hitched a ride from New Orleans, where they sold their goods for more than they had been able to sell them in Natchez. Saloons and brothels sprang up near the steamboat dock, creating a decadent nightlife.

More respectable residents wanted to distance themselves from the "riffraff" and built their homes in Natchez above the river area. Andrew bought a small tract of land where he and Susanna planned to build their townhome.

On April 8, 1812, with the help of Livingston's brother Edward, a New Orleans politician, Fulton and Livingston secured the exclusive rights and concession to the use of steam navigation on the new Louisiana Territory's rivers for eighteen years, provided that they charge a freight rate of no more than three quarters of the rate already charged by non-steam-powered boats. After New Orleans began navigating the lower Mississippi River, Fulton and Livingston attempted to prevent other steamboats from using the river until court decisions broke their monopoly on steamboat commerce in New York and Louisiana. As commercial shipping improved, land development also increased along the inland rivers below the "Falls of the Ohio" at Louisville. Like Nicholas Roosevelt had predicted, even though he paid more for his coal-laden land in Louisville, property values increased, and he sold the remaining coal for more than the land cost him. That same land was later sold and dug up for the canal to bypass the falls.

The New Orleans began the rapid development of the technology of the time. As the technology improved, more efficient steam engines, improvements in steamboats designed for western rivers, and lock and canal construction developed.

After New Orleans, several steamboats were quickly built in Pittsburgh over the next couple of years, including the Comet, commissioned in 1813. The Vesuvius was commissioned in 1814, and Aetna around 1817. By then, there were twelve steamboats on the midwestern rivers, and the public, once skeptical of steamboat navigation, was completely convinced that steamboat navigation would work. By 1819, over sixty steamboats traveled the western waters, and by 1826, 143 steamboats steamed up and down the river. Two hundred and thirty-three had existed up to that time, but many of these steamboats had been destroyed by overheated boiler explosions and wrecks from river obstructions.

As the steamboat traffic grew on the Mississippi River, new cities began to spring up along the river. Villages like New Madrid, decimated by the earthquakes, were replaced by other steamboat stops like Memphis. This city was founded in 1819 and named after the ancient capital of Egypt on the Nile River in North Africa.

Galena, an ore that formed the basis for the early lead mining economy, was founded north of St. Louis. Owing to these deposits, Galena was the site of the first major mineral rush in the United States. By 1828, the town's population was 10,000, rivaling the population of Chicago.

Galena developed as the largest steamboat hub on the Mississippi River north of St. Louis.

Andrew remained the New Orleans' pilot until the steamboat hit a snag, which punctured the hull. She sank near Baton Rouge, Louisiana, on July 14, 1814, two years after her first historic trip, setting the pattern for the average lifespan of a steamboat of about three years.

At that time, Fulton's steamboat company moved the engine and machinery of the New Orleans into a new hull, which they also named New Orleans, and she continued the Natchez steamboat trade.

Andrew had plans to help build more riverboats for the company, but the War of 1812 ended those plans.

On December 2, 1814, General Andrew Jackson marched from Mobile, Alabama, to New Orleans with orders to oppose an imminent military invasion by an overwhelming British force. Jackson made frequent requests for military supplies, especially small firearms and ammunition, that were in short supply. To this end, the shareholders decided to send the Enterprise.

To help defend the area, Andrew joined a local militia. If the British won here, they could claim the American territories gained from the 1803 Louisiana Purchase as void and not part of the US Territory. The Americans, as well as former French citizens, had every motivation not to let that happen.

He was on patrol on December 14 when he saw a British transport downriver from New Orleans. He alerted his commander that the British had come ashore. His commander then ordered him to report his findings to Old Hickory himself.

Everyone there called General Andrew Jackson "Old Hickory" because he was as tough as old hickory. Jackson is also known to carry a cane made of hickory, which he used to beat people who displeased him. Andrew did not want to be one of those people, so he proceeded to the general's tent cautiously.

The lieutenant at the desk ushered him into General Andrew Jackson's office tent. Andrew had never seen the general this close. The man had fiery red hair and a scar on his head. Everyone knew how he got that scar. The general ensured everyone knew that what happened to him during the American Revolution was why he hated the British.

During the Revolutionary War, 14-year-old Andrew Jackson and his older brother Robert had been captured by British soldiers in the Battle of Hanging Rock. The officer in command ordered Jackson to clean his boots, but Jackson refused. The officer raised his sword to strike a violent blow at the boy's head. Jackson ducked and threw up his left hand. It was cut to the bone, and a gash on his head left a white scar that Andrew Jackson still carried to remind him of his animosity. He hated everything English and every Englishman as well.

Now, as Andrew Mayford approached the general's desk, he saw the famous hickory cane leaning against it.

"Well, speak up, young man. I don't have all day," Old Hickory looked Andrew straight in the older man's eyes. The man's piercing blue eyes were intimidating. Andrew swallowed hard.

He feared that he would feel the hickory cane's strike. He blurted out his message.

Old Hickory rose to his feet. He stood six feet tall and was as thin as a pine log stripped of its bark. He began barking orders. He had dispatches written and sent to all the commanders. Andrew carried the message back to his commander. They would attack the enemy before the British could attack them.

Andrew knew that one of the Americans' major concerns was that the British and their Spanish allies wanted to reclaim the territories of the Louisiana Purchase because they did not recognize any land deals made by Napoleon. These land deals had started with the 1800 Spanish cession of Louisiana to France, followed by the 1804 French sale of Louisiana to the United States.

Andrew later learned that sixteen hundred British soldiers under the command of General John Keane had rowed 60 miles west from Cat Island to Pea Island, situated about 30 miles east of New Orleans. It took the British six days and nights to ferry the troops, each transit taking around ten hours. By then, the Americans knew they were there and were getting ready for them.

Andrew was among the dispatchers who met in Andrew Jackson's tent when he shared surveillance with the generals under Old Hickory. "There are three potential routes to the east of the Mississippi that the British could take, in addition to traversing up the Mississippi itself. Rather than a slow approach to New Orleans up the Mississippi River, I believe the British will choose to advance on an overland route. The first route would be to take the Rigolets passage into Lake Pontchartrain, and thence to disembark a few miles north of the city. Our one hindrance was the fort at Petit Coquilles at the Rigolets passage."

The dispatchers and generals vigorously wrote down the information while Old Hickory continued.

"The second option is to row to the Plain of Gentilly via the Chef Menteur Bayou and take the Chef Menteur Road that leads from the Rigolets to the city. This road is narrow and can easily be blocked. I have already sent troops so that it's heavily guarded."

Andrew wrote a quick note saying, *"Chef Menteur Road heavily guarded,"* and continued listening to the report.

"The third option is for them to head to Bayou Bienvenue, then Bayou Mazant, and via the Villeré Canal to disembark at a point one mile from the Mississippi and seven miles south of the city. I guess this option is the one the British general will take, but we have troops ready to engage in any of these scenarios."

As it turned out, the British command squandered a passing opportunity to succeed when it decided not to take the open road from the Rigolets to New Orleans by way of Bayou Chef Menteur. The British had received inaccurate map details and were bogged down by the shallow waters of the narrow passes of the Rigolets and the Chef Menteur, and could not take any vessel drawing eight feet or more.

On the morning of December 23, intelligence reported a vanguard of almost 2000 British soldiers had reached the east bank of the Mississippi River, nine miles south of New Orleans. They could have attacked the city by advancing a few hours up the undefended river road. However, they decided to camp at Lacoste's Plantation and wait for reinforcements. The British invaded the home of Major Gabriel Villeré. Villere escaped through a window and hastened to warn General Jackson of the approaching army and the position of their encampment.

On the evening of December 23, following Villeré's intelligence report, Andrew was among the 2,131 men that Jackson sent in a brief three-pronged assault from the north on the unsuspecting British troops. Those British troops had been resting in their camp. The action was consequential since, by December 25, British forces now had an effective strength of almost 6000 soldiers. The British won a "tactical victory", which enabled them to maintain their position, but they no longer had the illusion that they would have an easy conquest.

Because of the Americans' knowledge of the land and the advanced warning, they had time to transform the canal into a heavily fortified earthwork.

All night, Andrew Mayford and the other Americans shoveled dirt from the canal onto the bank nearest the direction from which the British would no doubt arrive.

Two days later, nine large naval artillery guns arrived along with a hot shot furnace to silence the two U.S. Navy warships, the sloop-of-war USS Louisiana and the schooner USS Carolina, that were harassing the army for 24 hours per day the past week from the Mississippi River.

The British cannons sank the Carolina in a massive explosion, but the Louisiana survived. The Louisiana was not able to sail northward under her own power due to damage during the attack. Quick-thinking Barataria pirates aboard the Louisiana lowered the ship's rowboats, tied the ship to the rowboats, and towed it further north and away from the British artillery.

These two vessels were now no longer a danger to the British, but Jackson ordered the ships' surviving guns and crew to be stationed on the west bank and provide covering fire for any British assault on the river road to Line Jackson, the name of the U.S. defensive line at the

Rodriguez Canal and New Orleans. After silencing the two ships, the British command ordered a reconnaissance-in-force on December 28 against the earthworks. The reconnaissance-in-force was designed to test Line Jackson and see how well-defended it was, and if any section of the line was weak, the British would take advantage of the situation, break through, and call for thousands of more soldiers to smash through the defenses.

To the right of Andrew Mayford's position in the trench, the British soldiers offensively and successfully sent the militia defenders panicking in retreat with the British's huge show of force, and were just a few hundred yards from breaching the defensive line.

The left side of the reconnaissance-in-force turned into a disaster for the British. The surviving artillery guns from the two neutralized warships successfully defended the section of Line Jackson closest to the Mississippi River with enfilading fire, making it look like the British offensive completely failed, even though on the section closest to the swamp, the British were on the verge of breaking through. The British command inexplicably decided to withdraw all the soldiers after seeing the left side of their reconnaissance-in-force collapsing and retreating in panic.

Luck saved Line Jackson on this day. This was the closest the British came to defeating Jackson.

In the subsequent battle, despite a British advantage in numbers, training, and experience, the American forces defeated a poorly executed assault in slightly more than 30 minutes. The Americans suffered 71 casualties, while the British suffered over 2,000, including the deaths of the commanding general, Major General Sir Edward Pakenham, and his second-in-command, Major General Samuel Gibbs.

While all of this was going on, another steamboat was making history. The Steamboat Enterprise traveled from Pittsburgh, Pennsylvania, to New Orleans to deliver the cargo of military supplies at the port of New Orleans on January 9, 1815.

Under normal circumstances, Enterprise's voyage into Louisiana's waters would have been a violation of the territorial steamboat monopoly granted to Robert R. Livingston and Robert Fulton. However, the steamboat was protected from the monopolists and free to navigate the state's waters by the martial law that General Andrew Jackson imposed on December 16.

Despite the military supplies delivered by the Enterprise, Jackson's forces were still in dire need, particularly for small firearms, gunpowder, and ammunition. Responding to reports that several flatboats laden with military supplies were near Natchez, Jackson sent the Enterprise. The boats were located, and the Enterprise took them in tow. The Enterprise delivered the flatboats and their cargo to New Orleans with much-needed supplies.

The Enterprise made another voyage to Natchez and returned to the port of New Orleans by February 12, 1815, when she entered for the first time in the New Orleans Wharf Register as "Steam Boat Captained by Shrive".

The Enterprise then steamed up the Red River to Alexandria with 250 troops in tow and returned to New Orleans.

The battle of New Orleans should never have been. As Andrew and the rest of the American soldiers learned. In August 1814, Britain and the United States had begun negotiations to end the War of 1812. However, the British Secretary of State for War and the Colonies, Henry Bathurst, issued Pakenham's secret orders on October 24, 1814, commanding him to continue the war even if he heard rumors of peace. Bathurst expressed concern that the United States might not ratify a treaty and did not want Pakenham either to endanger his forces or miss an opportunity for victory. Before that, in August 1814, Vice Admiral Cochrane had convinced the Admiralty that a campaign against New Orleans would weaken American resolve against Canada and hasten a successful end to the war. The battle had been a ruse, but the men of Louisiana didn't care. They had won the campaign, and "Old Hickory" was their hero.

After the War of 1812 ended, river traffic at Louisville, Kentucky, and Shippingport increased. Because of the "Falls of the Ohio" with its shallows, rapids, and rocky "white water" at Louisville, Kentucky, the entire length of the Ohio River could not be easily navigated by boat, so the partners of the fledgling steamboat industry divided the western steamboat commerce into two sections, where one section operated steamboats from Pittsburgh to the Falls at Louisville, and the other from Louisville downstream to New Orleans.

Andrew, himself, however, had decided to put the riverboat life behind him and move on. He ended his time piloting on the river and stayed closer to home because, at this time, Andrew discovered that he was going to be a father. Because his family was growing, he had to find a place for them to settle down. His focus changed from working on the river to starting a cotton plantation.

By this time, he and Susanna had saved up enough, and the time had come to build her a nice town home in Natchez above the hill, and Andrew could attend to business closer to home. The house overlooked the river and was built to take advantage of the cool breeze off the Mississippi.

Their home was Federal style. The house featured a distinctive roof shape created by surrounding shed roofs attached high on a central gable. This Anglo-American roof shape differs from the French Louisiana vernacular, where shed roofs extend from a central hipped roof. The house related to its French contemporaries in Louisiana in the use of bousillage, composed of mud and Spanish moss, in the exterior walls of the frame upper story.

The house was built on the side of a hill, and the house façade was two stories, including a raised brick basement. On the rear elevation, where the basement is beneath ground level, the house appeared to be a single story. A dry moat across the rear provided light and ventilation for the lower roof. It had a long gallery or piazza, partly enclosed by Venetian blinds.

The house's interior included the fan-lighted doorways of the front and rear elevations, which were among the earliest Mississippi expressions of this common hallmark of the federal style. The interior millwork of the principal room was finely executed and included a gouged-carved cornice and a matching pair of gouge-carved mantel pieces. The room included a unique ceiling dome unique to the region that provided extra height for a lighting fixture and was lined with tin to reflect light.

Susanna had planned to have fine furniture crafted or purchased. She was making plans for fine dining room furniture. However, she couldn't complete the dining room before she gave birth. Within two weeks after moving into her new house, Susanna gave birth to their first child.

"A handsome boy you have there," the midwife said as she held the baby for Andrew to take.

Andrew took the baby from the midwife and held him gingerly.

"He's not going to break," Susanna said.

"What shall we name him?" Andrew asked.

"I think that we should name him Andre," Susanna replied.

"Andre? Why Andre?" Andrew asked. The baby started to squirm.

"Let me take him," Susanna said.

Andrew handed the baby back to the midwife, and she gave the baby to Susanna.

"Why should we name him, Andre?"

"Andre is French for Andrew."

"I get it," Andrew replied. "This way he will be a little of you and a little of me," Andrew said. "I like it."

After the war, Jackson's men received access to purchase lands in Mississippi and Alabama at an extreme discount. This was perfect timing for Andrew. Now that he had a townhouse for his wife, he turned his attention to building his plantation. He bought a forested land along the Mississippi just south of Natchez. Because he participated in the Battle of New Orleans, Andrew purchased a large tract of land for less than he thought possible above Natchez. He now dedicated his time to clearing the land of oaks and milling them to sell to his friend PJ, who built steamboat hulls and the wooden parts of paddlewheels at Natchez under the Hill. PJ then sold them to other captains and pilots of the company who outfitted the steamboats with the boilers and the gear mechanisms for the paddlewheel.

Andrew couldn't find free laborers willing to help on his plantation, so with the money from the boat building, he purchased several male slaves who helped clear more land and prepare his land for growing cotton.

Susanna raised their children with the help of a Jamaican woman whom Susanna had taught as a housemaid. She then had the slave housekeeper train other maids not only to work in their house, but she also sold them to other plantations in Louisiana and Mississippi. She felt that it was her way of helping keep as many slave women out of the fields as possible.

Andrew's business flourished, and soon he became wealthy enough to build Susanna a house on his plantation. This grand Grecian-style house made his parents' home in the north seem small and dreary. They kept the house in town for when he made excursions into town for business, or she wanted to attend parties in town with other local women. Whenever they were in town, Andrew and Susanna would sit on their veranda and watch the moonrise over the Mississippi and reminisce about their steamboat adventure.

19

Separating Fact from Fiction

When I saw this story about the maiden voyage of the New Orleans from Pittsburgh to New Orleans, and that there was a love story involved, I knew I had to tell it. The 1810s were an exciting time for the early American frontier. Because of this new technology, steamboat travel on the rivers developed commerce in the frontier towns along the Mississippi and Ohio Rivers.

Western Life before Steamboat Travel

Before the introduction of steamboats on the Western waters, the means of transportation consisted of keelboats, barges, and flatboats. Those who pushed the creation of the steamboat were already reaching beyond the technical limits of the day. Traversing the Ohio and Mississippi by steam to reach Louisiana was almost akin to envisioning a trip to the moon. Once Nicholas Roosevelt and his crew set off from Pittsburgh, it probably would have taken far more than a few earthquakes and some sunken trees to dissuade them from staying on course. Their journey had already taken them too far to turn back.

During the decades preceding the first voyage of New Orleans, and after the Louisiana Purchase in 1803, settlers arrived in the western lands via the Ohio and Mississippi Rivers. However, with no practical way to go upstream, trade remained limited. To move upstream, a poleman had to row laboriously at low speeds to push a boat with poles or be pulled by men walking on shore, straining their backs while pulling towlines. Otherwise, the return trip required a sea voyage from New Orleans to an eastern port and crossing the Appalachian Mountains to reach an inland departure point.

The steamboat New Orleans, which achieved a downstream speed of eight to ten miles per hour and an upstream speed of three miles per hour, became the first of thousands of steamboats that converted river commerce from a one-way trip downstream to two-way traffic, opening the Mississippi River and Ohio River valleys to commercial trade. In her first year of business on the Mississippi River, between New Orleans and Natchez,

In the first couple of decades of the 1800s, the first major transportation revolution was underway in the United States. Innovations and internal improvements included canals, highways, and steamboats. Together, they made a truly national economy possible by allowing farmers to ship their goods to wider markets and allowing manufacturers to reach more consumers like the one that Charles Mayford would open at the end of the epilogue. When the New Orleans succeeded, it marked a turning point in transportation. Soon, steamboats were proliferating on the Ohio River, the Mississippi River, and their tributaries. Steamboat traffic opened markets for farm goods, increased the number of people, and increased commerce in cities along the rivers.

The development of the steamboat trade brought about other innovations as well. These internal improvements of the early nineteenth century included canals, highways, and steamboats. Together, they made a truly national economy possible by allowing farmers to ship their goods to wider markets and allowing manufacturers to reach more consumers.

The steam engines developed for steamboats eventually became the same technology developed a couple of decades later in the locomotive industry.

Natchez and the Natchez Trace

In the late 18th century, Natchez was the starting point of the Natchez Trace overland route. This Native American trail followed a path established by migrating animals, most likely buffalo.

Native Americans created and used the trail for centuries. Early European and American explorers, traders, and immigrants used it in the late 18th and early 19th centuries. European Americans founded inns, also known as "stands", along the Trace to serve food and lodging to travelers. Most of these stands closed as travel shifted to steamboats on the Mississippi and other rivers. The heyday of the Trace began in the 1770s and ended in the 1820s. By the 1830s, the route was already in disrepair, and its time as a major interregional commercial route ended.

The trail ran from Natchez to Nashville through what are now Mississippi, Alabama, and Tennessee. Flatboat and keelboat men transported produce and other goods on the Mississippi River. These men sold their wares at Natchez or New Orleans. When they arrived at their destination, they dismantled their boats and sold the materials as lumber.

The Natchez landing was the perfect location for unloading their goods. Natchez had a safe harbor for boats because the harbor was half-moon shaped. This harbor was ideal because the wind seldom disturbed it. Even in heavy winds, if boats were fastened properly, they would not likely be damaged.

The boatmen who made the long trek back north to their homes overland on the Natchez Trace were locally called "Kaintucks" because they were usually from Kentucky. Of course, not all the "Kaintucks" were from Kentucky. Many, like Andrew, originated from other parts of the Ohio River Valley.

Because the area was a mostly unsettled frontier, banditry regularly occurred along the Trace. Much of it centered around the river landing Natchez Under-The-Hill, where boatmen enjoyed whiskey, women, and song after they traded their wares for cash. This area was a hotbed of gamblers, prostitutes, and drunken crews from the boats.

Other dangers lurked along the Trace in the areas outside city boundaries. Highwaymen, like John Murrell and Samuel Mason, terrorized travelers along the road. They operated large gangs of organized brigands in one of the first examples of land-based organized crime in the United States.

Natchez was the center of economic activity for the young state. Its strategic location on the high bluffs on the eastern bank of the Mississippi River enabled it to develop into a bustling port.

In later years, many local plantation owners loaded their cotton onto steamboats at the Natchez Under-the-Hill to be transported downriver to New Orleans. Later, when the use of steamboat power became commonplace, cotton was also sent upriver to St. Louis or Cincinnati. This cotton was sold and shipped to New England, New York, and European spinning and textile mills.

The New Orleans Steamboat

The New Orleans was not the first commercially successful steamboat. Beginning in 1807, Robert Livingston and Robert Fulton offered services from New York City to Albany, New York. In 1809, they arranged with Nicholas Roosevelt to build a steamboat in Pittsburgh, take it down the Ohio and Mississippi Rivers, and establish service between New Orleans and Natchez.

The steamboat New Orleans journey down the Ohio and Mississippi Rivers to New Orleans in 1811-1812 marked a new chapter in American travel. After the New Orleans showed what was possible, steamboats proliferated on the Ohio and the Mississippi and their tributaries. Steamboat traffic helped create a national economy, opened markets for farm goods, and drew people and commerce to cities along the rivers. The New Orleans persevered through a combination of skill, luck, and sheer doggedness.

The New Orleans arrived in New Orleans on Jan. 10, 1812. During the same month, she began her profitable career providing transportation between New Orleans and Natchez. She averaged $2,400 in receipts per trip, making the round trip about once every three weeks. Factoring in expenses, this amounted to a net gain of at least $20,000. This revenue was superior to any other establishment in the United States at the time.

Even after the New Orleans' first successful voyage, the public doubted that steam navigation could succeed. They believed that it was still more expensive than other methods of river transport, and they doubted anyone would ever be able to afford it. As a result, carrying freight on flatboats and keels increased. Now, however, these boatmen could travel upriver to anywhere along the Ohio or Mississippi in the relative comfort of the steamboat and without the dangers of the Natchez Trace.

After the New Orleans showed that steamboat traffic on western waters was not only possible but profitable, steamboats proliferated on the Ohio and the Mississippi and their tributaries. Steamboat traffic helped create a national economy, opening markets for farm goods and drawing people and commerce to cities along the rivers.

Steamboat travel did not make river travel effortless. The "Falls of the Ohio" at Louisville effectively cut navigation into two sections. Travel by steamboat was still fraught with danger. Thanks to the effects of the earthquakes, the riverbed was dotted with dangerous snags, gravel, and sandbars. Eventually, the riverbed would be cleared, and later the Louisville and Portland Canal would be built, making it easier for travelers to navigate the 981-mile passage between Pittsburgh and the junction with the Mississippi River.

Nicholas and Lydia Roosevelt

Most of the credit for the New Orleans' success can be attributed to Nicholas Roosevelt and his plucky young wife, Lydia Latrobe Roosevelt.

Nicholas Roosevelt was born in 1767 and became an inventor and entrepreneur with an interest in steam engines. He had business connections with Robert Fulton, the developer of the first American commercially successful steamboat. Fulton and Robert Livingston, who assisted in drafting the Declaration of Independence, provided much of the capital for the venture.

Benjamin Henry Latrobe, architect of the U.S. Capitol and Lydia's father, helped finance the expedition, too. Lydia Latrobe was born in 1791.

Nicholas and Lydia had an unusual relationship. They first discussed marriage when he was 37 and she was 13, and they held off getting married until four years later. Despite the differences in their ages, they appeared to have a stable marriage.

In 1809, Nicholas Roosevelt suggested that Fulton introduce steamboats on the western waters. Fulton wanted to know the idea's viability, so he told Nicholas to research the project and get back to him with the details.

A few months after the wedding, the Roosevelts began a six-month flatboat trip from Pittsburgh to New Orleans to determine whether a steamboat could also travel that route. Pregnant during the journey, Lydia Roosevelt gave birth to their daughter, Rosetta Mark Roosevelt, shortly after returning to New York City.

The New Orleans was launched from Pittsburgh, Pennsylvania, for a company organized by Robert Livingston and Robert Fulton, her designer. She was a large, heavy side-wheeler with a deep draft. Her low-pressure Boulton and Watt steam engine operated a complex power train that was heavy and inefficient.

Nicholas had to rebuild the steam engine so that the steamboat could make the journey. Nicholas Roosevelt began supervising construction in Pittsburgh.

Although their neighbors thought that Lydia (who was pregnant again) should stay in Pittsburgh rather than accompany her husband on what might be dangerous journeys, the Roosevelts insisted on making the trip as a team and brought their toddler daughter with them. They left Pittsburgh on October 20, and ten days later, Lydia gave birth to their son, Henry Latrobe Roosevelt, shortly after the steamboat arrived in Louisville.

Nicholas died in 1854. Lydia died in 1878.

Decades later, their great-grand-nephew, Theodore Roosevelt, carried some of their adventurous spirit into the White House and beyond.

The Great Comet

The Great Comet of 1811, first observed in March and easily visible in the night sky during September and October, made a dramatic backdrop for the first weeks of the trip.

The appearance of this comet at the same time as the earthquakes in the New Madrid area of the Mississippi caused many to be superstitious.

Louisville

The New Orleans' arrival in Louisville gave its crew a taste of how their new technology might be received by those less familiar with the sights and sounds of the steam-powered boat. The New Orleans pulled in around midnight, and the roar of the boat's steam power proved so unsettling that crowds rushed down to the wharf to see what was happening, sure that something terrible had occurred.

The "Falls of the Ohio" had already made Louisville a portage for boats traveling downstream. Heavy-laden boats would unload in Louisville. Therefore, travelers had a reason to enjoy what Louisville offered before continuing their journey downstream.

Louisville's sister town, Shippingport, also benefited from the falls. The shipping industry's dilemma with the falls kept the citizens of the village employed. Shippingport reached its peak in the 1820s with a population of 600. Unfortunately, Shippingport frequently flooded. In

1825, engineers constructed the Louisville and Portland Canal across the peninsula. This left the settlement on an island. Using the canal, ships could bypass the Falls and, by extension, Shippingport.

Indian Relations

The New Orleans passed through territory occupied by the Chickasaw. At the time of this New Orleans adventure, Native Americans in much of what is now the Midwest resented the settlers who were encroaching on their land. Unsympathetic settlers fueled that resentment. The Shawnee war chief Tecumseh and his brother Tenskwatawa (known to Euro-Americans as the Prophet) organized Indian unity and resistance. Tensions between the Americans and British were also high, and not long after the New Orleans' maiden voyage, the War of 1812 broke out. To that end, the British recruited Indian allies and encouraged conflict between Native Americans and American settlers.

The Indians who lived along the riverbanks saw the Great Comet of 1811, along with the earthquakes and the roar of the steamboat down the Mississippi, as an ominous sign. Some Native American tribes who were already provoked by the United States' expansion into their territories were openly hostile toward the Americans. The Battle of Tippecanoe, November 1811, was evidence of this. Many of the spiritual leaders saw this as one more sign that the events that fall and winter foreshadowed disaster.

The Chickasaw Bluffs (where Memphis is now located) belonged to the Chickasaw until they ceded that territory in 1818. On one memorable occasion during the New Orleans' time in Chickasaw territory, Indians threatened and chased after the steamboat.

New Madrid and Surrounding Counties Before the Earthquakes

The first settlement in Mississippi County was made around 1800 by Joseph Johnson near Bird's Point. Other early settlements were made on Mathews Prairie. Johnson sold his land in 1805 to Abraham Bird. He gave his name to the settlement known as Bird's Point.

Before the earthquakes, the town of New Madrid had been a thriving village with a parklike feel. The banks of the Mississippi, throughout the territory, were considered a highway and kept open forever as such. The town had a policy of allowing certain trees to grow without being damaged or cut down, except if the Magistrates of the Police dictated that they be cut down for a road.

George Morgan secured a land grant from the Spanish government for New Madrid's settlement. Because of the well-known liberality of the Spanish government, land grants were very easy to secure. Anyone who performed a service for the government or who promised to perform such a service in the future could obtain a grant of land. These grants were also given to encourage industry development.

Many settlers were attracted by the generous conditions under which land was granted and by the real desirability of the site of New Madrid, and George Morgan accomplished much of what he desired. His plans, however, conflicted with Governor Miro, the Spanish governor of Louisiana's plans whose headquarters were in New Orleans and who was engaged in an intrigue with General James Wilkinson.

Wilkinson was an officer in the United States Army in command of the district along the Mississippi River. He planned with Miro to incite a rebellion among the people of the United States west of the Alleghenies, to separate this territory from the United States and join it to the Spanish territory. Wilkinson drew a pension from the Spanish government and hoped his efforts would secure that territory of the United States for Spain.

Morgan's plan of drawing settlers to New Madrid and making that a prosperous and flourishing center of trade for Upper Louisiana directly opposed Wilkinson's vision. Colonel Morgan was his rival, so Wilkinson sought to thwart his plans. He wrote Governor Miro that he had applied for a grant in the Yazoo country to destroy the place of a certain Colonel Morgan. He told Miro that Morgan was an educated and intelligent man, but a thorough speculator. He also told the governor that Morgan had twice been bankrupt and that he was poor but ambitious. He said that he had hired a spy to research Morgan's agreement with Don Diego Gardoqui. He said he was convinced that Morgan's scheme would be successful unless they took steps to counteract it.

Wilkinson assured Miro that their plans would be greatly hindered if Morgan carried out his plans for his settlement. Acting on this information, Governor Miro sought to end Morgan's operations. On May 20, 1789, he wrote to the Spanish government and protested against Morgan's grant. He said that it formed a state within a state and asked the government to cancel this grant.

At the same time, he wrote to Morgan and charged him with having exceeded his authority and acted in bad faith. He said that Morgan had no authority to lay out a town and provide for a government. He informed Morgan that he intended to construct a fort at New Madrid and place a detachment of soldiers to control the situation. Morgan saw that this interference would ruin his hopes. He apologized in the letter, saying that if he had exceeded his authority, his actions were because he was anxious to serve the King of Spain.

He could not conceal this fact from those colonists who had come and were still coming to New Madrid, that he had fallen out of favor with the government. The colonists complained about some of the regulations and finally sent an agent, John Ward, to present a petition to Governor Miro. Acting on this petition, Miro carried out his threat and sent a company of soldiers with orders to construct a fort at New Madrid and to take entire charge of the government of the post. This practically destroyed Morgan's influence, and with its loss went all his hope of making a settlement at New Madrid. The post continued under the government of Spanish officials.

Some of the other early settlers were John Summers, Joseph, and Louis Vandenbenden. These brothers were merchants, and the widow of Louis afterward married Richard Jones Waters.

Jacob Meyers, Joseph McCourtney, David Gray, and John La Valle were other early settlers. La Valle was the last commandant under the Spanish government; his descendants still live in New Madrid County. Doctor Robert D. Dawson, who was a native of Maryland, came to New Madrid at an early date and engaged in the practice of medicine. For several years, he was the leading physician of the town and was a very popular man. His activities were not confined to the practice of his profession, but he had a great interest in politics. For several years, he represented New Madrid County in the general assembly of the territory and was elected a member of the Constitutional Convention.

Because of their location on the Mississippi, the inhabitants of New Madrid saw that if they had harvested extensively, they could sell their surplus. The inhabitants desired to create farms to raise stock and to make crops.

Several American families came to New Madrid; some of them placed themselves at once on farms, and the Spanish clamored against the Americans, whom they thought too wonderful. Jealousy stimulated them, and they would also place themselves on farms.

An officer, Lieutenant Pierre Forcher, in charge of thirty soldiers, came to take charge of a post that was set up near the town between Bayou St. John and the Decyperi. The fort, built on the bank of the Mississippi River, was named after Governor Miro's wife and called Fort Celeste.

Commandant Forcher was a man of energy and administrative ability, and under his rule, order and prosperity reigned in the community. Eighteen months later, Thomas Portell took over the post. Portell was a man well suited to the place, governed with justice, and was able to satisfy most of the people.

Several American families came to New Madrid; some of them placed themselves at once on farms, and the Spanish schemed against the Americans. Jealousy stimulated them, and they would take over farmland.

The commandant managed everything according to the views of the government. He welcomed and encouraged activity and exhibited to the industrious men that he was distinguished above others and earned governmental protection. The Americans who obtained grants of land have nothing more at heart but to settle on them at once and improve them to the extent of their ability.

In 1799, De Lassus was transferred to St. Louis and became the lieutenant governor of Upper Louisiana. De Lassus was the most popular official ever in command at not just in New Madrid, but all of Louisiana territory. He was succeeded by Don Henri Peyroux, who was transferred to the post from Ste. Genevieve Peyroux landed in New Madrid in August 1799 and was in command for four years. He then resigned and returned to France.

John Lavalle succeeded Peyroux as commandant of the post and held the place until the transfer to the United States in March 1804.

Before the earthquakes, New Madrid contained about a hundred houses scattered on a fine plain two miles square on which, however, the river has so encroached during the twenty-three years since it was first settled, that the bank was half a mile behind its old bounds and the inhabitants had to move back away from the river. The inhabitants were a mixture of French Creoles from Illinois, United States Americans, and Germans. They have plenty of cattle, but in other respects seemed destitute. There is some trade with the Indian hunters of furs and pelts, but this was of little consequence. Dry goods and groceries are enormously high-priced, and the inhabitants charged travelers immense prices for common necessities like milk, butter, fowls, and eggs. The militia officers wore cockades to distinguish themselves, but underneath they wore dirty, ragged shirts and trousers.

Courts of Common Pleas and Quarter Sessions were held in New Madrid, but appeals would have had to go to the Supreme Court at St. Louis, the capital of the territory of Upper Louisiana. To get there, litigants had to travel by wagon two hundred and forty miles north and through Saint Genevieve, which was 180 miles away from New Madrid. Because of its distance from the capital, New Madrid had the right to have all trials for felony held and adjudged in their town without appeal. The inhabitants often regretted the change of government from Spanish to American, even though they complained a lot about the Spanish government.

Francois and Joseph LeSieur were the earliest French settlers in the New Madrid area. These two sons of Charles LeSieur, a native of southern France who emigrated to Three Rivers in Canada, came to St. Louis in 1785. A fur trader, Gabriel Cerre, employed him. Joseph died in 1796 and left no children. Francois married on May 13, 1791, Cecile Guilbeault, a native of Vincennes. Their descendants were still found in the New Madrid area in 1811.

In 1794, they moved to Little Prairie, remaining there until the earthquakes of 1811 and 1812, when they returned to New Madrid County and made their home at Point Pleasant. Francois LeSieur died in 1826. He had been married three times.

Another French settler was Pierre Antoine La Forge. He also came from France. La Forge was an aristocrat by birth, had been educated to be a priest, but fell in love with his cousin Margaret Champagne. He left Paris at the time of the French Revolution and moved to America. At first, he lived in Gallipolis, Ohio. He later moved to New Madrid, where he was appointed a public writer and interpreter. He was also an adjutant of militia, justice of the peace, and a notary public. De Lassus thought very highly of La Forge and considered him one of the best officers in the service of the Spanish.

One of the most prominent men in New Madrid was Captain McCoy. He had come to the settlement with Morgan and became an officer under the Spanish authorities. He was in command of a Spanish galley, or revenue boat. Several galleys were stationed in New Madrid and enforced Spanish commercial laws. All boats passing New Madrid were required to stop to give an account of themselves and to pay taxes to the government. It was while in command of one of these boats that McCoy captured the celebrated Mason gang of robber pirates who for many years committed depredations on the river commerce. Joseph Michel, who visited New Madrid in 1887, had a vivid recollection of the encounter between McCoy and the Mason gang. The Spanish governor at that time was Peyroux. He ordered McCoy to Little Prairie, where he found and captured Mason and his men. They were then brought to New Madrid, sent from there to New Orleans and were then ordered up the river again, and on the return while their boat was tied at the riverbank with most of the crew on the bank, Mason and his men seized the boat, shot and wounded Captain McCoy and they escaped. McCoy was commandant at the post of New Madrid in 1799, then he became commandant at Tywappity Bottom. He died in New Madrid in 1840.

One of the most prominent men who came with Morgan was Doctor Richard Jones Waters. Waters was a native of Maryland. He came to New Madrid about 1790 and began the practice of his profession. Besides being a physician, he was also a trader, mill owner, and land speculator. He married the widow of Louis Vandenbenden. The Waters family of New Madrid descended from Richard Jones Waters. He left a large estate and was an energetic, enterprising man. De Lassus rated him as a good officer but also considered him somewhat extravagant.

The first settlement in Pemiscot County was made at Little Prairie, a short distance below the present town of Caruthersville. The settlement was made in 1794 by Francois Le Sieur, who came to Little Prairie from New Madrid, where he had lived. He received a grant of land laid out about two hundred arpents (An arpent was a French unit of measurement used before the metric system. An arpent was equal to about 78.15470 yards) into a town divided into lots, each containing an arpent. Here, a fort, called Fort St. Fernando, was constructed. The site of Little Prairie was well chosen. It was situated on a great ridge along the Mississippi River, and the surrounding country was rich in soil, timber, and wild game. The town traded with the Indians, and therefore, it prospered. By 1803, Little Prairie's population had grown to 103 inhabitants. It continued to grow until the earthquakes of 1811 and 1812, when it was almost destroyed. This earthquake seems to have had its center about Little Prairie, and the shocks were probably more violent here than anywhere else. Most of the population moved away after the earthquake occurred. The village was practically deserted. The only conspicuous settler who remained in the vicinity was Colonel John Hardeman Walker.

In 1808, Cuming visited Little Prairie and gave the following account: *"We landed at the town of Little Prairie on the right, containing twenty-four little log cabins scattered on a fine, pleasant plain. Inhabitants, primarily French Creoles from Canada and Illinois, informed us that there were several Anglo-American farmers all around in a circle of ten miles. We stopped at a tavern and store kept by European Frenchmen, where we got some necessaries, everything is excessively dear (expensive) here as in New Madrid, butter a quarter of a dollar per pound, milk half a dollar per gallon, eggs a quarter of a dollar a dozen and fowls half to three-quarters of a dollar each."*

Besides this settlement at Little Prairie, several other settlements existed in Pemiscot County. One of them was near the town of Gayoso, which became the county seat. Another was in the western part of the county on Little River. A third was just north of the lake, called Big Lake, and the fourth was located on Portage Bay. All these settlements suffered greatly from the earthquake, and most were abandoned because of its effects.

Other settlements were established within the territory of New Madrid County. Some were made on Lake St. Ann, along the St. Johns Bayou, at Lake St. Mary, and on Bayou St. Thomas. The district of New Madrid included not only New Madrid County but also Pemiscot, Mississippi, Scott County, and even the counties lying further west.

With the opening of the King's Highway from Saint Genevieve to New Madrid in 1789 there sprung up several settlements along this road, some of them were in Scott County. One of the first of these was made near Sikeston by Edward Robertson and a son-in-law, Moses

Hurley. Robertson was a shrewd and capable man. He traded with the Indians and kept a stock of goods which he sold to other settlers. He accumulated most of his wealth by land speculation. At his death, he left a considerable amount of property.

Another of these early settlements was made in Scott County in 1796 near the present town of Benton by Captain Charles Friend, a Virginia native. He received a grant from the Spanish government near Benton and built a home there with his family. He had nine sons and two daughters in his family, and most of them remained near the land where the Spanish granted Friend his land. John Ramsay of Cape Girardeau came in 1811.

Settlers began to settle in Tywappity Bottoms as early as 1798. These settlers included James Brady, James Curran, Charles Findley, and Edmund Hogan. Others were Thomas, John, and James Wellborn, and the Quimby family. In 1802, Thomas W. Waters was the first settler on the site of Commerce. Here, he began the sale of goods in partnership with Robert Hall and also operated a ferry across the Mississippi.

The New Madrid Earthquake

I tried to make the events they experienced as realistic as possible, although I did rearrange some of the timeline of certain events to fit my story. The New Orleans journeyed down the Ohio and Mississippi rivers during another terrifying historical milestone. Between Dec. 16, 1811, and Feb. 7, 1812, a series of earthquakes struck along the New Madrid fault line near the Mississippi River in what is now Missouri and Arkansas. With magnitudes ranging from 7.5 to 8.0, they remain the strongest earthquakes ever to hit the eastern U.S. The impact of these quakes was felt as far away as Pennsylvania and Massachusetts.

Their effects were felt all over the territory, but especially in New Madrid and the adjoining region. The first major earthquake occurred on December 16, 1811, and its epicenter was in the town of New Madrid (now in the state of Missouri). The Roosevelts and the crew of the New Orleans were about 200 miles from the epicenter on December 16, and they felt the distinctive shock. (It was discernible as far away as Boston.) The earthquake caused enough damage to change the shape of the Mississippi River, meaning that the steamboat traveled through miles and miles of uncharted waters. The tremors continued for more than a year, with the three largest ones (with magnitudes between 7 and 8) occurring during the first three months.

The Mississippi temporarily ran backward. Two waterfalls briefly emerged as the river's bed shifted to accommodate the tremors. Whole islands disappeared while new ones were created. Channels were blocked by debris. Existing navigational charts became meaningless. Boats traversing the area braved miles of utterly uncharted waters.

Miraculously, as happened in the story, the New Orleans made it through the earthquake zone. Avoiding the banks, where trees continued to fall into the river, the boat somehow navigated through the disappearing islands, roiling waters, and unstable riverbed to reach its destination during the worst period of seismic activity the region has ever experienced.

Before the steamboat arrived in Natchez, some newspapers had speculated that there was no way that the New Orleans could have survived the devastation, and people had rumored that the steamboat must have been destroyed. Fortunately, the arrival of the New Orleans in Natchez and later New Orleans proved that those conspiracies were a myth.

At New Madrid, the shocks have been uncommonly violent. Chimneys and houses collapsed. This compelled one-third of the inhabitants to leave the area and escape to the adjacent hills. The remainder encamped in tents in open fields. The earth was so convulsed that people could not stand upright. The upward motion of the earthquake was estimated at approximately a foot. The shocks were accompanied by a partial darkness, tremendous noise, and a sulfurous smell. Sixty-seven shocks have been witnessed in all, which have split and cracked the earth in a hundred places in the neighborhood. During the violent shocks, the people, by their yells and shrieks, discovered their extreme alarm, and upon one of those occasions, a lady was known to faint and never recovered! The face of the country, below, about Little Prairie, has almost entirely changed — large lakes having been converted into dry land, and fields into lakes — the banks of the river fallen in — mills destroyed, and the earth cracked in every direction. The St. Francis was at one time very shallow at another time overflowing the surrounding country. At Little Prairie, the Mississippi was said to have formed an eddy, and presented a retrograde motion, and in 15 or 20 minutes afterward resumed its course and rose about 5 feet. Seven Indians were said to have been swallowed up in one of those apertures in the earth, one of which only made his escape, who stated that this quandary was foretold by the Shawnee Prophet [Tenskwatawa] to destroy the white man.

Several miles above the mouth of the Ohio, the current's diminished speed indicated a rise in the Mississippi. This was found to be the case. The bottom lands on either shore were underwater, and there was every sign of a flood.

The injury produced by the effects of the earthquakes in New Madrid was greater than in any other town. They caused most of the people in the area to move elsewhere. Plantations, stock of all kinds, cribs of corn, and smokehouses filled with meat were offered for horses to live on. Heavy losses at different times in Chicago and on the Mississippi River in produce went to New Orleans in flatboats, and by the earthquakes. Individuals were left destitute and without any capital to operate on. Friends up and downstream came forward to assist them.

The staple of this country from 1805 to 1812 had been cotton. The average yield of an acre was from 1000 to 1200 pounds of cottonseed. After 1812, a great change in the climate occurred. The winters grew colder and the other seasons more changeable. Raising cotton was entirely abandoned during the 35 years after 1812. The staple crop became corn.

In 1820, one visitor said that they had arrived before noon at New Madrid, where they found both sides of the river lined with logs, some remaining stationary and others in motion. New Madrid had become an insignificant French hamlet containing little more than about twenty log houses and stores miserably supplied. The goods sold there were retailed at exorbitant prices. The land seemed rich, but the people had been discouraged by the earthquakes, which were frequent experiences. Two or three oscillations were sometimes felt in a day. To compensate those who suffered in their property by the catastrophe, the United States Government granted the settlers an equivalent acreage in other parts of the territory.

Chickasaw Bluffs

The New Orleans passed the Chickasaw Bluffs on her maiden voyage. At the time, the area belonged to the Chickasaw tribe. The Chickasaw finally ceded the territory in 1818.

The Indians threatening and chasing the New Orleans was a recorded event. As stated in the story. As the New Orleans passed this area, canoes came and went among the boles of the trees. Sometimes, the Indians attempted to approach them, but they would immediately flee when the huge, loud steamboat approached them. In that one instance, a large canoe, fully manned, came out of the woods abreast of the steamboat. The Indians, outnumbering the crew of the vessel, paddled after it. Immediately, a race ensued. For a time, the contest was equal. The result, however, was what anyone might have anticipated. Steam had the advantage of endurance. The Indians, with wild shouts of defiance, gave up the pursuit and turned into the forest from whence they had emerged.

While the crew of the New Orleans was more amused than alarmed by this incident. Mr. Roosevelt was concerned about a visit they had on the flatboat on the preliminary exploration, when Indians came onboard the flatboat, demanding that Nicholas give them whiskey.

The kitchen fire I wrote about had occurred, too, but not exactly as I wrote in the story. In the real event, Lydia and Nicholas were still discussing the adventure when they retired to rest. They had scarcely fallen asleep when they were aroused by shouts on deck and the trampling of many feet. With the fear of Indians still predominant, Mr. Roosevelt sprang from his bed and seized a sword, the only weapon at hand. He ran from their cabin to join the battle against what he perceived must have been the Chickasaws. It was a more alarming enemy that he encountered. New Orleans was on fire. Flame and smoke poured from the forward cabin. The servant who attended there had placed some green wood too close to the stove in anticipation of the next day's wants. He had lain down beside the stove and had fallen sound asleep. The stove had become overheated, and the wood was on fire. The woodwork near the stove had caught fire. The entire cabin would soon have been in flames, had not the servant, half suffocated, rushed on deck and given the alarm. It took much exertion, but the fire, consuming the cabin, was extinguished. However, the interior woodwork had been defaced. Few eyes were closed for the remainder of the night. The accident did nothing to tranquilize the anxiety of the passengers and crew.

There was a conversation between one of the crew and a principal Chickasaw warrior called Indian Factor. He was named this because he had formerly been a kind of Agent for that nation. He was concerned that the Chickasaw would join other tribes in raising the long-buried tomahawk, which was another way of saying that they were contemplating the idea of breaking the treaty with the white men.

The Factor told the crew on wood gathering duty that their Prophet Tenskwatawa had suggested that the comet, the earthquakes, and the steamboat were all connected. His prophecy suggested that the reason for the earthquake and the sign of the comet was that the Great Spirit was displeased with the way the white man was destroying the earth, and the tribes needed to rid themselves of this evil force.

The Chickasaw did little more to avenge the white man's presence other than to steal a few horses at Bear Creek, about thirty miles from Colbert's Ferry on the Tennessee River.

The City of New Orleans

New Orleans in the 1800s was a bustling and culturally rich city with a dynamic economy and a diverse population. In 1810, the city had a population of 17,242. It was a melting pot of different ethnicities, resulting in a unique cultural tapestry. The city's French roots were evident in its architecture, language, and cuisine. The Spanish influence can be seen in the city's street names, such as Bourbon and Chartres, as well as in the preservation of the Spanish Colonial architecture style. African traditions and customs, brought by enslaved people, also played a significant role in shaping the city's culture.

The city was known for its narrow streets, ornate balconies, and unique Creole townhouses. The area buzzed with entertainment venues. It boasted of numerous theaters, opera houses, and galleries, attracting local and international artists alike. Dishes like gumbo, jambalaya, and beignets had already become synonymous with New Orleans, reflecting the city's diverse heritage and culinary ingenuity.

The New Orleans economy during the 19th century was heavily reliant on agriculture, with cotton its primary crop. The city served as a hub for shipping and processing cotton, making it a major player in the lucrative cotton trade. Additionally, sugar cane cultivation and the production of molasses were also major economic activities.

Yellow fever outbreaks were a recurring problem, causing significant loss of life and economic setbacks. Additionally, issues related to slavery and racial tensions were prevalent.

Once the New Orleans and other steamboats that followed, the city served as a gateway for goods going up and down the river from the vast interior of the United States. New Orleans also served as a point of entry for goods from abroad.

The War of 1812

Though it was not part of the main story, I felt I had to include the Battle of New Orleans in the War of 1812 in the epilogue. Andrew's participation in that war explains how he obtained a Mississippi plantation that I will include in a volume of *The Locket Saga* that I will be writing. This is simply a prequel to that story.

The Battle of New Orleans should not have been fought at all. In August 1814, Britain and the United States began negotiations to end the War of 1812. However, British Secretary of State for War and the Colonies Henry Bathurst issued Pakenham's secret orders on October 24, 1814, commanding him to continue the war even if he heard rumors of peace. Bathurst expressed concern that the United States might not ratify a treaty and did not want Pakenham either to endanger his forces or miss an opportunity for victory. Before that, in August 1814, Vice Admiral Cochrane had convinced the Admiralty that a campaign against New Orleans would weaken American resolve against Canada and hasten a successful end to the war.

There was a major concern that the British and their Spanish allies wanted to reclaim the territories of the Louisiana Purchase because they did not recognize any land deals made by Napoleon (starting with the 1800 Spanish cession of Louisiana to France, followed by the 1804 French sale of Louisiana to the United States). This is why the British invaded New Orleans during the Treaty of Ghent negotiations. It has been theorized that if the British had won the Battle of New Orleans, they would have likely interpreted that all territories gained from the 1803 Louisiana Purchase would be void and not part of U.S. territory.

The treaty had been signed, but the troops in New Orleans had no way of knowing this. Modern communication methods had not yet been invented, so news from across the Atlantic was slow. The battle occurred 15 days after the delegations signed the Treaty of Ghent, formally ending the War of 1812 on December 24, 1814. The United States Congress did not ratify the treaty until February 16, 1815.

In the epilogue, I included Andrew in the Battle of New Orleans with General Andrew Jackson on January 8, 1815. This battle was fought between the British Army under Major General Sir Edward Pakenham and the United States Army under Brevet Major General Andrew Jackson, roughly 5 miles southeast of the French Quarter of New Orleans.

The battle was the climax of the five-month Gulf Campaign by Britain to try to take New Orleans, West Florida, and possibly the Louisiana Territory, which began at the First Battle of Fort Bowyer. Britain started the New Orleans campaign on December 14, 1814, at the Battle of Lake Borgne, and numerous skirmishes and artillery duels happened in the weeks leading up to the final battle.

Despite a British advantage in numbers, training, and experience, the American forces defeated a poorly executed assault in slightly more than 30 minutes. The Americans suffered 71 casualties, while the British suffered over 2,000, including the deaths of the commanding general, Major General Sir Edward Pakenham, and his second-in-command, Major General Samuel Gibbs.

Under the command of General John Keane, 1600 British soldiers were rowed 60 miles west from Cat Island to Pea Island (possibly now Pearl Island), situated about 30 miles from New Orleans. It took six days and nights to ferry the troops, each transit taking around ten hours.

Keane squandered a passing opportunity to obtain his objective when he decided to not take the open road from the Rigolets to New Orleans. The shallow waters of the narrow passes of the Rigolets and the Chef Menteur could not take any vessel more than eight feet.

A further hindrance was the lack of shallow draft vessels, which Cochrane had requested, yet the Admiralty had refused. Because of this, even when they used shallow boats, they could not transport more than 2,000 men at a time.

On the morning of December 23, Keane and a vanguard of 1,800 British soldiers reached the east bank of the Mississippi River, 9 miles south of New Orleans. They could have attacked the city by advancing a few hours up the undefended river road. However, Keane decided to camp at Lacoste's Plantation and wait for the arrival of reinforcements. The British invaded the home of Major Gabriel Villeré, but he escaped through a window and quickly warned General Jackson of the approaching army and the location of their encampment. This information contributed to the British downfall.

After receiving Villeré's intelligence report, on the evening of December 23, Jackson led 2,131 men in a brief three-pronged assault from the north on the unsuspecting British troops resting in their camp. He pulled his forces back to the Rodriguez Canal, about 4 miles south of the city. The Americans suffered 24 killed, 115 wounded, and 74 missing, while the British reported their losses as 46 killed, 167 wounded, and 64 missing. The action was consequential since, by December 25, Pakenham's forces had an effective strength of 5,933 out of a headcount of 6,660 soldiers. The British won a "tactical victory," which enabled them to maintain their position, but they did not achieve the expected easy conquest. Because the Americans did not allow the British to advance, the Americans gained time to transform the canal into a heavily fortified earthwork.

On Christmas Day, General Edward Pakenham arrived on the battlefield. Two days later, he received nine large naval artillery guns from Admiral Cochrane along with a hot shot furnace to silence the two U.S. Navy warships, the sloop-of-war USS Louisiana and the schooner USS Carolina, that had harassed the army for 24 hours per day from the Mississippi River. The British sank the Carolina in a massive explosion, but the Louisiana survived thanks to the Barataria pirates. These men boarded rowboats and tied the ship to those rowboats. They rowed it further north and away from the British artillery. The Louisiana was not able to sail northward under her own power due to the attack. This vessel was no longer a danger to the British, but Jackson ordered the ships' surviving guns and crew to be stationed on the west bank to provide covering fire for any British assault on the river road to Line Jackson, the name of the U.S. defensive line at the Rodriguez Canal.

On December 28, after silencing the two ships, Pakenham ordered a reconnaissance-in-force to attack the earthworks that Jackson's men had erected. The reconnaissance-in-force was designed to test Line Jackson and see how well-defended it was, and if any section of the line was weak, the British would take advantage of the situation, break through, and call for thousands of more soldiers to smash through the defenses. On the right side of this offensive with their huge show of force, the British soldiers successfully sent the militia defenders into a hasty retreat. They were just a few hundred yards from breaching the defensive line, but the left side of the reconnaissance-in-force held. This led to disaster for the British. The surviving artillery guns from the two neutralized warships successfully defended with cannon fire the section of the line that Jackson had erected closest to the Mississippi River. This made it appear that the British offensive completely failed, even though on the section closest to the swamp, the British were on the verge of breaking through. Pakenham withdrew all the soldiers after seeing the left side of his reconnaissance-in-force collapsing and retreating in panic. The British suffered 16 killed and 43 wounded, and the Americans suffered 7 killed and 10 wounded. Luck saved Jackson's line that day. This was the closest the British came during the entire campaign to defeating Jackson.

After the operation failed, Pakenham met with General Keane and Admiral Cochrane that evening to update the situation. Pakenham wanted to use Chef Menteur Pass as the invasion route, but Admiral Cochran overruled him. Admiral Cochrane insisted that his boats provided everything they needed. Admiral Cochrane believed that the veteran British soldiers would easily destroy Jackson's ramshackle army, and he said that if the army did not do it, his sailors would. This meeting determined how and where the next attack would occur.

The main British army arrived on New Year's Day 1815 and began an artillery bombardment of the American earthworks. Jackson's headquarters, Macarty House, was fired at for the first 10 minutes of the skirmish while Jackson and his officers were eating breakfast. The house was destroyed, but Jackson and the officers escaped harm. The Americans recovered quickly and mobilized their artillery to fire back at the British artillery. This began an artillery exchange that continued for three hours. The British artillery exhausted its ammunition, and Pakenham canceled the attack.

The Battle of New Orleans on January 8 was remarkable both for its apparent brevity and its casualties, though some numbers are in dispute and contradict the official statistics. A combined force of Tennessee militia and Choctaw warriors used heavy small arms fire to repel this final barrage. The Tennessee and Choctaw soldiers even moved forward in front of Line Jackson and counterattacked, guerrilla-style, to guarantee the British withdrawal. After yet another failure to breach Line Jackson, Pakenham decided to wait for his entire force of 8,000 men to assemble before continuing his attack (the 40th Foot arrived too late, disembarking on 12 January 1815. The British lost 45 killed and 55 wounded in the artillery duel, and the Americans lost 11 killed and 23 wounded.

John James Audubon

I had Nicholas and Lydia Roosevelt meet John James Audubon in Louisville and later along a trail near the Mississippi River. I doubt that either of these events occurred, but I have always had a fondness for Audubon and his love of plants and animals, so I had to fit him into the book. Audubon was probably already in Missouri when the New Orleans steamboat came through Louisville. He lived in the Sait Genevieve area. As I learned when writing *Book VII: Two Rivers*, Saint Genevieve is upriver, not downriver, from the mouth of the Ohio River. Therefore, it's not possible that this meeting could have occurred.

John James Audubon (born Jean-Jacques Rabin, April 26, 1785 – January 27, 1851) was a French American self-trained artist, naturalist, and ornithologist. His combined interests in art and ornithology turned into a plan to make a complete pictorial record of all the bird species of North America. He was notable for his extensive studies documenting all types of American birds and for his detailed illustrations, which depicted the birds in their natural habitats. His major work, a color-plate book titled The Birds of America (1827–1839), is considered one of the finest ornithological works ever completed. Audubon is also known for identifying twenty-five new species. He is the eponym of the National Audubon Society, and many towns, neighborhoods, and streets across the United States are named after him. In addition, the scientific community still uses dozens of scientific names first published by Audubon. In recent years, his legacy has become controversial for his involvement in slavery and his racist writings, as well as allegations of dishonesty.

In 1808, Audubon moved to Kentucky, which was rapidly being settled. Six months later, he married Lucy Bakewell at her family estate, Fatland Ford, Pennsylvania, and took her the next day to Kentucky. The two shared many common interests and began to explore the natural world around them. Though their finances were tenuous, the Audubon family grew. They had two sons, Victor Gifford (1809–1860) and John Woodhouse Audubon (1812–1862), and two daughters who died while extremely young, Lucy at two years (1815–1817) and Rose at nine months (1819–1820). Both sons eventually helped publish their father's works. John W. Audubon became a naturalist, writer, and painter in his own right.

Audubon and Jean Ferdinand Rozier moved their merchant business partnership west at various stages. Audubon was moving to Saint Genevieve, Missouri, a former French colonial settlement west of the Mississippi River and south of St. Louis. Shipping goods ahead, Audubon and Rozier had started a general store in Louisville, Kentucky, on the Ohio River. The city had an increasingly important slave market and was the most important port between Pittsburgh and New Orleans. He was drawing bird specimens again. He regularly burned his earlier efforts to force continuous improvement. He made detailed field notes to document his drawings.

Due to rising tensions with the British, President Jefferson ordered an embargo on British trade in 1808. This hurt Audubon's trading business. In 1810, Audubon moved his business further west to the less competitive Henderson, Kentucky, area. He and his small family took over an abandoned log cabin. In the fields and forests, Audubon wore typical frontier clothes and moccasins, having "a ball pouch, a buffalo horn filled with gunpowder, a butcher knife, and a tomahawk on his belt".

When business slowed, he frequently turned to hunting and fishing to feed his family. On a prospecting trip down the Ohio River with a load of goods, Audubon joined Shawnee and Osage hunting parties and learned their methods. By the light of evening bonfires, he drew bird specimens and parted the tribe "like brethren". Audubon had great respect for Native Americans: "Whenever I meet Indians, I feel the greatness of our Creator in all its splendor, for there I see the man naked from His hand and yet free from acquired sorrow." Audubon also admired the skill of Kentucky riflemen and the "regulators". Regulators were citizen lawmen who managed vigilante justice on the Kentucky frontier. In his travel notes, he claims to have encountered Daniel Boone. The Audubon family owned several slaves while he lived in Henderson until they needed money, at which point the slaves were sold. Abolitionists condemned Audubon for holding slaves.

Audubon and Rozier mutually agreed to end their partnership at Saint Genevieve on April 6, 1811. Audubon had decided to work in ornithology and art and wanted to return to Lucy and their son in Kentucky.

Zadok Cramer

Zadok Cramer was an author, publisher, printer, and bookseller in Pittsburgh, Pennsylvania. His book, *The Navigator*, was an influential guide for settlers and travelers on the Ohio and Mississippi Rivers in the first half of the nineteenth century.

He was born in New Jersey in 1773. Years later, he would refer to his childhood in "the Pines of New Jersey". His family moved to Washington, Pennsylvania, and he spent his youth and early adulthood there.

Though born to a Quaker family, he left that faith. However, he continued to wear the characteristic clothing of the Quakers.

Having learned his trade as a bookbinder in Washington, PA, he moved to Pittsburgh in early 1800 and started as a bookbinder. He soon bought a bookstore on Market Street, founded by John Gilkison in 1798. He hung a sign with a Benjamin Franklin portrait and called his store the "Sign of the Franklin Head". He advertised that his store had nearly 800 volumes.

Cramer also established a successful circulating library, containing romances and a few periodicals. The library eventually grew to have two thousand volumes.

The Navigator

Cramer's most important work was The Navigator, a navigation guide and gazetteer for the Ohio and Mississippi Rivers. It served the need for detailed information about the rivers and surrounding country to the west and south for the thousands of merchants and immigrants who passed through Pittsburgh in the early nineteenth century. It also provided guidance for the journey's preparation, such as advice about where to buy a river boat and what to watch for in its purchase.

Zadok Cramer was an inexhaustible compiler of facts. He proved to a generation of river travelers that meticulously detailed maps and topographic descriptions are the foundation of progress. He demonstrated by updating his gazettes year after year that facts, like a river course, often adjust to new information.

He published the first edition of the Navigator in 1801, but it is now lost to time. In his 1802 edition, called The Ohio and Mississippi Navigator, the preface (dated February 1802) states that two previous editions had been issued, that they covered only the navigation of the Ohio River, and that they had sold out quickly.

Cramer updated The Navigator regularly. The book went through twelve editions in less than 25 years. The third edition contained a description of and directions for navigating the Ohio River, with only a description of the Mississippi. Directions for navigating the Mississippi came in later editions, after the Louisiana Purchase of 1803 gave the United States ownership of the western Mississippi basin. Based on accounts from the Lewis and Clark Expedition, the 1808 edition of The Navigator also included descriptions of the Missouri and Columbia Rivers. The largest edition was the eighth, published in 1814, with 360 pages. From then on, the volumes' sizes gradually got smaller until the last edition in 1824.

Cramer sold The Navigator for a dollar a copy at his bookstore and boatyards along the Monongahela River. The book's success made Cramer the best-known publisher in the United States of his day.

The Navigator was so popular that other authors plagiarized it. These authors included Thaddeus Mason Harris in his Journal of a Tour (Boston, 1805); Thomas Ash, who published a travel book in London in 1808, and Samuel Cumings with his Western Pilot (1825), as well as Lloyd's Steamboat Directory (1856).

Bookselling and publishing

In the first years of the 1800s, Cramer's store, which he advertised as the "Pittsburgh Bookstore" or "Zadok Cramer's Classical, Literary, and Law Bookstore", was the only business in Pittsburgh primarily dedicated to bookselling, and it prospered. He sold books in English, German, French, Greek, Latin, and Spanish, including dictionaries, almanacs, Bibles, schoolbooks, and books on music and law. He expanded his inventory to include stationery, playing cards, and patent medicines, and he was the first to sell wallpaper in Pittsburgh.

Cramer was not the first to publish a book in Pittsburgh, but he was the most important early book publisher by quantity and breadth of selection. At first, he did not have his own press but relied on the two newspaper printing offices in the same block. John Israel of the Tree of Liberty printed his first almanacs. John Scull of the *Pittsburgh Gazette* published the early editions of *The Navigator*. On August 14, 1805, he announced that he had purchased a press, and his publishing business grew. He published a wide range of books, including schoolbooks, religious texts, travel journals, collections of poetry, biographies, histories, books on philosophy and law, plays, belles-lettres, and books of local interest.

In 1808, Cramer partnered with John Spear, and the firm was renamed Cramer & Spear. In 1810, William Eichbaum Jr. became a partner after having served an apprenticeship of seven years, and the business became Cramer, Spear & Eichbaum. It kept this name until 1818, the year of the death of Zadok's widow, Elizabeth Cramer, when Eichbaum withdrew. The business later became Johnston & Stockton and lasted until 1850.

Travels and death

Cramer traveled extensively to gather information for The Navigator. He journeyed down the Ohio River in 1806. He visited Kentucky in 1810. The New Orleans, built in Pittsburgh and launched in 1811, was the first steamboat on the western rivers of the United States; Cramer traveled on it twice from Natchez, Mississippi, to New Orleans, and included information about the steamboat and its river route in The Navigator.

Cramer's health suffered from his intense dedication to his work, and he became ill with tuberculosis. His physician recommended that he travel to Havana, Cuba, to improve his health, but while traveling there, he died in Pensacola, Florida, on August 1, 1813. His body was buried there in an unmarked grave.

Cramer had been planning new business projects up to his death. His business was continued by his widow and his partners, who attempted to carry out his most cherished plan, the publication of a magazine. The first issue of *The Western Gleaner or Repository for Arts, Sciences, and Literature*, a monthly magazine of 64 pages, was published in December 1813. It ran until June 1814, when it was discontinued for financial reasons.

Other Early Steamboats on the Mississippi

The New Orleans was the first steamboat to travel down the Mississippi to New Orleans, but never made a return trip to Pittsburgh. This honor fell to the Enterprise, captained by Henry Miller Shreve. This boat demonstrated that upriver travel and shipping were not only practical between Natchez and New Orleans but also made upriver travel and shipping practical from Louisville to New Orleans.

The enthusiasm for another steamboat on the Mississippi was not embraced by everyone. The trip upriver to Louisville from New Orleans almost didn't happen because of legal reasons. John Livingston submitted a petition to the Federal Court accusing Captain Henry Shreve and the shareholders of the Monongahela and Ohio Steamboat Company of violating the territorial steamboat monopoly granted to Robert R. Livingston and Robert Fulton. John Livingston's petition requested restitution. Sheriff John H. Holland, acting on orders issued by the court, quickly arrested Henry Shreve and seized the Enterprise. Attorney Abner L. Duncan, representing the Monongahela and Ohio Steamboat Company's shareholders, posted bail and arranged for Shreve and the Enterprise to be released.

The Enterprise finally departed New Orleans and, after a voyage of 1,500 miles, reached Louisville on May 31. After that eventful trip, the Enterprise steamed to Pittsburgh and Brownsville. This voyage was performed against the powerful currents of the Mississippi, Ohio, and Monongahela Rivers, and the steamboat was the only one to tackle going up the Falls of the Ohio.

In August and autumn of 1815, Captain Lowns, Captain Shreve's replacement, commanded the Enterprise during voyages to Ohio River ports between Pittsburgh and Louisville.

In November 1815, the Monongahela and Ohio Steamboat Co. leased the Enterprise to shareholder James Tomlinson, and his son-in-law, Daniel Wehrley (also spelled Worley), became the captain of the Enterprise. Bound for New Orleans, the Enterprise arrived at Shippingport on January 21, 1816. On January 25, the Enterprise "with a full cargo of flour, whiskey, apples, &c. and many passengers" departed Shippingport bound for New Orleans. The Enterprise reached the port of New Orleans on February 27. The Enterprise completed a round-trip voyage when she returned to New Orleans on April 5.

Steaming from the city of New Orleans under the command of Daniel Wehrley, the Enterprise reached Shippingport by August 5, 1816. Because the Ohio River above the Falls was too shallow for the voyage to continue, the Enterprise anchored in Rock Harbor.

During August or early 1816, the Enterprise finally reached Shippingport, below the Falls of the Ohio River, and the river being low above, and freights dull, the captain anchored the boat in deep water and hired two men to take care of her. The main crew went by land to Pittsburgh. One of the men that they had hired went ashore, and the other got drunk and neglected the pumps; the weather was hot, and the seams of the boat opened. The Enterprise filled and sank to the bottom. In 1818, a man offered Elisha Hunt $1,000 for the wreck, as he thought he could get her engine out to run a sawmill. He must have refused because in 1851, Hunt said that the Enterprise remained at the bottom of the river.

After the Enterprise successfully navigated the upstream voyage of the Mississippi, steamboat travel flourished up and down the river. Before this could happen, though, they had to determine a few legal factors. Another steamboat, the Dispatch, owned by the Monongahela and Ohio Steamboat Company, steamed from Brownsville to Louisville under the command of Israel Gregg. At Louisville, he transferred command to Henry Bruce. Bruce navigated the Dispatch to the port of New Orleans by February 13, 1816.

While docked at the landing, an incident occurred aboard the Dispatch. Edward Livingston and the district marshal came on board to inform the captain that Fulton and Livingston had the exclusive right to navigate the waters in Louisiana with steamboats, and they did not allow their rights to be infringed. However, as the crew of the Dispatch pleaded ignorance of the law, the marshal and Livingston agreed to let them go if they would leave the Louisiana waters and not return. They took in a little freight and a few passengers and started for Alexandria, located at the Red River Rapids. After unloading their cargo, the Dispatch returned to the river's mouth and returned to Pittsburgh.

Within a decade, steamboats would link the nation's interior like nothing had before. With the coming of the riverboat, the cities of New Orleans, Natchez, Baton Rouge, and St. Louis grew in leaps and bounds. In addition, other cities began to pop up along the southern Mississippi River, including Vicksburg, Mississippi, in 1811, and Memphis, Tennessee, in 1819.

After the New Orleans voyage, the Vesuvius and then the Aetna followed the New Orleans, These two steamboats were followed by others, and again by others, until travelers on the Mississippi were rarely, if ever, out of sight of the white and feathery plumes that accompany the boats of the Western waters as their high-pressure engines urged them on their way.

The town of Shippingport reached its peak in the 1820s with a population of 600. In 1825, the Louisville and Portland Canal was constructed, leaving the settlement on an island. By using the canal, ships could bypass the Falls and, by extension, Shippingport. In the same way that a major highway causes detours around towns today and causes population declines, this canal ended the growth of that river port.

20

Sneak Peek: Book IX of the Locket Saga: The

"There's a wagon coming!" Robbie McCray announced. Robbie, the eight-year-old son of Robert and Judith McCray, dropped his wooden hoe and tugged on his uncle Joseph's hand, and drew the eighteen-year-old toward the road.

On this warm day at the end of June, the men and boys of Concord were working in the field. They stopped planting squash seeds among the corn and beans, which were already reaching their leaves toward the sun.

Joseph and the rest looked directly toward where Robbie pointed.

The road to Concord Township, Pennsylvania, was not perfect, but it was improving. When the first families arrived, they could only travel on the creeks and rivers. Since their arrival several years earlier, they widened the roads, and at least during the summer months, wagons traveled to their settlement.

"Well, whoever it is, he is no doubt coming here," Joseph stated the obvious. The road ended just beyond the settlement where the Miles homestead had been. After their daughter married their cousin Isaac Thorton, the older Miles couple moved to the Missouri Territory, where Isaac and Rebecca resided. Their land in Missouri adjoined Nathan Boone's property. From letters they received from Isaac, the families learned that Nathan was the son of the legendary Daniel Boone.

"It's cousin Jonathan!" Robert, Robbie's father, Joseph's older brother, announced. Jonathan Mayford was from another branch of the family. Jonathan, his wife, Lowri, and their youngest son, Charles, lived in Pittsburgh. He had helped provide resources for building the first steamboat on the western rivers, and his older son, Andrew, piloted that boat from Pittsburgh to New Orleans.

The men quickly planted a few more seeds each and leaned on their hoes as the wagon seemed to grow larger as it grew closer.

"Well, well, what brings you here, Jonathan?"

"You heard about the war, didn't you?" Jonathan asked.

"War? What war?"

"What? You don't know? We're at war with Britain! It was announced two weeks ago on the twelfth."

"Is that a fact?" Robert asked. "Well, what does it have to do with us? Are you commissioning us to join the army?"

"Well, the army is looking for men to join in the fight, but I am on a different mission."

"Really, what's that?"

"Since I grew up around a shipyard and helped build the New Orleans steamboat, the President of the United States wrote me asking me to help obtain labor and supplies to help build warships on the Great Lakes."

"I thought that you were planning to build steamboats?"

"I am, but duty calls, and I have been called to hire you and the boys to help obtain the tall timbers for building tall ships on Lake Erie!"

"Tall ships?" Lake Erie was a long way from the ship-building ports of New England. Jonathan himself had manned a privateer boat when he was younger, had run a series of mills on the Monongahela, and had helped build the steamboat. His father had been a shipbuilder.

"Why isn't Cousin Matthew taking on this project?" Robert asked. "Oh, you know how it is. He's been living high off the hog there, and his gout won't let him travel. That's why the government has seen fit to let him continue building ships and fishing boats on the east coast."

Matthew Thorton had taken over Jonathan's father's ship and fishing boat building business and for years had been managing the shipping business in Boston. He married Jonathan's daughter Lacey, and they had several children of their own.

As they walked back to their tiny community, Jonathan told them about the war.

The British had been goading the Americans into war for many years. By 1803, British ships had boarded American merchant ships and were forcing them to work on British ships. Jonathan told them that he was told that to date, they had taken almost ten thousand Americans into forced service.

In 1806, an American named James Monroe discovered what the British ships were doing. He tried to find a resolution, but Britain was at war with France. While sailing in neutral waters, British ships took over 1000 American ships. They claimed the Americans were trading with France, which the English had blockaded. This did little to ease tensions between the former mother country and the fledgling nation.

In 1807, tensions escalated when a British ship, the Leopard, fired on America's Chesapeake. Word spread quickly so that soon even people on the frontier had heard about this atrocity.

Finally, in 1812, the Americans had had enough. Their small country declared war on the English. A US ship, the USS Constitution, defeated the British ship, the HMS Guerriere.

"It's our second American Revolution," Jonathan declared to his cousins of Concord. "We will be able to free our French allies in Canada before this is over."

"Oh, and I brought this back," Jonathan held out the old locket box. Jonathan's wife had asked for the locket over a year earlier. "Lowri says it will be a few years before our family will need this, and your family has several young people of marrying age, so she made me bring it along."

Robert laughed. "We don't have anyone sparking right now, but I'm sure it will happen soon enough."

He looked over at his younger brother Joseph. Joseph rolled his eyes at Robert. "You're as bad as the womenfolk!"

"Yeah, I've got two married now," Jonathan replied. "I just have one at home, but he's not much older than your son, Robbie here."

"So, Andrew finally got himself hitched, huh?" Robert asked.

"Yes, he's married to a fine French girl named Susanna."

"Well, at least he picked someone from the right side," Robert replied. "Unlike some people that we know."

"Are you talking about me?" Jonathan asked.

"If the shoe fits!" Robert taunted.

Jonathan laughed. "I got myself the perfect wife, just like you did."

Jonathan's wife, Lowri, was from Wales. Her family had been on the British side of the Revolution.

"So, what can we do to help build those boats?"

"Not boats, tall ships," Jonathan replied. "We need some to harvest your tall trees for masts, hulls, and whatnot. I figured you could float them down French Creek to Waterford and then haul them up the Old French Road to Lake Erie."

"We do have a lot of tall trees," Robert replied. "We probably have enough wood for a thousand tall ships."

"Well, I don't think the United States has enough in its fund for a hundred ships, but the government does have enough for a few."

"We'll need help at the shipyard, too. We'll need people who know what they're doing at the sawpits," Jonathan continued.

"I'll go to Erie to help you," Joseph exclaimed.

"We'll have to discuss it with your father," Jonathan exclaimed.

"When we finish the ships, I'd like to become a sailor like you did," Joseph exclaimed.

"Now I understand how my parents felt when I wanted to go to war," Jonathan exclaimed. "I'm just glad I came to my senses during this war and am helping with the logistics rather than doing the actual fighting. I know what it's like to spend time on a prison ship. It is not a pleasant adventure, believe me."

That evening, Jonathan Mayford discussed with the Thorton and McCray families what they would need to do to get the tall trees to Great Lake Erie. Joseph would help in the sawpits in Erie while the others in the community helped buck the logs and deliver them to the port city.

The following morning, the men went to the forest, and Philip McCray showed Jonathan the tallest and straightest trees. Jonathan chose the choicest trees for the masts and hulls, and the community agreed to prepare them to float down French Creek to Waterford to be hauled overland to Erie.

Jonathan spent the night in Robert and Judith's cabin.

That night, Robert and Judith were awakened by chanting in the distance. Robert McCray got out of bed, and his wife Judith followed him to the front door. Robert opened the door to hear better.
"Is that the Indians?" Judith asked.

Young Robbie McCray jumped out of bed and ran, dressed in his nightshirt and cap. "Are we going to kill some Indians?"

"Land sakes, no," Judith exclaimed, then turned accusingly toward Robert. "Where does he get these ideas?"

Robert shrugged. "He's heard too many stories from Father."

"You still didn't answer my questions. "Were those Indians?"

Robert nodded. "I don't know what to make of it, but I would say that in the morning we need to do what we can to prepare for whatever might happen."

Robert went out to the woodshed to get a few pieces of wood. Across the field and toward his parents' house, he saw that his father was doing the same.

"What do you make of the Indian chants?"

"The Iroquois were on the side of the British during the Revolution," Philip McCray said. "I wouldn't be surprised if they weren't on their side now."

Robert furrowed his forehead. He thought of his wife and children. *What would happen to them if the Indians did attack? Would he be able to keep them safe?*

The Indians chanted throughout the night. Before dawn, Phillip McCray asked his son Joseph to go up to the top of Concord Ridge to discover the Indians' location. He looked out toward the hills beyond the farm. The Indian fires burned in the valley less than five miles to the northeast.

He rushed home to tell his father what he saw. Judith McCray rang the triangle that Robert, the community blacksmith, had made to call the community together. They weren't a big group, but they were as prepared as many.

They collected what gunpowder they could find and all the lead ammunition available to prepare for battle. Fortunately, the group's patriarchs, Luke Thorton and Philip McCray, had diplomatic relations with these Indians during the Revolution and beyond. They hoped they could negotiate with Chief Cornplanter and avoid bloodshed.

The women made bullets with all the available lead. Because there wasn't enough time to build a proper stockade. The men prepared a ditch along the road and a brushy roadblock along the Thorton property line on the northeast side of the community. There was nothing to keep the Indians from flanking the wall, but the wall should have been enough to at least give the settlers a chance to negotiate with the Indians.

They expected the Indians to act like Indians and sneak up to the settlement, but when they did arrive, they didn't sneak in through the woods. Instead, they entered the settlement via the road. The Indians were dressed in battle gear and wore war paint.

The Indians knew that there were only a few of them and that the settlers of Concord Ridge had few if any defensible positions. It didn't look good for the settlement.

An old, grizzled chief led the warrior band. Joseph McCray guessed that the old chief had to be Chief Cornplanter. Joseph's father and uncle had met with this Seneca warrior numerous times. Had he come to betray his old friends?

The old man stopped and stared at the brushworks and pit that the Concord community members erected.

The old Iroquois laughed. Joseph had not expected to hear the Indian laugh.

"Do you think I'd go to war against you, my friends? I would never betray our friendship."

The old man smiled, revealing a mouth full of rotting teeth. He raised his hands.

Philip came out from behind the brushwork and held out his hand. The two men clasped hands.

"I am going to Erie with you to defend our territory." Said the old Seneca. "We are going to Erie to help defend our territory from the English. We are friends with Head of Stone and you, Phillip. I want to keep living in peace with my white brothers."

Several years earlier, in northern Pennsylvania and southern New York, the Seneca Nation, led by Cornplanter, allied with the young United States, worked to bring the Native Americans of the Ohio Country to the negotiating table. For a young nation with a small army, this help was crucial. A wider war with even more Native American nations could have easily led to disaster for the young nation.

Joseph's father helped Cornplanter arrange numerous trips to Philadelphia and later Washington to strengthen relationships. He tried to understand Euro-American culture, as he felt it necessary for successful relations between the Iroquois and the United States. He even used his white man's name, John Abeel III, when dealing with many of the white men.

To reward Cornplanter for his support, the Pennsylvania and federal governments had gifted Cornplanter and his heirs, not the entire Seneca Nation, three tracts of land in Forest, Venango, and Warren Counties. Both Joseph's father, Phillip McCray, and Joseph's uncle, Luke, had helped secure that agreement with Cornplanter and his descendants so that the American government would leave them alone in peace.

Phillip said, "So you're going to fight the British, old man?"

"Who are you calling an old man, old man? I intend to live many more winters, but alas, no, I will not be fighting in this war. I am sending my son, Henry, and his cousin Chainbreaker to go to Fort Erie along the Niagara River to support the American cause."

"That's good to know, my friend. That is good to know."

The old Indian and the warriors with him headed north toward Erie.

Jonathan Mayford and young Joseph McCray left the next day to head up through Waterford for Erie.

"We'll be staying at Dobbins Landing," Jonathan said. "Newly commissioned Captain Daniel Dobbins has agreed to set up a shipyard on his property."

Joseph nodded. He had heard of Daniel Dobbins. Dobbins built boats for fishing on Lake Erie.

There, he saw the most beautiful girl he had ever seen. Her name was Rose. The Rose of Dobbins Landing.

Her hair was strawberry blonde. Her eyes were the most brilliant blue he had ever seen. She wore a bright blue gown and a white apron. Joseph couldn't keep his eyes off her. He barely noticed that she was surrounded by men of every age, shape, and size.

Could this be what they meant by love at first sight?

21

Cygnet Brown is the author's pen name. Cygnet chose the name Cygnet because "Swanson" was her maiden name (a cygnet is a baby swan)and she chose "Brown" because it was her married name. She grew up in North-western Pennsylvania, and began writing stories in Mrs. Watson's seventh grade English class.

Because of the experience, she wanted to become a professional writer, but life got in the way. She is a US Navy Veteran. She served six years active duty as a Hospital Corpsman with a specialty in neuro-psychology and another ten years as a reservist and participated in the First Gulf War. She married. Became a mother of three, became a stepmother to another, and is now grandmother of one grandson and three granddaughters. She worked as a nurse for a while. In October 2008, she resumed writing when she fell in love with her characters all over again. She went back to school and graduated magnum cum laud with a liberal arts degree in 2014.

Cygnet Brown currently lives in the Missouri Ozarks. She loves to write research and write history from a from a fictional perspective. She never knows when she will uncover another historical flame that sparks the creation of another story in *The Locket Saga*.

When God Turned His Head, the first volume of The Locket Saga was published in 2010. Other books in the series include: *Soldiers Don't Cry, A Coward's Solace, Sailing Under the Black Flag, In the Shadow of the Mill Pond, The Anvil, Two Rivers, and now Moonrise on the Mississippi.*

Cygnet has also written a contemporary romance called *Because of Ryan,* and wrote several nonfiction books. In 2013, she published her first nonfiction book *Simply Vegetable Gardening* based on her more than fifty years of gardening experience. She has also written *Help from Kelp, Using Diatomaceous Earth Around the House and Yard, Gourmet Weeds, Oregon County, Wild and Scenic, Living Today, The Power of Now, Write a Book and Ignite Your Business, and the Ultimate Keystone Habit.*

Mrs. Brown has written for The Mother Earth News magazine as well as several online sites. Discover more from Cygnet Brown on her website at https://authorcygnetbrown.com.